The Potter's Field

The Seventeenth Chronicle of Brother Cadfael

Ellis Peters

Brother CADFAEL

Stoddart

First published in 1989 by
Stoddart Publishing Co. Limited
34 Lesmill Road
Toronto, Canada
M3B 2T6

Published in Great Britain by
Headline Book Publishing PLC
Headline House
79 Great Titchfield Street
London W1P 7FN
England

Canadian Cataloguing in Publication Data

Peters, Ellis, 1913–
  The potters field

  ISBN 0–7737–2382–X

  I. Title.

PR6031.A49P68 1989   823'.914   89–094658–2

Typeset in 12/14½ pt English Times
by Colset Private Limited, Singapore

Printed and bound in Great Britain by
Richard Clay Ltd, Bungay, Suffolk

The Potter's Field

Chapter One

AINT PETER'S FAIR of that year, 1143, was one week past, and they were settling down again into the ordinary routine of a dry and favourable August, with the corn harvest already being carted into the barns, when Brother Matthew the cellarer first brought into chapter the matter of business he had been discussing for some days during the Fair with the prior of the Augustinian priory of Saint John the Evangelist, at Haughmond, about four miles to the north-east of Shrewsbury. Haughmond was a FitzAlan foundation, and FitzAlan was out of favour and dispossessed since he had held Shrewsbury castle against King Stephen, though rumour said he was back in England again from his refuge in France, and safe with the Empress's forces in Bristol. But many of his tenants locally had continued loyal to the king, and retained their lands, and Haughmond flourished in their patronage and gifts, a highly respectable neighbour with whom business could be done to mutual advantage at times. This, according to Brother Matthew, was one of the times.

'The proposal for this exchange of land came from Haughmond,' he said, 'but it makes good sense for both houses. I have already set the necessary facts before Father

1

Abbot and Prior Robert, and I have here rough plans of the two fields in question, both large and of comparable quality. The one which this house owns lies some mile and a half beyond Haughton, and is bounded on all sides by land gifted to Haughmond Priory. Clearly it will advantage them to add this piece to their holdings, for economy in use and the saving of time and labour in going back and forth. And the field which Haughmond wishes to exchange for it is on the hither side of the manor of Longner, barely two miles from us but inconveniently distant from Haughmond. Clearly it is good sense to consider this exchange. I have viewed the ground, and the bargain is a fair one. I recommend that we should accept.'

'If this field is on the hither side of Longner,' said Brother Richard, the sub-prior, who came from a mile or so beyond that manor and knew the outlines of the land, 'how does it lie with regard to the river? Is it subject to flooding?'

'No. It has the Severn along one flank, yes, but the bank is high, and the meadow climbs gradually from it to a headland and a windbreak of trees and bushes along the ridge. It is the field of which Brother Ruald was tenant until some fifteen months ago. There were two or three small claypits along the river bank, but I believe they are exhausted. The field is known as the Potter's Field.'

A slight ripple of movement went round the chapter-house, as all heads turned in one direction, and all eyes fastened for one discreet moment upon Brother Ruald. A slight, quiet, grave man, with a long, austere face, very regular of feature, of an ageless, classical comeliness, he still went about the devout hours of the day like one half withdrawn into a private rapture, for his final vows were only two months old, and his desire for the life of the cloister, recognised only after fifteen years of married life and twenty-five of plying the potter's craft, had burned into an acute agony before he gained admittance and entered into peace. A peace he never seemed to leave now, even for a moment. All eyes might turn on him, and his calm remained absolute. Everyone here knew his story, which was complex and strange enough, but that did not trouble him. He was where he wanted to be.

'It is good pasture,' he said simply. 'And could well be cultivated, if it is needed. It lies well above any common floodline. The other field, of course, I do not know.'

'It may be a little greater,' said Brother Matthew judicially, contemplating his parchments with head on one side, measuring with narrowed eyes. 'But at that distance we are spared time and labour. I have said, I judge it a fair exchange.'

'The Potter's Field!' said Prior Robert, musing. 'It was such a field that was bought with the silver of Judas's betrayal, for the burial of strangers. I trust there can be no ill omen in the name.'

'It was only named for my craft,' said Ruald. 'Earth is innocent. Only the use we make of it can mar it. I laboured honestly there, before I knew whither I was truly bound. It is good land. It may well be better used than for a workshop and kiln such as mine. A narrow yard would have done for that.'

'And access is easy?' asked Brother Richard. 'It lies on the far side of the river from the highroad.'

'There is a ford a little way upstream, and a ferry even nearer to the field.'

'That land was gifted to Haughmond only a year ago, by Eudo Blount of Longner,' Brother Anselm reminded them. 'Is Blount a partner to this exchange? He made no demur? Or has he yet been consulted?'

'You will remember,' said Brother Matthew, patiently competent at every point, as was his way, 'that Eudo Blount the elder died early this year at Wilton, in the rearguard that secured the king's retreat. His son, also Eudo, is now lord of Longner. Yes, we have talked with him. He has no objection. The gift is Haughmond's property, to be used to Haughmond's best advantage, which manifestly this exchange serves well. There is no obstacle there.'

'And no restriction as to the use we in our turn may make of it?' demanded the prior acutely. 'The agreement will be on the usual terms? That either party may make whatever use it wishes of the fields? To build, or cultivate, or keep as pasture, at will?'

'That is agreed. If we want to plough, there is no bar.'

'It seems to me,' said Abbot Radulfus, casting a long glance around at the attentive faces of his flock, 'that we have heard enough. If anyone has any other point to raise, do so now, by all means.'

In the considering silence that followed many eyes turned again, mildly expectant, to the austere face of Brother Ruald, who alone remained withdrawn and unconcerned. Who should know better the qualities of that field where he had worked for so many years, or be better qualified to state whether they would be doing well in approving the proposed exchange? But he had said all he had to say, in duty bound, and felt no need to add another word. When he had turned his back upon the world and entered into his desired vocation, field and cottage and kiln and kin had vanished for him. He never spoke of his former life, probably he never thought of it. All those years he had been astray and far from home.

'Very well!' said the abbot. 'Clearly both we and Haughmond gain by the exchange. Will you confer with the prior, Matthew, and draw up the charter accordingly, and as soon as a day can be fixed we will see it witnessed and sealed.

4

And once that is done, I think Brother Richard and Brother Cadfael might view the ground, and consider its most profitable use.'

Brother Matthew rolled up his plans with a brisk hand and a satisfied countenance. It was his part to keep a strict eye upon the property and funds of the house, to reckon up land, crops, gifts and legacies in the profits they could bring to the monastery of Saint Peter and Saint Paul, and he had assessed the Potter's Field with professional shrewdness, and liked what he saw.

'There is no other business?' asked Radulfus.

'None, Father!'

'Then this chapter is concluded,' said the abbot, and led the way out of the chapter-house into the sunbleached August grasses of the cemetery.

Brother Cadfael went up into the town after Vespers, in the cooling sunlight of a clear evening, to sup with his friend Hugh Beringar, and visit his godson Giles, three and a half years old, long and strong and something of a benevolent tyrant to the entire household. In view of the sacred duty such a sponsor has towards his charge, Cadfael had leave to visit the house with reasonable regularity, and if the time he spent with the boy was occupied more often in play than in the serious admonitions of a responsible godparent, neither Giles nor his own parents had any complaint to make.

'He pays more heed to you,' said Aline, looking on with smiling serenity, 'than he does to me. But he'll tire you out before you can do as much for him. Well for you it's near his bedtime.'

She was as fair as Hugh was black, primrose-fair, and fine-boned, and a shade taller than her husband. The child was built on the same long, slender lines, and flaxen like her. Some day he would top his father by a head. Hugh himself had foretold it, when first he saw his newborn heir, a winter child, come with the approach of Christmas, the finest of gifts for the festival. Now at three years old he had the boisterous energy of a healthy pup, and the same whole-hearted abandonment to sleep when energy was spent. He was carried away at length in Aline's arms to his bed, and Hugh and Cadfael were left to sit down companionably together over their wine, and look back over the events of the day.

'Ruald's field?' said Hugh, when he heard of the morning's business at chapter. 'That's the big field the near side of Longner, where he used to have his croft and his kiln? I remember the gift to Haughmond, I was a witness to it. Early October of last year, that was. The Blounts were always good patrons to Haughmond. Not that the canons ever made much use of that land when they had it. It will do better in your hands.'

'It's a long time since I passed that way close,' said Cadfael. 'Why is it so neglected? When Ruald came into the cloister there was no one to take over his craft, I know, but at least Haughmond put a tenant into the cottage.'

'So they did, an old widow woman, what could she do with the ground? Now even she is gone, to her daughter's household in the town. The kiln has been looted for stone, and the cottage is falling into decay. It's time someone took the place over. The canons never even bothered to take the hay crop in, this year, they'll be glad to get it off their hands.'

'It suits both sides very well,' said Cadfael thoughtfully. 'And young Eudo Blount at Longner has no objection, so Matthew reports. Though the prior of Haughmond must have asked his leave beforehand, since the gift came from his father

6

in the first place. A pity,' he said ruefully, 'the giver is gone to his maker untimely, and isn't here to say a word for himself in the matter.'

Eudo Blount the elder, of the manor of Longner, had left his lands in the charge of his son and heir only a few weeks after making the gift of the field to the priory, and gone in arms to join King Stephen's army, then besieging the Empress and her forces in Oxford. That campaign he had survived, only to die a few months later in the unexpected rout of Wilton. The king, not for the first time, had underestimated his most formidable opponent, Earl Robert of Gloucester, miscalculated the speed at which the enemy could move, and ridden with only his vanguard into a perilous situation from which he had extricated himself safely only by virtue of a heroic rearguard action, which had cost the king's steward, William Martel, his liberty, and Eudo Blount his life. Stephen, in honour bound, had paid a high price to redeem Martel. No one, in this world, could ransom back Eudo Blount. His elder son became lord of Longner in his place. His younger son, Cadfael recalled, a novice at the abbey of Ramsey, had brought his father's body home for burial in March.

'A fine, tall man he was,' Hugh recalled, 'no more than two or three years past forty. And handsome! There's neither of his lads can match him. Strange how the lot falls. The lady's some years older, and sick with some trouble that's worn her to a shadow and gives her no rest from pain, yet she lingers on here, and he's gone. Does she ever send to you for medicines? The lady of Longner? I forget her name.'

'Donata,' said Cadfael. 'Donata is her name. Now you mention it, there was a time when her maid used to come for draughts to help her with the pain. But not for a year or more now. I thought she might have been on the mend, and felt less

7

need of the herbs. Little enough I could ever do for her. There are diseases beyond any small skill of mine.'

'I saw her when they buried Eudo,' said Hugh, gazing sombrely out through the open hall door at the summer dusk gathering blue and luminous above his garden. 'No, there's no remission. So little flesh she has between her skin and bone, I swear the light shone through her hand when she raised it, and her face grey as lavender, and shrunken into deep lines. Eudo sent for me when he made up his mind to go to Oxford, to the siege. I did wonder how he could bear to leave her in such case. Stephen had not called him, and even if he had, there was no need for him to go himself. His only due was an esquire, armed and mounted, for forty days. Yet he saw his affairs in order, made over his manor to his son, and went.'

'It may well be,' Cadfael said, 'that he could no longer bear to stay, and look on daily at a distress he could neither prevent nor help.'

His voice was very low, and Aline, re-entering the hall at that moment, did not hear the words. The very sight of her, radiantly content in her fulfilment, happy wife and mother, banished all such thoughts, and caused them both to shake off in haste all trace of a solemnity that might have cast a shadow on her serenity. She came to sit with them, her hands for once empty, for the light was too far gone for sewing or even spinning, and the warm, soft evening too beautiful to be banished by lighting candles.

'He's fast asleep. He was nodding over his prayers. But still he could rouse enough to demand his story from Constance. He'll have heard no more than the first words, but custom is custom. And I want my story, too,' she said, smiling at Cadfael, 'before I let you leave us. What is the news with you, there at the abbey? Since the fair I've got no further afield than Saint Mary's for Mass. Do you find the fair a success this year? There were fewer Flemings there, I thought, but some excellent cloths, just the same. I bought well, some heavy Welsh woollen for winter gowns. The sheriff,' she said, and made an impish face at Hugh, 'cares nothing what he puts on, but I won't have my husband go threadbare and cold. Will you believe, his best indoor gown is ten years old, and twice relined, and still he won't part with it?'

'Old servants are the best,' said Hugh absently. 'Truth to tell, it's only habit sends me looking for it, you may clothe me new, my heart, whenever you wish. And for what else is new, Cadfael tells me there's an exchange of lands agreed between Shrewsbury and Haughmond. The field they call the Potter's Field, by Longner, will come to the abbey. In good time for the ploughing, if that's what you decide, Cadfael.'

'It may well be,' Cadfael conceded. 'At least on the upper part, well clear of the river. The lower part is good grazing.'

'I used to buy from Ruald,' said Aline rather ruefully. 'He was a good craftsman. I still wonder – what was it made him leave the world for the cloister, and all so suddenly?'

'Who can tell?' Cadfael looked back, as now he seldom did, to the turning-point of his own life, many years past. After all manner of journeying, fighting, endurance of heat and cold and hardship, after the pleasures and the pains of experience, the sudden irresistible longing to turn about and withdraw into quietness remained a mystery. Not a retreat, certainly. Rather an emergence into light and certainty. 'He never could explain it or describe it. All he could say was that he had had a revelation of God, and had turned where he was pointed, and come where he was called. It happens. I think Radulfus had his doubts at first. He kept him the full term and over in his novitiate. His desire was extreme, and our abbot suspects extremes. And then, the man had been fifteen years married, and his wife was by no means consenting. Ruald left her everything he had to leave, and all of it she scorned. She fought his resolve for many weeks, but he would not be moved. After he was admitted among us she did not stay long in the croft, or avail herself of anything he had left behind for her. She went away, only a few weeks later, left the door open and everything in its place, and vanished.'

'With another man, so all the neighbours said,' Hugh remarked cynically.

'Well,' said Cadfael reasonably, 'her own had left her. And very bitter she was about it, by all accounts. She might well take a lover by way of revenge. Did ever you see the woman?'

'No,' said Hugh, 'not that I recall.'

'I have,' said Aline. 'She helped at his booth on market days and at the fair. Not last year, of course, last year he was in the cloister and she was already gone. There was a lot of talk about Ruald's leaving her, naturally, and gossip is never very charitable. She was not well liked among the market women, she never went out of her way to make friends, never let them close to her. And then, you see, she was very beautiful, and a stranger. He brought her from Wales, years ago, and even after years she spoke little English, and never made any effort to be anything but a stranger. She seemed to want no one but Ruald. No wonder if she was bitter when he abandoned her. The neighbours said she turned to hating him, and claimed she had another lover and could do without such a husband. But she fought for him to the end. Women turn for ease to hate, sometimes, when love leaves them nothing but pain.' She had mused herself into another woman's anguish with unwonted gravity; she shook off the image with some dismay. 'Now *I* am the gossip! What will you think of me? And it's all a year past, and surely by now she's reconciled. No wonder if she took up her roots – they were shallow enough here, once Ruald was gone – and went away home to Wales without a word to a soul. With another man, or alone, what does it matter?'

'Love,' declared Hugh, at once touched and amused, 'you never cease to be a wonder to me. How did you ever come to know so much about the case? And feel so hotly about it?'

'I've seen them together, that was enough. From across a fairground stall it was plain to be seen how fond and wild she was. And you men,' said Aline, with resigned tolerance, 'naturally see the man's rights first, when he sets his heart on doing what he wants, whether it's entering the cloister or going off to war, but I'm a woman, and I see how deeply wronged the wife was. Had she no rights in the matter? And did you ever stop to think – *he* could have his freedom to go and become a monk, but his going didn't confer freedom on *her*. She could not take another husband, the one she had, monk or no, was still alive. Was that fair? Almost,' avowed Aline roundly, 'I hope she did go with a lover, rather than have to live and endure alone.'

Hugh reached a long arm to draw his wife to him, with something between a laugh and a sigh. 'Lady, there is much in what you say, and this world is full of injustice.'

'Still I suppose it was not Ruald's fault,' said Aline, relenting. 'I daresay he would have released her if he could. It's done, and I hope, wherever she is, she has some comfort in her life. And I suppose if a man really is overtaken by an act of God there's nothing he can do but obey. It may even have cost him almost as much. What kind of brother has he made, Cadfael? Was it really something that could not be denied?'

11

'Truly,' said Cadfael, 'it seems that it was. The man is wholly devoted. I verily believe he had no choice.' He paused reflectively, finding it hard to discover the appropriate words for a degree of self-surrender which was impossible to him. 'He has now that entire security that cannot be moved by well or ill, since to his present state everything is well. If martyrdom was demanded of him now, he would accept it with the same serenity as bliss. Indeed it would be bliss, he knows nothing less. I doubt if he gives a thought to any part of that life he led for forty years, or the wife he knew and abandoned. No, Ruald had no choice.'

Aline was regarding him steadily with her wide iris eyes, that were so shrewd in their innocence. 'Was it like that for you,' she asked, 'when your time came?'

'No, I had a choice. I made a choice. It was even a hard choice, but I made it, and I hold to it. I am no such elect saint as Ruald.'

'Is that a saint?' said Aline. 'It seems to me all too easy.'

The charter of the exchange of lands between Haughmond and Shrewsbury was drawn up, sealed and witnessed in the first week of September. Some days later Brother Cadfael and Brother Richard the sub-prior went to view the new acquisition, and consider its future use to the best advantage of the abbey. The morning was misty when they set out, but by the time they had reached the ferry just upstream from the field the sun was already coming through the haze, and their sandalled feet left dark tracks through the dewy grass above the shore. Across the river the further bank rose, sandy and steep, undercut here and there by the currents, and levelling off into a narrow plain of grass, with a rising ridge of bushes and trees beyond. When they stepped from the boats they had some minutes of walking along this belt of pasture, and then they stood at the corner of the Potter's Field, and had the whole expanse obliquely before them.

It was a very fair place. From the sandy escarpment of the river bank the slope of grass rose gradually towards a natural headland of bush and thorn and a filigree screen of birch trees against the sky. Backed into this crest in the far corner the shell of the empty cottage squatted, its garden unfenced and running wild into the embracing wildness of the unreaped grass. The crop Haughmond had not found worth its while to garner was bleaching into early autumn pallor, having ripened and seeded weeks earlier, and among the whitened standing stems all manner of meadow flowers still showed, harebell and archangel, poppy and daisy and centaury, with the fresh green shoots of new grass just breaking through the roots of the fading yield. Under the headland above, tangles of bramble offered fruit just beginning to blacken from red.

'We could still cut and dry this for bedding,' said Brother Richard, casting a judicial eye over the wild expanse, 'but would it be worth the labour? Or we could leave it to die down of itself, and plough it in. This land has not been under the plough for generations.'

'It would be heavy work,' said Cadfael, viewing with pleasure the sheen of sunlight on the distant white trunks of the birch trees on the ridge.

'Not so heavy as you might think. The soil beneath is good, friable loam. And we have a strong ox-team, and the field has length enough to get a team of six into the yoke. We need a deep, broad furrow for the first ploughing. I would recommend it,' said Brother Richard, secure in the experience of his farming stock, and set off up the field to the crest, by the same rural instinct keeping to the headland instead of wading through the grass. 'We should leave the lower strip for pasture, and plough this upper level.'

Cadfael was of the same mind. The field they had parted with, distant beyond Haughton, had been best left under stock, here they could very well take a crop of wheat or barley, and turn the stock from the lower pasture into the stubble afterwards, to manure the land for the next year. The place pleased him, and yet had an undefined sadness about it. The remnants of the garden fence, when they reached it, the tangled growth in which herb and weed contended for root and light and space, the doorless doorway and shutterless window, all sounded a note of humanity departed and human occupation abandoned. Without the remnants this would have been a scene wholly placid, gentle and content. But it was impossible to look at the deserted croft without reflecting that two lives had been lived there for fifteen years, joined in a childless marriage, and that of all the thoughts and feelings they had shared not a trace now remained here. Nor to note the bare, levelled site from which every stone had been plundered, without recalling that a craftsman had laboured here at loading his kiln and firing it, where now the hearth was barren and cold. There must surely have been human happiness here, satisfaction of the mind, fulfilment of the hands. There had certainly been grief, bitterness and rage, but only the detritus of that past life clung about the spot now, coldly, indifferently melancholy.

Cadfael turned his back upon the corner which had once been inhabited, and there before him lay the sweep of meadow, gently steaming as the sun drew off the morning mist and dew, and the sharp, small colours of the flowers brightened among the seeding grasses. Birds skimmed the bushes of the headland and flickered among the trees of the crest, and the uneasy memory of man was gone from the Potter's Field.

'Well, what's your judgement?' asked Brother Richard.

'I think we should do well to sow a winter crop. Deep-plough now, then do a second ploughing, and sow winter wheat, and some beans with it. So much the better if we can get some marl on to it for the second ploughing.'

'As good a use as any,' agreed Richard contentedly, and led the way down the slope towards the curve and glimmer of the river under its miniature cliffs of sand. Cadfael followed, the dry grasses rustling round his ankles in long, rhythmic sighs, as if for a tragedy remembered. As well, he thought, break the ground up there as soon as maybe, and get the soil to bear. Let's have young corn greening over where the kiln was, and either pull down the cottage or put a live tenant into it, and see to it he clears and tends the garden. Either that, or plough up all. Better forget it ever was a potter's croft and field.

In the first days of October the abbey's plough team of six oxen, with the heavy, high-wheeled plough, was brought over by the ford, and cut and turned the first sod in Ruald's field. They began at the upper corner, close to the derelict cottage, and drove the first furrow along beneath the ridge, under the strong growth of bushes and brambles that formed the head-land. The ox-driver urged his team, the oxen lumbered stolidly ahead, the coulter bit deep through turf and soil, the ploughshare sheared through the matted roots, and the furrow-board heaved the sod widely away like a sullenly breaking wave, turning up black soil and the strong scent of the earth. Brother Richard and Brother Cadfael had come to see the work begun, Abbot Radulfus had blessed the plough, and every augury was good. The first straight furrow drove

15

the length of the field, brightly black against the autumnal pallor of the grasses, and the ploughman, proud of his skill, swung his long team in a swooping curve to bring them about as neatly as possible on the return course. Richard had been right, the soil was not so heavy, the work would go briskly.

Cadfael had turned his back on the work, and stood in the gaping doorway of the cottage, gazing into the empty interior. A full year ago, after the woman had shaken off the dust of this place from her feet and walked away from the debris of her life to look for a new beginning elsewhere, all the movable belongings of Ruald's marriage had been removed, with the consent of his overlord at Longner, and given to Brother Ambrose the almoner, to be shared among his petitioners according to their needs. Nothing remained within. The hearthstone was still soiled with the last cold ashes, and leaves had been blown into corners and silted there into nesting-places for the hibernating hedge-pig and the dormouse. Long coils of bramble had found their way in at the vacant window from the bushes outside, and a branch of hawthorn nodded in over his shoulder, half its leaves shed, but starred with red berries. Nettle and groundsel had rooted and grown in the crevices of the flooring. It takes a very short time for earth to seal over the traces of humankind.

He heard the distant shout from across the field, but thought nothing of it but that the driver was bawling at his team, until Richard caught at his sleeve and said sharply into his ear: 'Something's amiss, over there! Look, they've stopped. They've turned up something – or broken something – Oh, surely not the coulter!' He had flashed easily into vexation. A plough is a costly machine, and an iron-shod coulter on new and untried ground might well be vulnerable.

Cadfael turned to stare towards the spot where the team

16

had halted, at the far edge of the field where the tangle of bushes rose. They had taken the plough close, making the fullest use possible of the ground, and now the oxen stood still and patient in their harness, only a few yards advanced into the new furrow, while teamster and ploughman were stooped with their heads together over something in the ground. And in a moment the ploughman came springing to his feet and running headlong for the cottage, arms pumping, feet stumbling in the tufted grasses.

'Brother . . . Brother Cadfael . . . Will you come? Come and see! There's something there . . .'

Richard had opened his mouth to question, in some irritation at so incoherent a summons, but Cadfael had taken a look at the ploughman's face, startled and disquieted, and was off across the field at a trot. For clearly this something, whatever it might be, was as unwelcome as it was unforeseen, and of a nature for which higher authority would have to take the responsibility. The ploughman ran beside him, blurting distracted words that failed to shed much light.

'The coulter dragged it up – there's more underground, no telling what . . .'

The teamster had risen to his feet and stood waiting for them with hands dangling helplessly.

'Brother, we could take no charge here, there's no knowing what we've come on.' He had led the team a little forward to leave the place clear and show what had so strangely interrupted the work. Close under the slight slope of the bank which marked the margin of the field, with broom bushes leaning over the curve of the furrow, where the plough had turned, the coulter had cut in more deeply, and dragged along the furrow after it something that was not root or stem. Cadfael went on his knees, and stooped close to see the better.

17

Brother Richard, shaken at last by the consternation that had rendered his fellows inarticulate and now chilled them into silence, stood back and watched warily, as Cadfael drew a hand along the furrow, touching the long threads that had entangled the coulter and been drawn upward into the light of day.

Fibres, but fashioned by man. Not the sinewy threads of roots gouged out of the bank, but half-rotted strands of cloth, once black, or the common dark brown, now the colour of the earth, but still with enough nature left in them to tear in long, frayed rags when the iron ripped through the folds from which they came. And something more, drawn out with them, perhaps from within them, and lying along the furrow for almost the length of a man's forearm, black and wavy and fine, a long thick tress of dark hair.

Chapter Two

ROTHER CADFAEL returned alone to the abbey, and asked immediate audience of Abbot Radulfus.

'Father, something unforeseen sends me back to you in this haste. I would not have troubled you for less, but in the Potter's Field the plough has uncovered something which must be of concern both to this house and to the secular law. I have not yet gone further. I need your sanction to report this also to Hugh Beringar, and if he so permits, to pursue what as yet I have left as we found it. Father, the coulter has brought into daylight rags of cloth and a coil of human hair. A woman's hair, or so it seems to me. It is long and fine, I think it has never been cut. And, Father, it is held fast under the earth.'

'You are telling me,' said Radulfus, after a long and pregnant pause, 'that it is still rooted in a human head.' His voice was level and firm. There were few improbable situations he had not encountered in his more than fifty years. If this was the first of its kind, it was by no means the gravest he had ever confronted. The monastic enclave is still contained and contingent upon a world where all things are possible. 'In this unconsecrated place there is some human creature buried. Unlawfully.'

19

'That is what I fear,' said Cadfael. 'But we have not gone on to confirm it, wanting your leave and the sheriff's attendance.'

'Then what have you done? How have you left things there in the field?'

'Brother Richard is keeping watch at the place. The ploughing continues, but with due care, and away from that spot. There seemed no need,' he said reasonably, 'to delay it. Nor would we want to call too much attention to what is happening there. The ploughing accounts for our presence, no one need wonder at seeing us busy there. And even if it proves true, this may be old, very old, long before our time.'

'True,' said the abbot, his eyes very shrewd upon Cadfael's face, 'though I think you do not believe in any such grace. To the best that I know from record and charter, there never at any time was church or churchyard near that place. I pray God there may be no more such discoveries to be made, one is more than enough. Well, you have my authority, do what needs to be done.'

What needed to be done, Cadfael did. The first priority was to alert Hugh, and ensure that the secular authority should be witness to whatever followed. Hugh knew his friend well enough to cast no doubts, ask no questions, and waste no time in demur, but at once had horses saddled up, taking one sergeant of the garrison with him to ride messenger should he be needed, and set off with Cadfael for the ford of Severn and the Potter's Field.

The plough team was still at work, lower down the slope, when they rode along the headland to the spot where Brother Richard waited by the bank of broom bushes. The long, attenuated, sinuous S-shapes of the furrows shone richly dark against the thick, matted pallor of the meadow. Only this corner under the headland had been left virgin, the plough drawn well aside after the first ominous turn. The scar the coulter had left ended abruptly, the long, dark filaments drawn along the gr ove. Hugh stooped to look, and to touch. The threads of cloth disintegrated under his fingers, the long strands of hair curled and clung. When he lifted them tentatively they slid through his hold, still rooted in earth. He stood back, and stared down sombrely into the deep scar.

'Whatever you've found here, we'd best have it out. Your ploughman was a little too greedy for land, it seems. He could have spared us trouble if he'd turned his team a few yards short of the rise.'

But it was already too late, the thing was done and could not be covered again and forgotten. They had brought spades with them, a mattock to peel off, with care, the matted root-felt of long undisturbed growth, and a sickle to cut back the overhanging broom that hampered their movements and had partially hidden this secret burial place. Within a quarter of an hour it became plain that the shape beneath had indeed the length of a grave, for the rotted shreds of cloth appeared here and there in alignment with the foot of the bank, and Cadfael abandoned the spade to kneel and scoop away earth with his hands. It was not even a deep grave, rather this swathed bundle had been laid in concealment under the slope, and the thick sod restored over it, and the bushes left to veil the place. Deep enough to rest undisturbed, in such a spot; a less efficient plough would not have turned so tightly as to reach it, nor the coulter have driven deep enough to penetrate it.

Cadfael felt along the exposed swathes of black cloth, and knew the bones within. The long tear the coulter had made slit the side distant from the bank from middle to head, where it had dragged out with the threads the tress of hair. He brushed away soil from where the face should be. Head to foot, the body was swathed in rotting woollen cloth, cloak or brychan, but there was no longer any doubt that it was a human creature, here laid underground in secret. Unlawfully, Radulfus had said. Buried unlawfully, dead unlawfully.

With their hands they scooped away patiently the soil that shrouded the unmistakable outline of humanity, worked their way cautiously beneath it from either side, to ease it out of its bed, and hoisted it from the grave to lay it upon the grass. Light, slender and fragile it rose into light, to be handled with held breath and careful touch, for at every friction the woollen threads crumbled and disintegrated. Cadfael eased the folds apart, and turned back the cloth to lay bare the withered remains.

Certainly a woman, for she wore a long, dark gown, ungirdled, unornamented, and strangely it seemed that the fullness of the skirt had been drawn out carefully into orderly folds, still preserved by the brychan in which she had been swathed for burial. The face was skeletal, the hands that emerged from the long sleeves were mere bone, but held in shape by her wrappings. Traces of dried and shrunken flesh showed at the wrists and at her bared ankles. The one last recollection of abundant life left to her was the great crown of black, braided hair, from which the one disordered coil had been drawn out by the coulter from beside her right temple. Strangely, she had clearly been stretched out decently for burial, her hands drawn up and crossed on her breast. More strangely still they were clasped upon a crude cross, made from two trimmed sticks bound together with a strip of linen cloth.

Cadfael drew the edges of the rotting cloth carefully back

22

over the skull, from which the dark hair burgeoned in such strange profusion. With the death's-head face covered she became even more awe-inspiring, and they drew a little back from her, all four, staring down in detached wonder, for in the face of such composed and austere death, pity and horror seemed equally irrelevant. They did not even feel any will to question, or admit to notice, what was strange about her burial, not yet; the time for that would come, but not now, not here. First, without comment or wonder, what was needful must be completed.

'Well,' said Hugh drily, 'what now? Does this fall within my writ, Brothers, or yours?'

Brother Richard, somewhat greyer in the face than normally, said doubtfully: 'We are on abbey land. But this is hardly in accordance with law, and law is your province. I don't know what the lord abbot will wish, in so strange a case.'

'He will want her brought back to the abbey,' said Cadfael with certainty. 'Whoever she may be, however long buried unblessed, it's a soul to be salved, and Christian burial is her due. We shall be bringing her from abbey land, and to abbey land he'll want her returned. When,' said Cadfael with deliberation, 'she has received what else is her due, if that can ever be determined.'

'It can at least be attempted,' said Hugh, and cast a considering glance along the bank of broom bushes and round the gaping pit they had cut through the turf. 'I wonder is there anything more to be found here, put in the ground with her. Let's at least clear a little further and deeper, and see.' He stooped to draw the disintegrating brychan again round the body, and his very touch parted threads and sent motes of dust floating into the air. 'We shall need a better shroud if

23

we're to carry her back with us, and a litter if she's to be carried whole and at rest, as we see her. Richard, take my horse and ride back to the lord abbot, tell him simply that we have indeed found a body buried here, and send us litter and decent covering to get her home. No need for more, not yet. What more do we know? Leave any further report until we come.'

'I will so!' agreed Brother Richard, so warmly that his relief was plain. His easy-going nature was not made for such discoveries, his preference was for an orderly life in which all things behaved as they should, and spared him too much exertion of body or mind. He made off with alacrity to where Hugh's raw-boned grey stood peacefully cropping the greener turf under the headland, heaved a sturdy foot into the stirrup, and mounted. There was nothing the matter with his horsemanship but recent lack of practice. He was a younger son from a knightly family, and had made the choice between service in arms and service in the cloister at only sixteen. Hugh's horse, intolerant of most riders except his master, condescended to carry this one along the headland and down into the water-meadow without resentment.

'Though he may spill him at the ford,' Hugh allowed, watching them recede towards the river, 'if the mood takes him. Well, let's see what's left us to find here.'

The sergeant was cutting back deeply into the bank, under the rustling broom bushes. Cadfael turned from the dead to descend with kilted habit into her grave, and cautiously began to shovel out the loose loam and deepen the hollow where she had lain.

'Nothing,' he said at last, on his knees upon a floor now packed hard and changing to a paler colour, the subsoil revealing a layer of clay. 'You see this? Lower, by the river,

Ruald had two or three spots where he got his clay. Worked out now, they said, at least where they were easy to reach. This has not been disturbed, in longer time than she has lain here. We need go no deeper, there is nothing to find. We'll sift around the sides a while, but I doubt not this is all.'

'More than enough,' said Hugh, scouring his soiled hands in the thick, fibrous turf. 'And not enough. All too little to give her an age or a name.'

'Or a kinship or a home, living,' Cadfael agreed sombrely, 'or a reason for dying. We can do no more here. I have seen what there is to be seen of how she was laid. What remains to be done can better be done in privacy, with time to spare, and trusted witnesses.'

It was an hour more before Brother Winfrid and Brother Urien came striding along the headland with their burden of brychans and litter. Carefully they lifted the slender bundle of bones, folded the rugs round them and covered them decently from sight. Hugh's sergeant was dismissed, back to the garrison at the castle. In silence and on foot the insignificant funeral cortège of the unknown set off for the abbey.

'It is a woman,' said Cadfael, reporting in due course to Abbot Radulfus in the privacy of the abbot's parlour. 'We have bestowed her in the mortuary chapel. I doubt if there is anything about her that can ever be recognised by any man, even if her death is recent, which I take to be unlikely. The gown is such as any cottage wife might wear, without ornament, without girdle, once the common black, now drab. She wears no shoes, no jewellery, nothing to give her a name.'

'Her face . . .?' wondered the abbot, but dubiously, expecting nothing.

'Father, her face is now the common image. There is nothing

25

left to move a man to say: This is wife, or sister, or any woman ever I knew. Nothing, except, perhaps, that she had a wealth of dark hair. But so have many women. She is of moderate height for a woman. Her age we can but guess, and that very roughly. Surely by her hair she was not old, but I think she was no young girl, either. A woman in her prime, but between five-and-twenty and forty who can tell?'

'Then there is nothing singular about her at all? Nothing to mark her out?' said Radulfus.

'There is the manner of her burial,' said Hugh. 'Without mourning, without rites, put away unlawfully in unconsecrated ground. And yet – Cadfael will tell you. Or if you so choose, Father, you may see for yourself, for we have left her lying as we found her.'

'I begin to see,' said Radulfus with deliberation, 'that I must indeed view this dead woman for myself. But since so much has been said, you may tell me what it is that outdoes in strangeness the circumstances of her secret burial. And yet . . .?'

'And yet, Father, she was laid out straight and seemly, her hair braided, her hands folded on her breast, over a cross banded together from two sticks from a hedgerow or a bush. Whoever put her into the ground did so with some show of reverence.'

'The worst of men, so doing, might feel some awe,' said Radulfus slowly, frowning over this evidence of a mind torn two ways. 'But it was a deed done in the dark, secretly. It implies a worse deed, also done in the dark. If her death was natural, without implication of guilt to any man, why no priest, no rites of burial? You have not so far argued, Cadfael, that this poor creature was killed as unlawfully as she was buried, but I do so argue. What other reason can there be for laying her underground in secrecy, and unblessed? And even the cross her grave-digger gave her, it seems, was cut from hedgerow twigs, never to be known as any man's property, to point a finger at the murderer! For from what you say, everything that might have given her back her identity was removed from her body, to keep a secret a secret still, even now that the plough has brought her back to light and to the possibility of grace.'

'It does indeed seem so,' Hugh said gravely, 'but for the fact that Cadfael finds no mark of injury upon her, no bone broken, nothing to show how she died. After so long in the ground, a stroke from dagger or knife might escape finding, but we've seen no sign of such. Her neck is not broken, nor her skull. Cadfael does not think she was strangled. It is as if she had died in her bed – even in her sleep. But no one would then have buried her by stealth and hidden everything that marked her out from all other women.'

'No, true! No one would so imperil his own soul but for desperate reasons.' The abbot brooded some moments in silence, considering the problem which had fallen into his hands thus strangely. Easy enough to do right to the wronged dead, as due to her immortal soul. Even without a name prayers could be said for her and Mass sung; and the Christian burial once denied her, and the Christian grave, these could be given at last. But the justice of this world also clamoured for recognition. He looked up at Hugh, one office measuring the other. 'What do you say, Hugh? Was this a murdered woman?'

'In the face of what little we know, and of the much more we do not know,' said Hugh carefully, 'I dare not assume that she is anything else. She is dead, she was thrust into the ground unshriven. Until I see reason for believing better of the deed, I view this as murder.'

'It is clear to me, then,' said Radulfus, after a moment's measuring silence, 'that you do not believe she has been long in her grave. This is no infamy from long before our time, or nothing need concern us but the proper amendment of what was done wrong to her soul. The justice of God can reach through centuries, and wait its time for centuries, but ours is helpless outside our own generation. How long do you judge has passed since she died?'

'I can but hazard, and with humility,' said Cadfael. 'It may have been no more than a year, it may have been three or four, even five years, but no more than that. She is no victim from old times. She lived and breathed only a short time ago.'

'And I cannot escape her,' said Hugh wryly.

'No. No more than I can.' The abbot flattened his long, sinewy hands abruptly on his desk, and rose. 'The more reason I must see her face to face, and acknowledge my duty towards her. Come let's go and look at our demanding guest. I owe her that, before we again commit her to the earth, with better auguries this time. Who knows, there may be something, some small thing, to call the living woman to mind, for someone who once knew her.'

It seemed to Cadfael, as he followed his superior out across the great court and in at the southern porch to the cloister and the church, that there was something unnatural in the way they were all avoiding one name. It had not yet been spoken, and he could not choose but wonder who would be the first to utter it, and why he himself had not already precipitated the inevitable. It could not go unspoken for much longer. But in the meantime, as well the abbot should be the first to assay. Death, whether old or new, could not disconcert him.

In the small, chilly mortuary chapel candles burned at head and foot of the stone bier, on which the nameless woman was laid, with a linen sheet stretched over her. They had disturbed her bones as little as possible in examining the remains for some clue to the means of her death, and composed them again as exactly as they could when that fruitless inspection was over. So far as Cadfael could determine, there was no mark of any injury upon her. The odour of earth clung heavy about her in the enclosed space, but the cold of stone tempered it, and the composure and propriety of her repose overcame the daunting presence of old death, thus summarily exposed again to light, and the intrusion of eyes.

Abbot Radulfus approached her without hesitation, and drew back the linen that covered her, folding it practically over his arm. He stood for some minutes surveying the remains narrowly, from the dark, luxuriant hair to the slender, naked bones of the feet, which surely the small secret inhabitants of the headland had helped to bare. At the stark white bone of her face he looked longest, but found nothing there to single her out from all the long generations of her dead sisters.

'Yes. Strange!' he said, half to himself. 'Someone surely felt tenderness towards her, and respected her rights, if he felt he dared not provide them. One man to kill, perhaps, and another to bury? A priest, do you suppose? But why cover up her death, if he had no guilt in it? Is it possible the same man both killed and buried her?'

'Such things have been known,' said Cadfael.

'A lover, perhaps? Some fatal mischance, never intended? A moment of violence, instantly regretted? But no, there would be no need to conceal, if that were all.'

'And there is no trace of violence,' said Cadfael.

'Then how did she die? Not from illness, or she would have been in the churchyard, shriven and hallowed. How else? By poison?'

29

'That is possible. Or a stab wound that reached her heart may have left no trace now in her bones, for they are whole and straight, never deformed by blow or fracture.'

Radulfus replaced the linen cloth, smoothing it tidily over her. 'Well, I see there is little here a man could match with a living face or a name. Yet I think even that must be tried. If she has been here, living, within the past five years, then someone has known her well, and will know when last she was seen, and have marked her absence afterwards. Come,' said the abbot, 'let us go back and consider carefully all the possibilities that come to mind.'

It was plain to Cadfael then that the first and most ominous possibility had already come to the abbot's mind, and brought deep disquiet with it. Once they were all three back in the quiet of the parlour, and the door shut against the world, the name must be spoken.

'Two questions wait to be answered,' said Hugh, taking the initiative. 'Who is she? And if that cannot be answered with certainty, then who may she be? And the second: Has any woman vanished from these parts during these last few years, without word or trace?'

'Of one such,' said the abbot heavily, 'we certainly know. And the place itself is all too apt. Yet no one has ever questioned that she went away, and of her own choice. That was a hard case for me to accept, as the wife never accepted it. Yet Brother Ruald could no more be barred from following his soul's bent than the sun from rising. Once I was sure of him, I had no choice. To my grief, the woman never was reconciled.'

So now the man's name had been spoken. Perhaps no one even recalled the woman's. Many within the walls could never have set eyes on her, or heard mention of her until her husband had his visitation and came to stand patiently at the gates and demand entry.

'I must ask your leave,' said Hugh, 'to have him view this body. Even if she is indeed his wife, truly he may not be able to say so now with any certainty, yet it must be asked of him that he make the assay. The field was theirs, the croft there was her home after he left it.' He was silent for a long moment, steadily eyeing the abbot's closed and brooding face. 'After Ruald entered here, until the time when she is said to have gone away with another man, was he ever at any time sent back there? There were belongings he gave over to her, there could be agreements to be made, even witnessed. Is he known to have met with her, after they first parted?'

'Yes,' said Radulfus at once. 'Twice in the first days of his novitiate he did visit her, but in company with Brother Paul. As master of the novices Paul was anxious for the man's peace of mind, no less than for the woman's, and tried his best to bring her to acknowledge and bless Ruald's vocation. Vainly! But with Paul he went, and with Paul he returned. I know of no other occasion when he could have seen or spoken with her.'

'Nor ever went out to field work or any other errand close to that field?'

'It is more than a year,' said the abbot reasonably. 'Even Paul would be hard put to it to say where Ruald served in all that time. Commonly, during his novitiate he would always be in company with at least one other brother, probably more, whenever he was sent out from the enclave to work. But doubtless,' he said, returning Hugh's look no less fixedly, 'you mean to ask the man himself.'

'With your leave, Father, yes.'

'And now, at once?'

'If you permit, yes. It will not yet be common knowledge what we have found. Best he should be taken clean, with no

31

warning, and knowing no need for deception. In his own defence,' said Hugh emphatically, 'should he later find himself in need of defence.'

'I will send for him,' said Radulfus. 'Cadfael, will you find him, and perhaps, if the sheriff sees fit, bring him straight to the chapel? As you say, let him come to the proof in innocence, for his own sake. And now I remember,' said the abbot, 'a thing he himself said when first this exchange of land was mooted. Earth is innocent, he said. Only the use we make of it mars it.'

Brother Ruald was the perfect example of obedience, the aspect of the Rule which had always given Cadfael the most trouble. He had taken to heart the duty to obey instantly any order given by a superior as if it were a divine command, 'without half-heartedness or grumbling', and certainly without demanding 'Why?' which was Cadfael's first instinct, tamed now but not forgotten. Bidden by Cadfael, his elder and senior in vocation, Ruald followed him unquestioning to the mortuary chapel, knowing no more of what awaited him than that abbot and sheriff together desired his attendance.

Even on the threshold of the chapel, suddenly confronted by the shape on the bier, the candles, and Hugh and Radulfus conferring quietly on the far side of the stone slab, Ruald did not hesitate, but advanced and stood awaiting what should be required of him, utterly docile and perfectly serene.

'You sent for me, Father.'

'You are a man of these parts,' said the abbot, 'and until recently well acquainted with all of your neighbours. You may be able to help us. We have here, as you see, a body found by chance, and none of us here can by any sign set a name to the dead. Try if you can do better. Come closer.'

Ruald obeyed, and stood faithfully staring upon the shrouded shape as Radulfus drew away the linen in one sharp motion, and disclosed the rigidly ordered bones and the flesh-less face in its coils of dark hair. Certainly Ruald's tranquillity shook at the unexpected sight, but the waves of pity, alarm and distress that passed over his face were no more than ripples briefly stirring a calm pool, and he did not turn away his eyes, but continued earnestly viewing her from head to foot, and again back to the face, as if by long gazing he could build up afresh in his mind's eye the flesh which had once clothed the naked bone. When at last he looked up at the abbot it was in mild wonder and resigned sadness.

'Father, there is nothing here that any man could recognise and name.'

'Look again,' said Radulfus. 'There is a shape, a height, colouring. This was a woman, someone must once have been near to her, perhaps a husband. There are means of recognition, sometimes, not dependent on the features of a face. Is there nothing about her that stirs any memory?'

There was a long silence while Ruald in duty repeated his careful scrutiny of every rag that clothed her, the folded hands still clasping the improvised cross. Then he said, with a sorrow rather at disappointing the abbot than over a distant death: 'No, Father. I am sorry. There is nothing. Is it so grave a matter? All names are known to God.'

'True,' said Radulfus, 'as God knows where all the dead are laid, even those hidden away secretly. I must tell you, Brother Ruald, where this woman was found. You know the ploughing of the Potter's Field was to begin this morning. At the turn of the first furrow, under the headland and partly screened by bushes, the abbey plough team turned up a rag of woollen cloth and a lock of dark hair. Out of the field that

33

once was yours, the lord sheriff has disinterred and brought home here this dead woman. Now, before I cover her, look yet again, and say if there is nothing cries out to you what her name should be.'

It seemed to Cadfael, watching Ruald's sharp profile, that only at this moment was its composure shaken by a tremor of genuine horror, even of guilt, though guilt without fear, surely not for a physical death, but for the death of an affection on which he had turned his back without ever casting a glance behind. He stooped closer over the dead woman, staring intently, and a fine dew of sweat broke out on his forehead and lip. The candlelight caught its sheen. This final silence lasted for long moments, before he looked up pale and quivering, into the abbot's face.

'Father, God forgive me a sin I never understood until now. I do repent what now I find a terrible lack in me. There is nothing, nothing cries out to me. I feel nothing in beholding her. Father, even if this were indeed Generys, my wife Generys, I should not know her.'

Chapter Three

I N THE ABBOT'S parlour, some twenty minutes later, he had regained his calm, the calm of resignation even to his own shortcomings and failures, but he did not cease to accuse himself.

'In my own need I was armed against hers. What manner of man can sever an affection half a lifetime long, and within the year feel nothing? I am ashamed that I could stand by that bier and look upon the relics of a woman, and be forced to say: I cannot tell. It may be Generys, for all I know. I cannot see why it should, or how it could so happen, but nor can I say: It is not so. Nothing moved in me from the heart. And for the eyes and the mind, what is there now in those bones to speak to any man?'

'Except,' said the abbot austerely, 'inasmuch as it speaks to all men. She was buried in unconsecrated ground, without rites, secretly. It is but a short step to the conclusion that she came by her death in a way equally secret and unblessed, at the hands of man. She requires of me due if belated provision for her soul, and from the world justice for her death. You have testified, and I believe it, that you cannot say who she is. But since she was found on land once in your possession, by the croft from which your wife departed, and to which she has

35

never returned, it is natural that the sheriff should have questions to ask you. As he may well have questions to ask of many others, before this matter is resolved.'

'That I do acknowledge,' said Ruald meekly, 'and I will answer whatever may be put to me. Willingly and truthfully.'

And so he did, even with sorrowful eagerness, as if he wished to flagellate himself for his newly realised failings towards his wife, in rejoicing in his own fulfilment while she tasted only the poison of bitterness and deprivation.

'It was right that I should go where I was summoned, and do what it was laid on me to do. But that I should embrace my joy and wholly forget her wretchedness, that was ill done. Now the day is come when I cannot even recall her face, or the way she moved, only the disquiet she has left with me, too long unregarded, now come home in full. Wherever she may be, she has her requital. These six months past,' he said grievously, 'I have not even prayed for her peace. She has been clean gone out of mind, because I was happy.'

'You visited her twice, I understand,' said Hugh, 'after you were received here as a postulant.'

'I did, with Brother Paul, as he will tell you. I had goods which Father Abbot allowed me to give over to her, for her living. It was done lawfully. That was the first occasion.'

'And when was that?'

'The twenty-eighth day of May, of last year. And again we went there to the croft in the first days of June, after I had made up the sum I had from selling my wheel and tools and what was left of use about the croft. I had hoped that she might have become reconciled, and would give me her forgiveness and goodwill, but it was not so. She had contended with me all those weeks to keep me at her side as before. But that day she turned upon me with hatred and anger, scorned to touch any part of what was mine, and cried out at me that I might go, for she had a lover worth the loving, and every tenderness ever she had had for me was turned to gall.'

'She told you that?' said Hugh sharply. 'That she had another lover? I know that was the gossip, when she left the cottage and went away secretly. But you had it from her own lips?'

'Yes, she said so. She was bitter that after she had failed to keep me at her side, neither could she now be rid of me and free in the world's eyes, for still I was her husband, a millstone about her neck, and she could not slough me off. But that should not prevent, she said, but she would take her freedom by force, for she had a lover, a hundred times my worth, and she would go with him, if he beckoned, to the ends of the earth. Brother Paul was witness to all,' said Ruald simply. 'He will tell you.'

'And that was the last time you saw her?'

'That was the last time. By the end of that month of June she was gone.'

'And since that time, have you ever been back to that field?'

'No. I have worked on abbey land, in the Gaye for the most part, but that field has only now become abbey land. Early in October, a year ago now, it was given to Haughmond. Eudo Blount of Longner, who was my overlord, made the gift to them. I never thought to see or hear of the place again.'

'Or of Generys?' Cadfael interjected mildly, and watched the lines of Ruald's thin face tighten in a brief spasm of pain and shame. And even these he would endure faithfully, mitigated and rendered bearable by the assurance of joy that now never deserted him. 'I have a question to ask,' said Cadfael, 'if Father Abbot permits. In all the years you spent with her, had you ever cause to complain of your wife's loyalty and fidelity, or the love she bore to you?'

Without hesitation Ruald said: 'No! She was always true and fond. Almost too fond! I doubt I ever could match her devotion. I brought her out of her own land,' said Ruald, setting truth before his own eyes and scarcely regarding those who overheard, 'into a country strange to her, where her tongue was alien and her ways little understood. Only now do I see how much more she gave me than I ever had it in me to repay.'

It was early evening, almost time for Vespers, when Hugh reclaimed the horse Brother Richard had considerately stabled, and rode out from the gatehouse into the Foregate, and for a moment hesitated whether to turn left, and make for his own house in the town, or right, and continue the pursuit of truth well into the dusk. A faint blue vapour was already rising over the river, and the sky was heavily veiled, but there was an hour or more of light left, time enough to ride to Longner and back and have a word with young Eudo Blount. Doubtful if he had paid any attention to the Potter's Field since it was deeded away to Haughmond, but at least his manor lay close to it, over the crest and in among the woodlands of his demesne, and someone among his people might almost daily have to pass that way. It was worth an enquiry.

He made for the ford, leaving the highway by the hospital of Saint Giles, and took the field path along the waterside, leaving the partially ploughed slope high on his left-hand side. Beyond the headland that bordered the new ploughland a gentle slope of woodland began above the water meadows, and in a cleared space within this belt of trees the manor of Longner stood, well clear of any flooding. The low undercroft was cut back into the slope, and stone steps led steeply up to the hall door of the living floor above. A groom was crossing the yard from the stable as Hugh rode in at the open gateway, and came blithely to take his bridle and ask his business with the master.

Eudo Blount had heard the voices below, and came out to his hall door to see who his visitor might be. He was already well acquainted with the sheriff of the shire, and greeted him warmly, for he was a young man cheerful and open by nature, a year established now in his lordship, and comfortable in his relationship with his own people and the ordered world around him. The burial of his father, seven months past now, and the heroic manner of his death, though a grief, had also served to ground and fortify the mutual trust and respect the new young lord enjoyed with his tenants and servants. The simplest villein holding a patch of Blount land felt a share in the pride due to Martel's chosen few who had covered the king's retreat from Wilton, and died in the battle. Young Eudo was barely twenty-three years old, and inexperienced, untravelled, as firmly bound to this soil as any villein in his holding, a big, comely, fair-skinned fellow with a shock of thick brown hair. The right management of a potentially prosperous manor, somewhat depleted in his grandfather's time, would be an absorbing joy to him, and he would make a good job of it, and leave it to his eventual heir richer than he had inherited it from his father. At this stage, Hugh recalled, this young man was only three months married, and the gloss of fulfilment was new and shiny upon him.

'I'm on an errand that can hardly be good news to you,' said Hugh without preamble, 'though no reason it should cause you any trouble, either. The abbey put in its plough team this morning in the Potter's Field.'

'So I've heard,' said Eudo serenely. 'My man Robin saw them come. I'll be glad to see it productive, though it's no business of mine now.'

'We're none of us overjoyed at the first crop it's produced,' said Hugh bluntly. 'The plough has turned up a body from under the headland. We have a dead woman in the mortuary chapel at the abbey – or her bones, at least.'

The young man had halted in the act of pouring wine for his visitor, so abruptly that the pitcher shook and spilled red over his hand. He turned upon Hugh round, blue, astonished eyes, and stared open-mouthed.

'A dead woman? What, buried there? Bones, you say – how long dead then? And who can it be?'

'Who's to know that? Bones is all we have, but a woman it is. Or was once. Dead perhaps as long as five years, so I'm advised, but no longer, and perhaps much less. Have you ever seen strangers there, or anything happening to make a man take notice? I know you had no need to keep a watch on the place, it has been Haughmond's business for the past year, but since it's so close, some of your men may have noted if there were intruders about. You've no inkling of anything untoward?'

Eudo shook his head vehemently. 'I haven't been up there since my father, God rest him, gave the field to the priory. They tell me there have been vagabonds lying up there in the cottage now and then, during the fair, or overnight last winter if they were travelling, but who or what I don't know. There was no harm ever reported or threatened, that I know of. This comes very strangely to me.'

'To all of us,' Hugh agreed ruefully, and took the offered cup. It was growing dim in the hall, and there was a fire already laid. Outside the open door the light showed faintly

blue with mist, shot through with the faded gold of sunset.
'You never heard of any woman going astray from her home
in these parts, these last few years?'

'No, none. My people live all around, they would have
known, and it would have come to my ears soon enough. Or
to my father's, in his time. He had a good hold on everything
that went on here, they brought everything to him, knowing
he would not willingly let any man of his miscarry.'

'I know that for truth,' said Hugh heartily. 'But you'll not
have forgotten, there was one woman who walked out of her
house and went away without a word. And from that very
croft.'

Eudo was staring at him again in open disbelief, great-eyed,
even breaking into a broad grin at the very idea. 'Ruald's
woman? You can't mean it! Everyone knew about her going,
that was no secret. And do you truly mean it could be so
recent? But even if it could, and this poor wench bones
already, that's folly! Generys took herself off with another
man, and small blame to her, when she found that if he was
free to follow his bent, she was still bound. We would have
seen to it that she would not want, but that was not enough for
her. Widows can wed again, but she was no widow. You can't
surely believe, in good earnest, that this is *Generys* you have
in the mortuary?'

'I am at a total loss,' Hugh admitted. 'But the place and the
time and the way they tore themselves apart must make a man
wonder. As yet there are but the few of us know of this, but in
a little while it must out, and then you'll hear what every
tongue will be whispering. Better if you should make enquiry
among your own men for me, see if any of them has noted
furtive things going on about that field, or doubtful fellows
lurking in the cottage. Especially if any had women with them.

41

If we can find some way of putting a name to the woman we shall be a long stride on the way.'

It seemed that Eudo had come to terms with the reality of death by this time, and was taking it seriously, though not as a factor which could or should be allowed to disturb the tenor of his own ordered existence. He sat thoughtfully gazing at Hugh over the wine cups, and considering the widening implications. 'You think this woman was done to death secretly? Could *Ruald* be in any real danger of such a suspicion? I cannot believe ill of him. Certainly I will ask among my fellows, and send you word if I find out anything of note. But had there been anything, surely it would have found its way to me before.'

'Nevertheless, do me that service. A trifle that a man might let slip out of his mind lightly, in the ordinary way, could come to have a weighty meaning once there's a death in the matter. I'll be putting together all I can about Ruald's end of it, and asking questions of many a one besides. He has seen what we found,' said Hugh sombrely, 'and could not say yes or no to her, and no blame to him, for it would be hard indeed for any man, if he lived with her many years, to recognise her face now.'

'He cannot have harmed his wife,' Eudo avowed sturdily. 'He was already in the cloister, had been for three or four weeks, maybe more, while she was still there in the croft, before she went away. This is some other poor soul who fell foul of footpads, or some such scum, and was knifed or stabbed to death for the clothes she wore.'

'Hardly that,' said Hugh wryly. 'She was clothed decently, laid out straight, and her hands folded on her breast over a little rough cross, cut from a hedge. As for the manner of her death, there's no mark on her, no bone broken. There *may*

42

have been a knife. Who's to tell, now? But she was buried with some care and respect. That's the strangeness of it.'

Eudo shook his head, frowning, over this growing wonder. 'As a priest might?' he hazarded doubtfully. 'If he found her dead? But then he would have cried it aloud, and had her taken to church, surely.'

'There are some,' said Hugh, 'will soon be saying, "As a husband might," if they were in bitter contention, and she drove him to violence first, and remorse afterwards. No, no need to fret yet for Ruald, he has been in the company of a host of brothers since before his wife was last seen whole and well. We'll be patching together from their witness all his comings and goings since he entered his novitiate. And going back over the past few years in search of other women gone astray.' He rose, eyeing the gathering dusk outside the door. 'I'd best be getting back. I've taken too much of your time.'

Eudo rose with him, willing and earnest. 'No, you did right to look this way first. And I'll ask among my men, be sure. I still feel sometimes as though that field is my ground. You don't let go of land, even to the Church, without feeling you've left stray roots in it. I think I've stayed away from it to avoid despite, that it was left waste. I was glad to hear of the exchange, I knew the abbey would make better use of it. To tell the truth, I was surprised when my father made up his mind to give it to Haughmond, seeing the trouble they'd have turning it to account.' He had followed Hugh towards the outer door, to see his guest out and mounted, when he halted suddenly, and looked back at the curtained doorway in a corner of the great hall.

'Would you look in for a moment, and say a neighbourly word to my mother, Hugh, while you're here. She can't get out at all now, and has very few visitors. She hasn't been out of the door since my father's burial. If you'd look in for a moment, it would please her.'

'I will, surely,' said Hugh, turning at once.

'But don't tell her anything about this dead woman, it would only upset her, land that was ours so lately, and Ruald being our tenant . . . God knows she has enough to endure, we try to keep the world's ill news away from her, all the more when it comes so near home.'

'Not a word!' agreed Hugh. 'How is it with her since I saw her last?'

The young man shook his head. 'Nothing changes. Only day by day she grows a little thinner and paler, but she makes no complaint. You'll see. Go in to her!' His hand was at the curtain, his voice lowered, to be heard only by Hugh. Plainly he was reluctant to go in with the guest, his vigorous youth was uneasy and helpless in the presence of illness, he could be excused for turning his eyes away. As soon as he opened the door of the solar and spoke to the woman within, his voice became unnaturally gentle and constrained, as to a stranger difficult to approach, but to whom he owed affection. 'Mother, here's Hugh Beringar paying us a visit.'

Hugh passed by him, and entered a small room, warmed by a little charcoal brazier set on a flat slab of stone, and lit by a torch in a sconce on the wall. Close under the light the dowager lady of Longner sat on a bench against the wall, propped erect with rugs and cushions, and in her stillness and composure dominating the room. She was past forty-five and long, debilitating illness had aged her into a greyness and emaciation beyond her years. She had a distaff set up before her, and was twisting the wool with a hand that looked frail as a withered leaf, but was patient and competent as it teased out and twirled the strands. She looked up, at Hugh's entrance, with a startled smile, and let down the spindle to rest against the foot of the bench.

'Why, my lord, how good of you! It's a long time since I saw you last.' That had been at her husband's funeral, seven months past now. She gave him her hand, light as a windflower in his, and as cold when he kissed it. Her eyes, which were huge and dusky blue, and sunk deeply into her head, looked him over with measured and shrewd intelligence. 'Your office becomes you,' she said. 'You look well on responsibility. I am not so vain as to think you made the journey here to see me, when you have such weighty burdens on your time. Had you business with Eudo? Whatever brought you, a glimpse of you is very welcome.'

'They keep me busy,' he said, with considered reserve. 'Yes, I had business of a sort with Eudo. Nothing that need trouble you. And I must not stay to tire you too long, and with you I won't talk business. How are you? And is there anything you need, or any way I can serve you?'

'All my needs are met before I can even ask,' said Donata. 'Eudo is a good soul, and I'm lucky in the daughter he's brought me. I have no complaints. Did you know the girl is already pregnant? And sturdy and wholesome as good bread, sure to get sons. Eudo has done well for himself. Perhaps I do miss the outside world now and then. My son is wholly taken up with making his manor worth a little more every harvest, especially now he looks forward to a son of his own. When my lord was alive, he looked beyond his own lands. I got to hear of every move up or down in the king's fortunes. The wind blew from wherever Stephen was. Now I labour behind the times. What *is* going on in the world outside?'

She did not sound to Hugh in need of any protection from the incursions of the outside world, near or far, but he stepped cautiously in consideration of her son's anxieties. 'In our part of it, very little. The Earl of Gloucester is busy turning the south-west into a fortress for the Empress. Both factions are conserving what they have, and for the moment neither side is for fighting. We sit out of the struggle here. Lucky for us!'

'That sounds,' she said, attentive and alert, 'as if you have very different news from elsewhere. Oh, come, Hugh, now you are here you won't deny me a little fresh breeze from beyond the pales of Eudo's fences? He shrouds me in pillows, but you need not.' And indeed it seemed to Hugh that even his unexpected company had brought a little wan colour to her fallen face, and a spark to her sunken eyes.

He admitted wryly: 'There's news enough from elsewhere, a little too much for the king's comfort. At St Albans there's been the devil to pay. Half the lords at court, it seems, accused the Earl of Essex of having traitorous dealings with the Empress yet again, and plotting the king's overthrow, and he's been forced to surrender his constableship of the Tower, and his castle and lands in Essex. That or the gallows, and he's by no means ready to die yet.'

'And he *has* surrendered them? That would go down very bitterly with such a man as Geoffrey de Mandeville,' she said, marvelling. 'My lord never trusted him. An arrogant, over-bearing man, he said. He has turned his coat often enough before, it may very well be true he had plans to turn it yet again. It's well that he was brought to bay in time.'

'So it might have been, but once he was stripped of his lands they turned him loose, and he's made off into his own country and gathered the scum of the region about him. He's sacked Cambridge. Looted everything worth looting, churches and all, before setting light to the city.'

'Cambridge?' said the lady, shocked and incredulous. '*Dare* he attack a city like Cambridge? The king must surely move against him. He cannot be left to pillage and burn as he pleases.'

'It will not be easy,' said Hugh ruefully. 'The man knows the Fen country like the lines of his hand, it's no simple matter to bring him to a pitched battle in such country.'

She leaned to retrieve the spindle as a movement of her foot set it rolling. The hand with which she re-coiled the yarn was languid and translucent, and the eyelids half-lowered over her hollow eyes were marble-white, and veined like the petals of a snowdrop. If she felt pain, she betrayed none, but she moved with infinite care and effort. Her lips had the strong set of reticence and durability.

'My son is there among the fens,' she said quietly. 'My younger son. You'll remember, he chose to take the cowl, in September of last year, and entered Ramsey abbey.'

'Yes, I remember. When he brought back your lord's body for burial, in March, I did wonder if he might have thought better of it by then. I wouldn't have said your Sulien was meant for a monk, from all I'd seen of him he had a good, sound appetite for living in the world. I thought six months of it might have changed his mind for him. But no, he went back, once that duty was done.'

She looked up at him for a moment in silence, the arched lids rolling back from still lustrous eyes. The faintest of smiles touched her lips and again faded. 'I hoped he might stay, once he was home again. But no, he went back. It seems there's no arguing with a vocation.'

It sounded like a muted echo of Ruald's inexorable departure from world and wife and marriage, and it was still ringing in Hugh's ears as he took his leave of Eudo in the darkening courtyard, and mounted and rode thoughtfully home. From

47

Cambridge to Ramsey is barely twenty miles, he was reckoning as he went. Twenty miles, to the north-west, a little further removed from London and the head of Stephen's strength. A little deeper into the almost impenetrable world of the Fens, and with winter approaching. Let a mad wolf like de Mandeville once establish a base, islanded somewhere in those watery wastes, and it will take all Stephen's forces ever to flush him out again.

Brother Cadfael went up to the Potter's Field several times while the ploughing continued, but there were no more such unexpected finds to be made. The ploughman and his ox-herd had proceeded with caution at every turn under the bank, wary of further shocks, but the furrows opened one after another smooth and dark and innocent. The word kept coming to mind. Earth, Ruald had said, is innocent. Only the use we make of it can mar it. Yes, earth and many other things, knowledge, skill, strength, all innocent until use mars them. Cadfael considered in absence, in the cool, autumnal beauty of this great field, sweeping gently down from its ridge of bush and bramble and tree, hemmed on either side by its virgin headlands, the man who had once laboured here many years, and had uttered that vindication of the soil on which he laboured, and from which he dug his clay. Utterly open, decent and of gentle habit, a good workman and an honest citizen, so everyone who knew him would have said. But how well can man ever know his fellow-man? There were already plenty of very different opinions being expressed concerning Ruald, sometime potter, now a Benedictine monk of Shrewsbury. It had not taken long to change their tune.

For the story of the woman found buried in the Potter's Field had soon become common knowledge, and the talk of the district, and where should gossip look first but to the woman who had lived there fifteen years, and vanished without a word to anyone at the end of it? And where for the guilty man but to her husband, who had forsaken her for a cowl?

The woman herself, whoever she might be, was already reburied, by the abbot's grace, in a modest corner of the graveyard, with all the rites due to her but the gift of a name. Parochially, the situation of the whole demesne of Longner was peculiar, for it had belonged earlier to the bishops of Chester, who had bestowed all their local properties, if close enough, as outer and isolated dependencies of the parish of Saint Chad in Shrewsbury. But since no one knew whether this woman was a parishioner or a passing stranger, Radulfus had found it simpler and more hospitable to give her a place in abbey ground, and be done with one problem, at least, of the many she had brought with her.

But if she was finally at rest, no one else was.

'You've made no move to take him in charge,' said Cadfael to Hugh, in the privacy of his workshop in the herb garden, at the close of a long day. 'Nor even to question him hard.'

'No need yet,' said Hugh. 'He's safe enough where he is, if ever I should need him. He'll not move. You've seen for yourself, he accepts all as, at worst, a just punishment laid on him by God – oh, not necessarily for murder, simply for all the faults he finds newly in himself – or at best as a test of his faith and patience. If we all turned on him as guilty he would bear it meekly and with gratitude. Nothing would induce him to avoid. No, rather I'll go on piecing together all his comings and goings since he entered here. If ever it reaches the case where I have cause to suspect him in good earnest, I know where to find him.'

'And as yet you've found no such cause?'

'No more than I had the first day, and no less. And no other woman gone from where she should be. The place, the possible time, the contention between them, the anger, all speak against Ruald, and urge that this was Generys. But Generys was well alive after he was here within the enclave, and I have found no occasion when he could have met with her again, except with Brother Paul, as both have told us. Yet is it impossible that he should, just once, have been on some errand alone, and gone to her, against all orders, for I'm sure Radulfus wanted an end to the bitterness. The frame,' said Hugh, irritated and weary, 'is all too full of Ruald and Generys, and I can find no other to fit into it.'

'But you do not believe it,' Cadfael deduced, and smiled.

'I neither believe nor disbelieve. I go on looking. Ruald will keep. If tongues are wagging busily against him, he's safe within from anything worse. And if they wag unjustly, he may take it as Christian chastisement, and wait patiently for his deliverance.'

Chapter Four

N THE EIGHTH day of October the morning began in a grey drizzle, hardly perceptible on the face, but wetting after a while. The working folk of the Foregate went about their business hooded in sacking, and the young man trudging along the highway past the horsefair ground had his cowl drawn well forward over his forehead, and looked very much like any other of those obliged to go out this labouring morning despite the weather. The fact that he wore the Benedictine habit excited no attention. He was taken for one of the resident brothers on some errand between the abbey and Saint Giles, and on his way back to be in time for High Mass and chapter. He had a long stride, but trod as though his sandalled feet were sore, as well as muddy, and his habit was kilted almost to the knee, uncovering muscular, well-shaped legs, smooth and young, mired to the ankles. It seemed he must have walked somewhat further than to the hospital and back, and on somewhat less frequented and seemly roads than the Foregate.

He was moderately tall, but slender and angular in the manner of youth still not quite accomplished in the management of a man's body, as yearling colts are angular and springy, and to see such a youngster putting his feet down

51

resolutely but tenderly, and thrusting forward with effort, struck Brother Cadfael as curious. He had looked back from the turn of the path into the garden, on his way to his workshop, just as the young man turned in at the gatehouse wicket, and his eye was caught by the gait before he noticed anything else about the newcomer. Belated curiosity made him take a second glance, in time to observe that the man entering, though manifestly a brother, had halted to speak to the porter, in the manner of a stranger making civil enquiry after someone in authority. Not a brother of this house, seemingly. And now that Cadfael was paying attention, not one that he knew. One rusty black habit is much like another, especially with the cowl drawn close against the rain, but Cadfael could have identified every member of this extensive household, choir monk, novice, steward or postulant, at greater distance than across the court, and this lad was none of them. Not that there was anything strange in that, since a brother of another house of the Order might very well be sent on some legitimate business here to Shrewsbury. But there was something about this visitor that set him apart. He came on foot: official envoys from house to house more often rode. And he had come on foot a considerable distance, to judge by his appearance, shabby, footsore and weary.

It was not altogether Cadfael's besetting sin of curiosity that made him abandon his immediate intent and cross the great court to the gatehouse. It was almost time to get ready for Mass, and because of the rain everyone who must venture out did so as briefly and quickly as possible and scurried back to shelter, so that there was no one else visible at this moment to volunteer to bear messages or escort petitioners. But it must be admitted that curiosity also had its part. He approached the pair at the gate with a bright eye and a ready tongue.

'You need a messenger, Brother? Can I serve?'

'Our brother here says he's instructed,' said the porter, 'to report himself first to the lord abbot, in accordance with his own abbot's orders. He has matter to report, before he can take any rest.'

'Abbot Radulfus is still in his lodging,' said Cadfael, 'for I left him there only a short while since. Shall I be your herald? He was alone. If it's so grave he'll surely see you at once.'

The young man put back the wet cowl from his head, and shook the drops that had slowly penetrated it from a tonsure growing somewhat long for conformity, and a crown covered with a strange fuzz of new growth, curly and of a dark, brownish gold. Yes, he had certainly been a long time on the way, pressing forward doggedly on foot from that distant cloister of his, wherever it might be. His face was oval, tapering slightly from a wide brow and wide-set eyes to a stubborn, probing jaw, covered at this moment by a fine golden down to match his unshaven crown. Weary and foot-sore he might be, but his long walk seemed to have done him no harm otherwise, for his cheeks had a healthy flush, and his eyes were of a clear, light blue, and confronted Cadfael with a bright, unwavering gaze.

'I shall be glad if he will,' he said, 'for I do need to get rid of the dirt of travel, but I'm charged to unburden to him first, and must do as I'm bid. And yes, it's grave enough for the Order – and for me, though that's of small account,' he added, shrugging off with the moisture of his cowl and scapular the present consideration of his own problems.

'He may not think it so,' said Cadfael. 'But come, and we'll put it to the test.' And he led the way briskly down the great court towards the abbot's lodging, leaving the porter to retire into the comfort of his own lodge, out of the clinging rain.

'How long have you been on the road?' asked Cadfael of the young man limping at his elbow.

'Seven days.' His voice was low-pitched and clear, and matched every other evidence of his youth. Cadfael judged he could not yet be past twenty, perhaps not even so much.

'Sent out alone on so long an errand?' said Cadfael, marvelling.

'Brother, we are all sent out, scattered. Pardon me if I keep what I have to say, to deliver first to the lord abbot. I would as soon tell it only once, and leave all things in his hands.'

'That you may do with confidence,' Cadfael assured him, and asked nothing further. The implication of crisis was there in the words, and the first note of desperation, quietly constrained, in the young voice. At the door of the abbot's lodging Cadfael let them both in without ceremony into the ante-room, and knocked at the half-open parlour door. The abbot's voice, preoccupied and absent, bade him enter. Radulfus had a folder of documents before him, and a long forefinger keeping his place, and looked up only briefly to see who entered.

'Father, there is here a young brother, from a distant house of our Order, come with orders from his own abbot to report himself to you, and with what seems to be grave news. He is here at the door. May I admit him?'

Radulfus looked up with a lingering frown, abandoning whatever had been occupying him, and gave his full attention to this unexpected delivery.

'From what distant house?'

'I have not asked,' said Cadfael, 'and he has not said. His instructions are to deliver all to you. But he has been on the road seven days to reach us.'

'Bring him in,' said the abbot, and pushed his parchments aside on the desk.

The young man came in, made a deep reverence to authority, and as though some seal on his mind and tongue had been broken, drew a great breath and suddenly poured out words, crowding and tumbling like a gush of blood.

'Father, I am the bearer of very ill news from the abbey of Ramsey. Father, in Essex and the Fens men are become devils. Geoffrey de Mandeville has seized our abbey to be his fortress, and cast us out, like beggars on to the roads, those of us who still live. Ramsey abbey is become a den of thieves and murderers.'

He had not even waited to be given leave to speak, or to allow his news to be conveyed by orderly question and answer, and Cadfael had barely begun to close the door upon the pair of them, admittedly slowly and with pricked ears, when the abbot's voice cut sharply through the boy's breathless utterance.

'Wait! Stay with us, Cadfael. I may need a messenger in haste.' And to the boy he said crisply: 'Draw breath, my son. Sit down, take thought before you speak, and let me hear a plain tale. After seven days, these few minutes will scarcely signify. Now, first, we here have had no word of this until now. If you have been so long afoot reaching us, I marvel it has not been brought to the sheriff's ears with better speed. Are you the first to come alive out of this assault?'

The boy submitted, quivering, to the hand Cadfael laid on his shoulder, and subsided obediently on to the bench against the wall. 'Father, I had great trouble in getting clear of de Mandeville's lines, and so would any other envoy have. In particular a man on horseback, such as might be sent to take the word to the king's sheriffs, would hardly get through alive. They are taking every horse, every beast, every bow or sword, from three shires, a mounted man would bring them down on him like wolves. I may well be the first, having nothing on me worth the trouble of killing me for it. Hugh Beringar may not know yet.'

The simple use of Hugh's name startled both Cadfael and Radulfus. The abbot turned sharply to take a longer look at the young face confidingly raised to his. 'You know the lord sheriff here? How is that?'

'It is the reason – it is one reason – why I am sent here, Father. I am native here. My name is Sulien Blount. My brother is lord of Longner. You will never have seen me, but Hugh Beringar knows my family well.'

So this, thought Cadfael, enlightened, and studying the boy afresh from head to foot, this is the younger brother who chose to enter the Benedictine Order just over a year ago, and went off to become a novice at Ramsey in late September, about the time his father made over the Potter's Field to Haughmond Abbey. Now why, I wonder, did he choose the Benedictines rather than his family's favourite Augustinians? He could as well have gone with the field, and lived quietly and peacefully among the canons of Haughmond. Still, reflected Cadfael, looking down upon the young man's tonsure, with its new fuzz of dark gold within the ring of damp brown hair, should I quarrel with a preference that flatters my own choice? He liked the moderation and good sense and human kindliness of Saint Benedict, as I did. It was a little disconcerting that this comfortable reflection should only raise other and equally pertinent questions. Why all the way to Ramsey? Why not here in Shrewsbury?

'Hugh Beringar shall know from me, without delay,' said the abbot reassuringly, 'all that you can tell me. You say de Mandeville has seized Ramsey. When did this happen? And how?'

Sulien moistened his lips and put together, sensibly and calmly enough, the picture he had carried in his mind for seven days.

'It was the ninth day back from today. We knew, as all that countryside knew, that the earl had returned to lands which formerly were his own, and gathered together those who had served him in the past and all those living wild, or at odds with law, willing to serve him now in his exile. But we did not know where his forces were, and had no warning of any intent towards us. You know that Ramsey is almost an island, with only one causeway dryshod into it? It is why it was first favoured as a place of retirement from the world.'

'And undoubtedly the reason why the earl coveted it,' said Radulfus grimly. 'Yes, that we knew.'

'But what need had we ever had to guard that causeway? And how could we, being brothers, guard it in arms even if we had known? They came in thousands,' said Sulien, clearly considering what he said of numbers, and meaning his words, 'crossed and took possession. They drove us out into the court and out from the gate, seizing everything we had but our habits. Some part of our enclave they fired. Some of us who showed defiance, though without violence, they beat or killed. Some who lingered in the neighbourhood though outside the island, they shot at with arrows. They have turned our house into a den of bandits and torturers, and filled it with weapons and armed men, and from that stronghold they go forth to rob and pillage and slay. No one for miles around has the means to till his fields or keep anything of value in his house. This is how it happened, Father, and I saw it happen.'

'And your abbot?' asked Radulfus.

'Abbot Walter is a valiant man indeed, Father. The next day he went alone into their camp and laid about him with a

brand out of their fire, burning some of their tents. He has pro-
nounced excommunication against them all, and the marvel is
they did not kill him, but only mocked him and let him go
unharmed. De Mandeville has seized all those of the abbey's
manors that lie near at hand, and given them to his fellows to
garrison, but some that lie further afield he has left
unmolested, and Abbot Walter has taken most of the brothers
to refuge there. I left him safe when I broke through as far as
Peterborough. That town is not yet threatened.'

'How came it that he did not take you also with him?' the
abbot questioned. 'That he would send out word to any of the
king's liegemen I well understand, but why to this shire in particular?'

'I have told it everywhere as I came, Father. But my abbot
sent me here to you for my own sake, for I have a trouble of my
own. I had taken it to him, in duty bound,' said Sulien, with
hesitant voice and lowered gaze, 'and since this disruption fell
upon us before it could be resolved, he sent me here to submit
myself and my burden to you, and take from you counsel or
penance or absolution, whatever you may judge my due.'

'Then that is between us two,' said the abbot briskly, 'and
can wait. Tell me whatever more you can concerning the scope
of this terror in the Fens. We knew of Cambridge, but if the
man now has a safe base in Ramsey, what places besides may be
in peril?'

'He is but newly installed,' said Sulien, 'and the villages
nearby have been the first to suffer. There is no cottage too
mean but they will wring some tribute out of the tenant, or take
life or limb if he has nothing besides. But I do know that Abbot
Walter feared for Ely, being so rich a prize, and in country the
earl knows so well. He will stay among the waters, where no
army can bring him to battle.'

This judgement was given with a lift of the head and a glint of the eye that bespoke rather the apprentice to arms than the monastic novice. Radulfus had observed it, too, and exchanged a long, mute glance with Cadfael over the young man's shoulder.

'So, we have it! If that is all you can furnish, let's see it fully delivered to Hugh Beringar at once. Cadfael, will you see that done? Leave Brother Sulien here with me, and send Brother Paul to us. Take a horse, and come back to us here when you return.'

Brother Paul, master of the novices, delivered Sulien again to the abbot's parlour in a little over half an hour, a different youth, washed clean of the muck of the roads, shaven, in a dry habit, his hair, if not yet properly trimmed of its rebellious down of curls, brushed into neatness. He folded his hands submissively before the abbot, with every mark of humility and reverence, but always with the same straight, confident stare of the clear blue eyes.

'Leave us, Paul,' said Radulfus. And to the boy, after the door had closed softly on Paul's departure: 'Have you broken your fast? It will be a while yet before the meal in the frater, and I think you have not eaten today.'

'No, Father, I set out before dawn. Brother Paul has given me bread and ale. I am grateful.'

'We are come, then, to whatever it may be that troubles you. There is no need to stand, I would rather you felt at ease, and able to speak freely. As you would with Abbot Walter, so speak with me.'

Sulien sat, submissive to orders, but still stiff within his own youthful body, unable quite to surrender from the heart what he offered ardently in word and form. He sat with straight back and eyes lowered now, and his linked fingers were white at the knuckles.

'Father, it was late September of last year when I entered Ramsey as a postulant. I have tried to deliver faithfully what I promised, but there have been troubles I never foresaw, and things asked of me that I never thought to have to face. After I left my home, my father went to join the king's forces, and was with him at Wilton. It may be all this is already known to you, how he died there with the rearguard, protecting the king's retreat. It fell to me to go and redeem his body and bring him home for burial, last March. I had leave from my abbot, and I returned strictly to my day. But . . . It is hard to have two homes, when the first is not yet quite relinquished, and the second not yet quite accepted, and then to be forced to make the double journey over again. And lately there have also been contentions at Ramsey that have torn us apart. For a time Abbot Walter gave up his office to Brother Daniel, who was no way fit to step into his sandals. That is resolved now, but it was disruption and distress. Now my year of novitiate draws to an end, and I know neither what to do, nor what I want to do. I asked my abbot for more time, before I take my final vows. When this disaster fell upon us, he thought it best to send me here, to my brothers of the order here in Shrewsbury. And here I submit myself to your rule and guidance, until I can see my way before me plain.'

'You are no longer sure of your vocation,' said the abbot.

'No, Father, I am no longer sure. I am blown by two conflicting winds.'

'Abbot Walter has not made it simpler for you,' remarked Radulfus, frowning. 'He has sent you where you stand all the more exposed to both.'

'Father, I believe he thought it only fair. My home is here, but he did not say: Go home. He sent me where I may still be within the discipline I chose, and yet feel the strong pull of place and family. Why should it be made simple for me,' said Sulien, suddenly raising his wide blue stare, unwaveringly gallant and deeply troubled, 'so the answer at the end is the right one? But I cannot come to any decision, because the very act of looking back makes me ashamed.'

'There is no need,' said Radulfus. 'You are not the first, and will not be the last, to look back, nor the first nor the last to turn back, if that is what you choose. Every man has within him only one life and one nature to give to the service of God, and if there was but one way of doing that, celibate within the cloister, procreation and birth would cease, the world would be depeopled, and neither within nor without the Church would God receive worship. It behoves a man to look within himself, and turn to the best dedication possible those endowments he has from his Maker. You do no wrong in questioning what once you held to be right for you, if now it has come to seem wrong. Put away all thought of being bound. We do not want you bound. No one who is not free can give freely.'

The young man fronted him earnestly in silence for some moments, eyes as limpidly light as harebells, lips very firmly set, searching rather his mentor than himself. Then he said with deliberation: 'Father, I am not sure even of my own acts, but I think it was not for the right reasons that I ever asked admission to the Order. I think that is why it shames me to think of abandoning it now.'

'That in itself, my son,' said Radulfus, 'may be good reason why the Order should abandon you. Many have entered for the wrong reasons, and later remained for the right ones, but to remain against the grain and against the truth, out of obstinancy and pride, that would be a sin.' And he smiled to see the boy's level brown brows draw together in despairing bewilderment. 'Am I confusing you still more? I do not ask why you entered, though I think it may have been to escape the world without rather than to embrace the world within. You are young, and of that outer world you have seen as yet very little, and may have misjudged what you did see. There is no haste now. For the present take your full place here among us, but apart from the other novices. I would not have them troubled with your trouble. Rest some days, pray constantly for guidance, have faith that it will be granted, and then choose. For the choice must be yours, let no one take it from you.'

'First Cambridge,' said Hugh, tramping the inner ward of the castle with long, irritated strides as he digested the news from the Fen country, 'now Ramsey. And Ely in danger! Your young man's right there, a rich prize that would be for a wolf like de Mandeville. I tell you what, Cadfael, I'd better be going over every lance and sword and bow in the armoury, and sorting out a few good lads ready for action. Stephen is slow to start, sometimes, having a vein of laziness in him until he's roused, but he'll have to take action now against this rabble. He should have wrung de Mandeville's neck while he had him, he was warned often enough.'

'He's unlikely to call on you,' Cadfael considered judicially, 'even if he does decide to raise a new force to flush out the wolves. He can call on the neighbouring shires, surely. He'll want men fast.'

'He shall have them fast,' said Hugh grimly, 'for I'll be ready to take the road as soon as he gives the word. True, he may not need to fetch men from the border here, seeing he trusts Chester no more than he did Essex, and Chester's turn will surely come. But whether or no, I'll be ready for him. If you're bound back, Cadfael, take my thanks to the abbot for his news. We'll set the armourers and the fletchers to work, and make certain of our horses. No matter if they turn out not to be needed, it does the garrison no harm to be alerted in a hurry now and then.' He turned towards the outer ward and the gatehouse with his departing friend, still frowning thoughtfully over this new complexity in England's already confused and troublous situation. 'Strange how great and little get their lives tangled together, Cadfael. De Mandeville takes his revenge in the east, and sends this lad from Longner scurrying home again here to the Welsh border. Would you say fate had done him any favour? It could well be. You never knew him until now, did you? He never seemed to me a likely postulant for the cloister.'

'I did gather,' said Cadfael cautiously, 'that he may not yet have taken his final vows. He said he came with a trouble of his own unresolved, that his abbot charged him bring with him here to Radulfus. It may be he's taken fright, now the time closes upon him. It happens! I'll be off back and see what Radulfus intends for him.'

What Radulfus had in mind for the troubled soul was made plain when Cadfael returned, as bidden, to the abbot's parlour. The abbot was alone at his desk by this time, the new entrant sent away with Brother Paul to rest from his long journey afoot and take his place, with certain safeguards, among his peers, if not of them.

'He has need of some days of quietude,' said Radulfus, 'with time for prayer and thought, for he is in doubt of his vocation, and truth to tell, so am I. But I know nothing of his state of mind and his behaviour when he conceived his desire for the cloister, and am in no position to judge how genuine were his motives then, or are his reservations now. It is something he must resolve for himself. All I can do is ensure that no further shadow or shock shall fall upon him, to distract his mind when most he needs a clear head. I do not want him perpetually reminded of the fate of Ramsey, nor, for that matter, upset by any talk of this matter of the Potter's Field. Let him have stillness and solitude to think out his own deliverance first. When he is ready to see me again, I have told Brother Vitalis to admit him at once. But in the meantime, it may be as well if you would take him to help you in the herb garden, apart from the brothers except at worship. In frater and dortoir Paul will keep a watchful eye on him, during the hours of work he will be best with you, who already know his situation.'

'I have been thinking,' said Cadfael, scrubbing reflectively at his forehead, 'that he knows Ruald is here among us. It was some months after Ruald's entry that this young fellow made up his mind for the cloister. Ruald was Blount's tenant life-long, and close by the manor, and Hugh tells me this boy Sulien was in and out of that workshop from a child, and a favourite with them, seeing they had none of their own. He has not spoken of Ruald, or asked to see him? How if he seeks him out?'

'If he does, well. He has that right, and I do not intend to hedge him in for long. But I think he is too full of Ramsey and his own trouble to have any thought to spare for other matters as yet. He has not yet taken his final vows,' said Radulfus, pondering with resigned anxiety over the complex agonies of the young. 'All we can do is provide him a time of shelter and calm. His will and his acts are still his own. And as for this shadow that hangs over Ruald – what use would it be to ignore the threat? – if the relations between them were as

64

Hugh says, that will be one more grief and disruption to the young man's mind. As well if he is spared it for a day or so. But if it comes, it comes. He is a man grown, we cannot take his rightful burdens from him.'

It was on the morning of the second day after his arrival that Sulien encountered Brother Ruald face to face at close quarters and with no one else by except Cadfael. At every service in church he had seen him among all the other brothers, once or twice had caught his eye, and smiled across the dim space of the choir, but received no more acknowledgement than a brief, lingering glance of abstracted sweetness, as if the older man saw him through a veil of wonder and rapture in which old associations had no place. Now they emerged at the same moment into the great court, converging upon the south door of the cloister, Sulien from the garden, with Cadfael ambling a yard or two behind him, Ruald from the direction of the infirmary. Sulien had a young man's thrusting, impetuous gait, now that his blistered feet were healed, and he rounded the corner of the tall box hedge so precipitately that the two almost collided, their sleeves brushing, and both halted abruptly and drew back a step in hasty apology. Here in the open, under a wide sky still streaked with trailers of primrose gold from a bright sunrise, they met like humble mortal men, with no veil of glory between them.

'Sulien!' Ruald opened his arms with a warm, delighted smile, and embraced the young man briefly cheek to cheek. 'I saw you in church the first day. How glad I am that you are here, and safe!'

Sulien stood mute for a moment, looking the older man over earnestly from head to foot, captivated by the serenity of his thin face, and the curious air he had of having found his way home, and being settled and content here as he had never been before, in his craft, in his cottage, in his marriage, in his community. Cadfael, holding aloof at the turn of the box hedge, with a shrewd eye on the pair of them, saw Ruald briefly as Sulien was seeing him, a man secure in the rightness of his choice, and radiating his unblemished joy upon all who drew near him. To one ignorant of any threat or shadow hanging over this man, he must seem the possessor of perfect happiness. The true revelation was that, indeed, so he was. A marvel!

'And you?' said Sulien, still gazing and remembering. 'How is it with you? You are well? And content? But I see that you are!'

'All is well with me,' said Ruald. 'All is very well, better than I deserve.' He took the young man by the sleeve, and the pair of them turned together towards the church. Cadfael followed more slowly, letting them pass out of earshot. From the look of them, as they went, Ruald was talking cheerfully of ordinary things, as brother to brother. The occasion of Sulien's flight from Ramsey he knew, as the whole household knew it, but clearly he knew nothing as yet of the boy's shaken faith in his vocation. And just as clearly, he did not intend to say a word of the suspicion and possible danger that hung over his own head. The rear view of them, springy youth and patient, plodding middle age jauntily shoulder to shoulder, was like father and son in one craft on their way to work, and, fatherly, the elder wanted no part of his shadowed destiny to cloud the bright horizons of faith that beckoned his son.

'Ramsey will be recovered,' said Ruald with certainty. 'Evil will be driven out of it, though we may need long patience. I have been praying for your abbot and brothers.'

'So have I,' said Sulien ruefully, 'all along the way. I'm

lucky to be out of that terror. But it's worse for the poor folk there in the villages, who have nowhere to run for shelter.'

'We are praying for them also. There will be a return, and a reckoning.'

The shadow of the south porch closed over them, and they halted irresolutely on the edge of separating, Ruald to his stall in the choir, Sulien to his obscure place among the novices, before Ruald spoke. His voice was still level and soft, but from some deeper well of feeling within him it had taken on a distant, plangent tone like a faraway bell.

'Did you ever hear word from Generys, after she left? Or do you know if any other did?'

'No, never a word,' said Sulien, startled and quivering.

'No, nor I. I deserved none, but they would have told me, in kindness, if anything was known of her. She was fond of you from a babe, I thought perhaps . . . I should dearly like to know that all is well with her.'

Sulien stood with lowered eyes, silent for a long moment. Then he said in a very low voice: 'And so should I, God knows how dearly!'

Chapter Five

T DID NOT PLEASE Brother Jerome that anything should be going on within the precinct of which he was even marginally kept in ignorance, and he felt that in the matter of the refugee novice from Ramsey not quite everything had been openly declared. True, Abbot Radulfus had made a clear statement in chapter concerning the fate of Ramsey and the terror in the Fens, and expressed the hope that young Brother Sulien, who had brought the news and sought refuge here, should be allowed a while of quietness and peace to recover from his experiences. There was reason and kindness in that, certainly. But everyone in the household, by now, knew who Sulien was, and could not help connecting his return with the matter of the dead woman found in the Potter's Field, and the growing shadow hanging over Brother Ruald's head, and wondering if he had yet been let into all the details of that tragedy, and what effect it would have on him if he had. What must he be thinking concerning his family's former tenant? Was that why the abbot had made a point of asking for peace and quietness for him, and seeing to it that his daily work should be somewhat set apart from too much company? And what would be said, what would be noted in the bearing of the two, when Sulien and Ruald met?

And now everyone knew that they had met. Everyone had seen them enter the church for Mass side by side, in quiet conversation, and watched them separate to their places without any noticeable change of countenance on either part, and go about their separate business afterwards with even step and unshaken faces. Brother Jerome had watched avidly, and was no wiser. That aggrieved him. He took pride in knowing everything that went on within and around the abbey of Saint Peter and Saint Paul, and his reputation would suffer if he allowed this particular obscurity to go unprobed. Moreover, his status with Prior Robert might feel the draught no less. Robert's dignity forbade him to point his own aristocratic nose into every shadowy corner, but he expected to be informed of what went on there, just the same. His thin silver brows might rise, with unpleasant implications, if he found his trusted source, after all, fallible.

So when Brother Cadfael sallied forth with a full scrip to visit a new inmate at the hospital of Saint Giles, that same afternoon, and to replenish the medicine cupboard there, leaving the herb garden to his two assistants, of whom Brother Winfrid was plainly visible digging over the depleted vegetable beds ready for the winter, Brother Jerome seized his opportunity and went visiting on his own account.

He did not go without an errand. Brother Petrus wanted onions for the abbot's table, and they were newly lifted and drying out in trays in Cadfael's store-shed. In the ordinary way Jerome would have delegated this task to someone else, but this day he went himself.

In the workshop in the herb garden the young man Sulien was diligently sorting beans dried for next year's seed, discarding those flawed or suspect, and collecting the best into a pottery jar almost certainly made by Brother Ruald in his former life. Jerome looked him over cautiously from the doorway before entering to interrupt his work. The sight only deepened his suspicion that things were going on of which he, Jerome, was insufficiently informed. For one thing, Sulien's crown still bore its new crop of light brown curls, growing more luxuriant every day, and presenting an incongruous image grossly offensive to Jerome's sense of decorum. Why was he not again shaven-headed and seemly, like all the brothers? Again, he went about his simple task with the most untroubled serenity and a steady hand, apparently quite unmoved by what he must have learned by now from Ruald's own lips. Jerome could not conceive that the two of them had walked together from the great court into the church before Mass, without one word being said about the murdered woman, found in the field once owned by the boy's father and tenanted by Ruald himself. It was the chief subject of gossip, scandal and speculation, how could it be avoided? And this boy and his family might be a considerable protection to a man threatened with the charge of murder, if they chose to stand by him. Jerome, in Ruald's place, would most heartily have enlisted that support, would have poured out the story as soon as the chance offered. He took it for granted that Ruald had done the same. Yet here this unfathomable youth stood earnestly sorting his seed, apparently without anything else on his mind, even the tension and stress of Ramsey already mastered.

Sulien turned as the visitor's shadow fell within, and looked up into Jerome's face, and waited in dutiful silence to hear what was required of him. One brother was like another to him here as yet, and with this meagre little man he had not so far exchanged a word. The narrow, grey face and stooped shoulders made Jerome look older than he was, and it was the duty of young brothers to be servicable and submissive to their elders.

Jerome requested onions, and Sulien went into the store-shed and brought what was wanted, choosing the soundest and roundest, since these were for the abbot's own kitchen. Jerome opened benevolently: 'How are you faring now, here among us, after all your trials elsewhere? Have you settled well here with Brother Cadfael?'

'Very well, I thank you,' said Sulien carefully, unsure yet of this solicitous visitor whose appearance was not precisely reassuring, nor his voice, even speaking sympathy, particularly sympathetic. 'I am fortunate to be here, I thank God for my deliverance.'

'In a very proper spirit,' said Jerome wooingly. 'Though I fear that even here there are matters that must trouble you. I wish that you could have come back to us in happier circumstances.'

'Indeed, so do I!' agreed Sulien warmly, still harking back in his own mind to the upheaval of Ramsey.

Jerome was encouraged. It seemed the young man might, after all, be in a mood to confide, if sympathetically prompted. 'I feel for you,' he said mellifluously. 'A shocking thing it must be, after such terrible blows, to come home to yet more ill news here. This death that has come to light, and worse, to know that it casts so black a shadow of suspicion upon a brother among us, and one well known to all your family – '

He was weaving his way so confidently into his theme that he had not even noticed the stiffening of Sulien's body, and the sudden blank stillness of his face.

'Death?' said the boy abruptly. 'What death?'

Thus sharply cut off in full flow, Jerome blinked and

gaped, and leaned to peer more intently into the young, frowning face before him, suspecting deception. But the blue eyes confronted him with a wide stare of such crystal clarity that not even Jerome, himself adept at dissembling and a cause of defensive evasion in others, could doubt the young man's honest bewilderment.

'Do you mean,' demanded Jerome incredulously, 'that Ruald has not told you?'

'Told me of what? Nothing of a death, certainly! I don't know what you mean, Brother!'

'But you walked with him to Mass this morning,' protested Jerome, reluctant to relinquish his certainty. 'I saw you come, you had some talk together . . .'

'Yes, so we did, but nothing of ill news, nothing of a death. I have known Ruald since I could first run,' said Sulien. 'I was glad to meet with him, and see him so secure in his faith, and so happy. But what is this you are telling me of a death? I beg you, let me understand you!'

Jerome had thought to be eliciting information, but found himself instead imparting it. 'I thought you must surely know it already. Our plough-team turned up a woman's body, the first day they broke the soil of the Potter's Field. Buried there unlawfully, without rites – the sheriff believes killed unlawfully. The first thought that came to mind was that it must be the woman who was Brother Ruald's wife when he was in the world. I thought you knew from him. Did he never say a word to you?'

'No, never a word,' said Sulien. His voice was level and almost distant, as though all his thoughts had already grappled with the grim truth of it, and withdrawn deep into his being, to contain and conceal any immediate consideration of its full meaning. His blue, opaque stare held Jerome at gaze, unwavering. 'That *it must be* – you said. Then it is not *known*? Neither he nor any can name the woman?'

'It would not be possible to name her. There is nothing left that could be known to any man. Mere naked bones is what they found.' Jerome's faded flesh shrank at the mere thought of contemplating so stark a reminder of mortality. 'Dead at least a year, so they judge. Maybe more, even as much as five years. Earth deals in many different ways with the body.'

Sulien stood stiff and silent for a moment, digesting this knowledge with a face still as a mask. At last he said: 'Did I understand you to say also that this death casts a black shadow of suspicion upon a brother of this house? You mean by that, on Ruald?'

'How could it be avoided?' said Jerome reasonably. 'If this is indeed she, where else would the law look first? We know of no other woman who frequented that place, we know that this one disappeared from there without a word to any. But whether living or dead, who can be certain?'

'It is impossible,' said Sulien very firmly. 'Ruald had been a month and more here in the abbey before she vanished. Hugh Beringar knows that.'

'And acknowledges it, but that does not make it impossible. Twice he visited her afterwards, in company with Brother Paul, to settle matters about such possessions as he left. Who can be sure that he never visited her alone? He was not a prisoner within the enclave, he went out with others to work at the Gaye, and elsewhere on our lands. Who can say he never left the sight of his fellows? At least,' said Jerome, with mildly malicious satisfaction in his own superior reasoning, 'the sheriff is busy tracing every errand Brother Ruald has had outside the gates during those early days of his novitiate. If he satisfies himself they never did meet and come to conflict,

74

well. If not, he knows that Ruald is here, and will be here, waiting. He cannot evade.'

'It is foolishness,' said the boy with sudden quiet violence. 'If there were proof from many witnesses, I would not believe he ever harmed her. I should know them liars, because I know him. Such a thing he could not do. He *did not* do!' repeated Sulien, staring blue challenge like daggers into Jerome's face.

'Brother, you presume!' Jerome drew his inadequate length to its tallest, though he was still topped by almost a head. 'It is sin to be swayed by human affection to defend a brother. Truth and justice are preferred before mere fallible inclination. In chapter sixty-nine of the Rule that is set down. If you know the Rule as you should, you know such partiality is an offence.'

It cannot be said that Sulien lowered his embattled stare or bent his head to this reproof, and he would certainly have been in for a much longer lecture if his superior's sharp ear had not caught, at that moment, the distant sound of Cadfael's voice, some yards away along the path, halting to exchange a few cheerful words with Brother Winfrid, who was just cleaning his spade and putting away his tools. Jerome had no wish to see this unsatisfactory colloquy complicated by a third party, least of all Cadfael, who, upon consideration, might have been entrusted with this ill-disciplined assistant precisely in order to withdraw him from too much knowledge too soon. As well leave things as they stood.

'But you may be indulged,' he said, with hasty magnanimity, 'seeing this comes so suddenly on you, and at a time when you have already been sorely tried. I say no more!'

And forthwith he took a somewhat abrupt but still dignified leave, and was in time to be a dozen paces outside the door when Cadfael met him. They exchanged a brief word in passing, somewhat to Cadfael's surprise. Such brotherly civility in Jerome argued a slight embarrassment, if not a guilty conscience.

Sulien was collecting his rejected beans into a bowl, to be added to the compost, when Cadfael came into the workshop. He did not look round as his mentor came in. He had known the voice, as he knew the step.

'What did Jerome want?' Cadfael asked, with only mild interest.

'Onions. Brother Petrus sent him.'

No one below Prior Robert's status sent Brother Jerome anywhere. He kept his services for where they might reflect favour and benefit upon himself, and the abbot's cook, a red-haired and belligerent northerner, had nothing profitable to bestow, even if he had been well-disposed towards Jerome, which he certainly was not.

'I can believe Brother Petrus wanted onions. But what did Jerome want?'

'He wanted to know how I was faring, here with you,' said Sulien with deliberation. 'At least, that's what he asked me. And, Cadfael, you know how things are with me. I am not quite sure yet how I am faring, or what I ought to do, but before I commit myself either to going or staying, I think it is time I went to see Father Abbot again. He said I might, when I felt the need.'

'Go now, if you wish,' said Cadfael simply, eyeing with close attention the steady hands that swept the bench clear of fragments, and the head so sedulously inclined to keep the young, austere face in shadow. 'There's time before Vespers.'

Abbot Radulfus examined his petitioner with a detached and tolerant eye. In three days the boy had changed in under-

76

standable ways, his exhaustion cured, his step now firm and vigorous, the lines of his face eased of their tiredness and strain, the reflection of danger and horror gone from his eyes. Whether the rest had resolved his problem for him was not yet clear, but there was certainly nothing indecisive in his manner, or in the clean jut of a very respectable jaw.

'Father,' he said directly. 'I am here to ask your leave to go and visit my family and my home. It is only fair that I should be equally open to influences from within and without.'

'I thought,' said Radulfus mildly, 'that you might be here to tell me that your trouble is resolved, and your mind made up. You have that look about you. It seems I am previous.'

'No, Father, I am not yet sure. And I would not offer myself afresh until I am sure.'

'So you want to breathe the air at Longner before you stake your life, and allow household and kin and kind to speak to you, as our life here has spoken. I would not have it otherwise,' said the abbot. 'Certainly you may visit. Go freely. Better, sleep again at Longner, think well upon all you stand to gain there, and all you stand to lose. You may need even more time. When you are ready, when you are certain, then come and tell me which way you have chosen.'

'I will, Father,' said Sulien. The tone was the one he had learned to take for granted in the year and more of his novitiate in Ramsey, submissive, dutiful and reverent, but the disconcerting eyes were fixed on some distant aim visible only to himself, or so it seemed to the abbot, who was as well versed in reading the monastic face as Sulien was in withdrawing behind it.

'Go then, at once if you wish.' He considered how long a journey afoot this young man had recently had to make, and added a concession. 'Take a mule from the stable, if you

77

intend to leave now. The daylight will see you there if you ride. And tell Brother Cadfael you have leave to stay until tomorrow.'

'I will, Father!' And Sulien made his reverence and departed with a purposeful alacrity which Radulfus observed with some amusement and some regret. The boy would have been well worth keeping, if that had truly been his bent, but Radulfus was beginning to judge that he had already lost him. He had been home once before, since electing for the cloister, to bring home his father's body for burial after the rout of Wilton, had stayed several days on that occasion, and still chosen to return to his vocation. He had had seven months since then to reconsider, and this sudden urge now to visit Longner, with no unavoidable filial duty this time to reinforce it, seemed to the abbot significant evidence of a decision as good as made.

Cadfael was crossing the court to enter the church for Vespers when Sulien accosted him with the news.

'Very natural,' said Cadfael heartily, 'that you should want to see your mother and your brother, too. Go with all our goodwill, and whatever you decide, God bless the choice.'

His expectation, however, as he watched the boy ride out at the gatehouse, was the same that Radulfus had in mind. Sulien Blount was not, on the face of it, cut out for the monastic life, however hard he had tried to believe in his misguided choice. A night at home now, in his own bed and with his kin around him, would settle the matter.

Which conclusion left a very pertinent question twitching all through Vespers in Cadfael's mind. What could possibly have driven the boy to make for the cloister in the first place?

Sulien came back next day in time for Mass, very solemn of countenance and resolute of bearing, for some reason looking years nearer to a man's full maturity than when he had arrived from horrors and hardships, endured with all a man's force and determination. A youth, resilient but vulnerable, had spent two days in Cadfael's company; a man, serious and purposeful, returned from Longner to approach him after Mass. He was still wearing the habit, but his absurd tonsure, the crest of dark gold curls within the overgrown ring of darker brown hair, created an incongruous appearance of mockery, just when his face was at its gravest. High time, thought Cadfael, observing him with the beginning of affection, for this one to go back where he belongs.

'I am going to see Father Abbot,' said Sulien directly.

'So I supposed,' agreed Cadfael.

'Will you come with me?'

'Is that needful? What I feel sure you have to say is between you and your superior, but I do not think,' Cadfael allowed, 'that he will be surprised.'

'There is something more I have to tell him,' said Sulien, unsmiling. 'You were there when first I came, and you were the messenger he sent to repeat all the news I brought to the lord sheriff. I know from my brother that you have always access to Hugh Beringar's ear, and I know now what earlier I did not know. I know what happened when the ploughing began, I know what was found in the Potter's Field. I know what everyone is thinking and saying, but I know it cannot be true. Come with me to Abbot Radulfus. I would like you to be by as a witness still. And I think he may need a messenger, as he did before.'

His manner was so urgent and his demand so incisive that Cadfael shrugged off immediate enquiry. 'As you and he wish, then. Come!'

They were admitted to the abbot's parlour without question.

79

No doubt Radulfus had been expecting Sulien to seek an audience as soon as Mass was over. If it surprised him to find the boy bringing a sponsor with him, whether as advocate to defend his decision, or in mere meticulous duty as the mentor to whom he had been assigned in his probation, he did not allow it to show in face or voice.

'Well, my son? I hope you found all well at Longner? Has it helped you to find your way?'

'Yes, Father.' Sulien stood before him a little stiffly, his direct stare very bright and solemn in a pale face. 'I come to ask your permission to leave the Order and go back to the world.'

'That is your considered choice?' said the abbot in the same mild voice. 'This time you are in no doubt?'

'No doubt, Father. I was at fault when I asked admission. I know that now. I left duties behind, to go in search of my own peace. You said, Father, that this must be my own decision.'

'I say it still,' said the abbot. 'You will hear no reproach from me. You are still young, but a good year older than when you sought refuge within the cloister, and I think wiser. It is far better to do whole-hearted service in another field than remain half-hearted and doubting within the Order. I see you did not yet put off the habit,' he said, and smiled.

'No, Father!' Sulien's stiff young dignity was a little affronted at the suggestion. 'How could I, until I have your leave? Until you release me I am not free.'

'I do release you. I would have been glad of you, if you had chosen to stay, but I believe that for you it is better as it is, and the world may yet be glad of you. Go, with my leave and blessing, and serve where your heart is.'

He had turned a little towards his desk, where more mundane matters waited for his attention, conceiving that the audience was over, though without any sign of haste or dismissal: but Sulien held his ground, and the intensity of his gaze checked the abbot's movement, and made him look again, and more sharply, at the son he had just set free.

'There is something more you have to ask of us? Our prayers you shall certainly have.'

'Father,' said Sulien, the old address coming naturally to his lips, 'now that my own trouble is over, I find I have blundered into a great web of other men's troubles. At Longner my brother has told me what was spared me here, whether by chance or design. I have learned that when ploughing began on the field my father granted to Haughmond last year, and Haughmond exchanged for more convenient land with this house two months ago now, the coulter turned up a woman's body, buried there some while since. But not so long since that the manner, the time, the cause of her death can go unquestioned. They are saying everywhere that this was Brother Ruald's wife, whom he left to enter the Order.'

'It may be *said* everywhere,' the abbot agreed, fronting the young man with a grave face and drawn brows, 'but it is not *known* anywhere. There is no man can say who she was, no way of knowing, as yet, how she came by her death.'

'But that is not what is being said and believed outside these walls,' Sulien maintained sturdily. 'And once so terrible a find was made known, how could any man's mind escape the immediate thought? A woman found where formerly a woman vanished, leaving no word behind! What else was any man to think but that this was one and the same? True, they may all be in error. Indeed, they surely are! But as I heard it, that is the thought even in Hugh Beringar's mind, and who is to blame him? Father, that means that the finger points at Ruald. Already, so they have told me, the common talk has him guilty of murder, even in danger of his own life.'

'Gossip does not necessarily speak with any authority,' said the abbot patiently. 'Certainly it cannot speak for the lord sheriff. If he examines the movements and actions of Brother Ruald, he is but doing his duty, and will do as much by others, as the need arises. I take it that Brother Ruald himself has said no word of this to you, or you would not have had to hear it for the first time at home in Longner. If he is untroubled, need you trouble for him?'

'But, Father, that is what I have to tell!' Sulien flushed into ardour and eagerness. 'No one need be troubled for him. Truly, as you said, there is no man can say who this woman is, but here is one who can say with absolute certainty who she is *not*! For I have proof that Ruald's wife Generys is alive and well – or was so, at least, some three weeks ago.'

'You have seen her?' demanded Radulfus, reflecting back half-incredulously the burning glow of the boy's vehemence.

'No, not that! But I can do better than that.' Sulien plunged a hand deep inside the throat of his habit, and drew out something small that he had been wearing hidden on a string about his neck. He drew it over his head, and held it out to be examined in the palm of his open hand, still warm from his flesh, a plain silver ring set with a small yellow stone such as were sometimes found in the mountains of Wales and the border. Of small value in itself, marvellous for what he claimed for it. 'Father, I know I have kept this unlawfully, but I promise you I never had it in Ramsey. Take it up, look within it!'

Radulfus gave him a long, searching stare before he extended a hand and took up the ring, turning it to catch the light on its inner surface. His straight black brows drew together. He had found what Sulien wanted him to find.

'G and R twined together. Crude, but clear. And old work. The edges are blunted and dulled, but whoever engraved it cut deep.' He looked up into Sulien's ardent face. 'Where did you get this?'

'From a jeweller in Peterborough, after we fled from Ramsey, and Abbot Walter charged me to come here to you. It was mere chance. There were some tradesmen in the town who feared to stay, when they heard how near de Mandeville was, and what force he had about him. They were selling and moving out. But others were stout-hearted, and meant to stay. It was night when I reached the town, and I was commended to this silversmith in Priestgate who would shelter me overnight. He was a stout man, who would not budge for outlaws or robbers, and he had been a good patron to Ramsey. His valuables he had hidden away, but among the lesser things in his shop I saw this ring.'

'And knew it?' said the abbot.

'From old times, long ago when I was a child. I could not mistake it, even before I looked for this sign. I asked him where and when it came into his hands, and he said a woman had brought it in only some ten days earlier, to sell, because, she said, she and her man thought well to move further away from the danger of de Mandeville's marauders, and were turning what they could into money to resettle them in safety elsewhere. So were many people doing, those who had no great stake in the town. I asked him what manner of woman she was, and he described her to me, beyond mistaking. Father, barely three weeks ago Generys was alive and well in Peterborough.'

'And how did you acquire the ring?' asked Radulfus mildly, but with a sharp and daunting eye upon the boy's face. 'And why? You had then no possible reason to know that it might be of the highest significance here.'

'No, none.' The faintest flush of colour had crept upward in Sulien's cheeks, Cadfael noted, but the steady blue gaze was as wide and clear as always, even challenging question or reproof. 'You have returned me to the world, I can and will speak as one already outside these walls. Ruald and his wife were the close friends of my childhood, and when I was no longer a child that fondness grew and came to ripeness with my flesh. They will have told you, Generys was beautiful. What I felt for her touched her not at all, she never knew of it. But it was after she was gone that I thought and hoped, I admit vainly, that the cloister and the cowl might restore me my peace. I meant to pay the price faithfully, but you have remitted the debt. But when I saw and handled the ring I knew for hers, I wanted it. So simple it is.'

'But you had no money to buy it,' Radulfus said, in the same placid tone, withholding censure.

'He gave it to me. I told him what I have now told you. Perhaps more,' said Sulien, with a sudden glittering smile that lasted only an instant in eyes otherwise passionately solemn. 'We were but one night companions, I should never see him again, nor he me. Such a pair encountering confide more than ever they did to their own mothers. And he gave me the ring.'

'And why,' enquired the abbot as directly, 'did you not restore it, or at least show it, to Ruald and tell him that news, as soon as you met with him here?'

'It was not for Ruald I begged it of the silversmith,' said Sulien bluntly, 'but for my own consolation. And as for showing it, and telling him how I got it, and where, I did not know until now that any shadow hung over him, nor that there was a dead woman, newly buried here now, who was held to be Generys. I have spoken with him only once since I came, and that was for no more than a few minutes on the

84

way to Mass. He seemed to me wholly happy and content, why should I hurry to stir old memories? His coming here was pain as well as joy, I thought well to let his present joy alone. But now indeed he must know. It may be I was guided to bring back the ring, Father. I deliver it to you willingly. What I needed it has already done for me.'

There was a brief pause, while the abbot brooded over all the implications for those present and those as yet uninvolved. Then he turned to Cadfael. 'Brother, will you carry my compliments to Hugh Beringar, and ask him to ride back with you and join us here? Leave word if you cannot find him at once. Until he has heard for himself, I think nothing should be said to any other, not even Brother Ruald. Sulien, you are no longer a brother of this house, but I hope you will remain as its guest until you have told your story over again, and in my presence.'

Chapter Six

UGH WAS AT THE castle, where Cadfael found him in the armoury, telling over the stores of steel, with the likelihood of a foray against the anarchy in Essex very much in mind. He had taken the omen seriously, and was bent on being ready at a day's notice if the king should call. But Hugh's provision for action was seldom wanting, and on the whole he was content with his preparations. He could have a respectable body of picked men on the road within hours when the summons came. There was no certainty that it would, to the sheriff of a shire so far removed from the devastated Fen country, but the possibility remained. Hugh's sense of order and sanity was affronted by the very existence of Geoffrey de Mandeville and his like.

He greeted Cadfael with somewhat abstracted attention, and went on critically watching his armourer beating a sword into shape. He was giving only the fringes of his mind to the abbot's pressing invitation, until Cadfael nudged him into sharp alertness by adding: 'It has to do with the body we found in the Potter's Field. You'll find the case is changed.'

That brought Hugh's head round sharply enough. 'How changed?'

'Come and hear it from the lad who changed it. It seems

young Sulien Blount brought more than bad news back from the Fens with him. The abbot wants to hear him tell it again to you. If there's a thread of significance in it he's missed, he's certain you'll find it, and you can put your heads together afterwards, for it looks as if one road is closed to you. Get to horse and let's be off.'

But on the way back through the town and over the bridge into the Foregate he did impart one preliminary piece of news, by way of introduction to what was to follow. 'Brother Sulien, it seems, has made up his mind to return to the world. You were right in your judgement, he was never suited to be a monk. He has come to the same conclusion, without wasting too much of his youth.'

'And Radulfus agrees with him?' wondered Hugh.

'I think he was ahead of him. A good boy, and he did try his best, but he says himself he came into the Order for the wrong reasons. He'll go back to the life he was meant for, now. You may have him in your garrison before all's done, for if he's quitting one vocation he'll need another. He's not the lad to lie idle on his brother's lands.'

'All the more,' said Hugh, 'as Eudo is not long married, so in a year or two there may be sons. No place there for a younger brother, with the line secured. I might do worse. He looks a likely youngster. Well made, and a good long reach, and he always shaped well on a horse.'

'His mother will be glad to have him back, surely,' Cadfael reflected. 'She has small joy in her life, from what you told me; a son come home may do much for her.'

The likely youngster was still closeted with the abbot when Hugh entered the parlour with Cadfael at his heels. The two seemed to be very easy together, but for a slight sense of tension in the way Sulien sat, very erect and braced, his shoulders flattened against the panelling of the wall. His part here was still only half done; he waited, alert and wide-eyed, to complete it.

'Sulien here,' said the abbot, 'has something of importance to tell you, I thought best you should hear it directly from him, for you may have questions which have not occurred to me.'

'That I doubt,' said Hugh, seating himself where he could have the young man clear in the light from the window. It was a little past noon, and the brightest hour of an overcast day. 'It was good of you to send for me so quickly. For I gather this has to do with the matter of the dead woman. Cadfael has said nothing beyond that. I am listening, Sulien. What is it you have to tell?'

Sulien told his story over again, more briefly than before, but in much the same words where the facts were concerned. There were no discrepancies, but neither was it phrased so exactly to pattern as to seem studied. He had a warm, brisk way with him, and words came readily. When it was done he sat back again with a sharp sigh, and ended: 'So there can be no suspicion now against Brother Ruald. When did he ever have ado with any other woman but Generys? And Generys is alive and well. Whoever it is you have found, it cannot be she.'

Hugh had the ring in his palm, the scored initials clear in the light. He sat looking down at it with a thoughtful frown. 'It was your abbot commended you to take shelter with this silversmith?'

'It was. He was known for a good friend to the Benedictines of Ramsey.'

'And his name? And where does his shop lie in the town?'

'His name is John Hinde, and the shop is in Priestgate, not

far from the minster.' The answers came readily, even eagerly.

'Well, Sulien, it seems you have delivered Ruald from all concern with this mystery and this death, and robbed me of one suspect, if ever the man really became suspect in earnest. He was never a very likely malefactor, to tell the truth, but men are men – even monks are men – and there are very few of us who could not kill, given the occasion, the need, the anger and the solitude. It was possible! I am not sorry to see it demolished. It seems we must look elsewhere for a woman lost. And has Ruald yet been told of this?' he asked, looking up at the abbot.

'Not yet.'

'Send for him now,' said Hugh.

'Brother,' said the abbot, turning to Cadfael, 'will you find Ruald and ask him to come?'

Cadfael went on his errand with a thoughtful mind. For Hugh this deliverance meant a setback to the beginning, and a distraction from the king's affairs at a time when he would much have preferred to be able to concentrate upon them. No doubt he had been pursuing a search for any other possible identities for the dead woman, but there was no denying that the vanished Generys was the most obvious possibility. But now with this unexpected check, at least the abbey of Saint Peter and Saint Paul could rest the more tranquilly. As for Ruald himself, he would be glad and grateful for the woman's sake rather than his own. The wholeness of his entranced peace, so far in excess of what most fallible human brothers could achieve, was a perpetual marvel. For him whatever God decreed and did, for him or to him, even to his grief and humiliation, even to his life, was done well. Martyrdom would not have changed his mind.

Cadfael found him in the vaulted undercroft of the refectory, where Brother Matthew the cellarer had his most commodious stores. To him Ruald had been allotted, as a practical man whose skills were manual rather than scholarly or artistic. Summoned to the abbot's parlour, he dusted his hands, abandoned his inventory, reported his errand and destination to Brother Matthew in his little office at the end of the south range, and followed Cadfael in simple, unquestioning obedience. It was not for him to ask or to wonder, though in his present circumstances, Cadfael reflected, he might well feel his heart sink a little at the sight of the secular authority closeted side by side with the monastic, and both with austerely grave faces, and their eyes fixed upon him. If the vision of this double tribunal waiting for his entry did shake his serenity on the threshold of the parlour, there was no sign of it in his bearing or countenance. He made his reverence placidly, and waited to be addressed. Behind him, Cadfael closed the door.

'I sent for you, Brother,' said the abbot, 'because something has come to light, something you may recognise.'

Hugh held out the ring in his palm. 'Do you know this, Ruald? Take it up, examine it.'

It was hardly necessary, he had already opened his lips to answer at the mere sight of it in Hugh's hand. But obediently he took it, and at once turned it to bring the light sidewise upon the entwined initials cut crudely within. He had not needed it as identification, he wanted and accepted it gratefully as a sign both of remembered accord and of hope for future reconciliation and forgiveness. Cadfael saw the faint quiver of warmth and promise momentarily dissolve the patient lines of the lean face.

'I know it well, my lord. It is my wife's. I gave it to her

before we married, in Wales, where the stone was found. How did it come here?'

'First let me be clear – you are certain this was hers? There cannot be another such?'

'Impossible. There could be other pairs having these initials, yes, but these I myself cut, and I am no engraver. I know every line, every irregularity, every fault in the work, I have seen the bright cuts dull and tarnish over years. This I last saw on the hand of Generys. There is nothing more certain under the sun. Where is she? Has she come back? May I speak with her?'

'She is not here,' said Hugh. 'The ring was found in the shop of a jeweller in the city of Peterborough, and the jeweller testified that he had bought it from a woman only some ten days previously. The seller was in need of money to help her to leave that town for a safer place to live, seeing the anarchy that has broken out there in the Fens. He described her. It would seem that she was indeed the same who was formerly your wife.'

The radiance of hope had made but a slow and guarded sunrise on Ruald's plain middle-aged face, but by this time every shred of cloud was dispersed. He turned on Abbot Radulfus with such shining eagerness that the light from the window, breaking now into somewhat pale sunrays, seemed only the reflection of his joy.

'So she is not dead! She is alive and well! Father, may I question further? For this is wonderful!'

'Certainly you may,' said the abbot. 'And wonderful it is.'

'My lord sheriff, how came the ring here, if it was bought and sold in Peterborough?'

'It was brought by one who recently came to this house from those parts. You see him here, Sulien Blount. You know him. He was sheltered overnight in his journey by the jeweller, and saw and knew the ring there in his shop. For old kindness,' said Hugh with deliberation, 'he wished to bring it with him, and so he has, and there you hold it in your hand.'

Ruald had turned to look steadily and long at the young man standing mute and still, a little apart, as though he wished to withdraw himself from sight, and being unable to vanish in so small a room, at least hoped to escape too close observance by being motionless, and closing the shutters over his too transparent face and candid eyes. A strange and searching look it was that passed between them, and no one moved or spoke to break its intensity. Cadfael heard within his own mind the questions that were not being asked: Why did you not show me the ring? If, for reasons I guess at, you were unwilling to do that, could you not at least have told me that you had had recent word of her, that she was alive and well? But all Ruald said, without turning away his eyes from Sulien's face, was: 'I cannot keep it. I have forsworn property. I thank God that I have seen it, and that he has pleased to keep Generys safe. I pray that he may have her in his care hereafter.'

'Amen!' said Sulien, barely audibly. The sound was a mere sigh, but Cadfael saw his taut lips quiver and move.

'It is yours to give, Brother, if not to keep,' said the abbot, watching the pair of them with shrewd eyes that weighed and considered, but refrained from judging. The boy had already confessed to him why he had obtained the ring, and why it was his intent to keep it. A small thing in itself, great in what it could accomplish, it had played its part, and was of no further significance. Unless, perhaps, in its disposal? 'You may bestow it where you think fit,' said Radulfus.

'If the lord sheriff has no further need of it,' said Ruald, 'I give it back to Sulien, who reclaimed it. He has brought me the best news I could have received, and that morsel of my peace of mind that even this house could not restore.' He smiled suddenly, the plain, long face lighting up, and held out the ring to Sulien. The boy advanced a hand very slowly, almost reluctantly, to receive it. As they touched, the vivid colour rose in his cheeks in a fiery flush, and he turned his face haughtily away from the light to temper the betrayal.

So that is how the case goes, Cadfael thought, enlightened. No questions asked because none are needed. Ruald must have watched his lord's younger son running in and out of his workshop and house almost since the boy was born, and seen him grow into the awkward pains of adolescence and the foreshadowing of manhood, and always close about the person of this mysterious and formidable woman, the stranger, who was no stranger to him, the one who kept her distance, but not from him, the being of whom every man said that she was very beautiful, but not for everyone was she also close and kind. Children make their way by right where others are not admitted. It touched her not at all, Sulien maintained, she never knew of it. But Ruald had known. No need now for the boy to labour his motives, or ask pardon for the means by which he defended what was precious to him.

'Very well,' said Hugh briskly, 'be it so. I have nothing further to ask. I am glad, Ruald, to see your mind set at rest. You, at least, need trouble no further over this matter, there remains no shadow of a threat to you or to this house, and I must look elsewhere. As I hear, Sulien, you have chosen to leave the Order. You will be at Longner for the present, should I need a word with you hereafter?'

'Yes,' said Sulien, still a little stiff and defensive of his own dignity. 'I shall be there when you want me.'

Now I wonder, thought Cadfael, as the abbot dismissed both Ruald and Sulien with a brief motion of benediction, and they went out together, what trick of the mind caused the boy to use the word 'when'? I should rather have expected '*if* you want me'. Has he a premonition that some day, for some reason, more will be demanded of him?

'It's plain he was in love with the woman,' said Hugh, when the three of them were left alone. 'It happens! Never forget his own mother has been ill some eight years, gradually wasting into the frail thing she is now. How old would this lad be when that began? Barely ten years. Though he was fond and welcome at Ruald's croft long before that. A child dotes on a kind and handsome woman many innocent years, and suddenly finds he has a man's stirrings in his body, and in his mind too. Then the one or the other wins the day. This boy, I fancy, would give his mind the mastery, set his love up on a pedestal – an altar, rather, if you'll allow me the word, Father – and worship her in silence.'

'So, he says, he did,' agreed Radulfus drily. 'She never knew of it. His words.'

'I am inclined to believe it. You saw how he coloured like a peony when he realised Ruald could see clean through him. Was he never jealous of his prize, this Ruald? The world seems to be agreed she was a great beauty. Or is it simply that he was used to having the boy about the place, and knew him harmless?'

'Rather, from all accounts,' Cadfael suggested seriously, 'he knew his wife immovably loyal.'

'Yet rumour says she told him she had a lover, at the last, when he was set on leaving her.'

'Not only rumour says so,' the abbot reminded them firmly. 'He says so himself. On the last visit he made to her, with Brother Paul to confirm it, she told him she had a lover better worth loving, and all the tenderness she had ever had for him, her husband, he himself had destroyed.'

'She said it,' agreed Cadfael. 'But was it true? Yet I recall she also spoke to the jeweller of herself and her man.'

'Who's to know?' Hugh threw up his hands. 'She might well strike out at her husband with whatever came to hand, true or false, but she had no reason to lie to the silversmith. The one thing certain is that our dead woman is not Generys. And I can forget Ruald, and any other who might have had ado with Generys. I am looking for another woman, and another reason for murder.'

'Yet it sticks in my craw,' said Hugh, as he walked back towards the gatehouse with Cadfael at his side, 'that he did not blurt it out the second they met that the woman was alive and well. Who had a better right to know it, even if he had turned monk, than her husband? And what news could be more urgent to tell, the instant the boy clapped eyes on him?'

'He did not then know anything about a dead woman, nor that Ruald was suspected of anything,' Cadfael suggested helpfully, and was himself surprised at the tentative sound it had, even in his own ears.

'I grant it. But he did know, none better, that Ruald must have her always in his mind, wondering how she does, whether she lives or dies. The natural thing would have been to cry it out on sight: "No need to fret about Generys, she's well enough." It was all he needed to know, and his contentment would have been complete.'

'The boy was in love with her himself,' Cadfael hazarded, no less experimentally. 'Perhaps when it came to the point he grudged Ruald that satisfaction.'

'Does he seem to you a grudging person?' demanded Hugh.

'Let's say, then, his mind was still taken up with the sack of Ramsey and his escape from it. That was enough to put all lesser matters out of his mind.'

'The reminder of the ring came after Ramsey,' Hugh reminded him, 'and was weighty enough to fill his mind then.'

'True. And to tell the truth, I wonder about it myself. Who's to account for any man's reasoning under stress? What matters is the ring itself. She owned it; Ruald, who gave it to her, knew it instantly for hers. She sold it for her present needs. Whatever irregularities there may be in young Sulien's nature and actions, he did bring the proof. Generys is alive, and Ruald is free of all possible blame. What more do we need to know?'

'Where to turn next,' said Hugh ruefully.

'You have nothing more? What of the widow woman set up by Haughmond as tenant after Eudo made his gift to them?'

'I have seen her. She lives with her daughter in the town now, not far from the western bridge. She was there only a short while, for she had a fall, and her daughter's man fetched her away and left the place empty. But she left all in good order, and never saw nor heard anything amiss while she was there, or any strangers drifting that way. It's off the highways. But there have been tales of travelling folk bedding there at times, mainly during the fair. Eudo at Longner promised to ask all his people if ever they'd noticed things going on up there without leave, but I've heard nothing to the purpose from him yet.'

'Had there been any rumours come to light there,' said

Cadfael reasonably, 'Sulien would have brought them back with him, along with his own story.'

'Then I must look further afield.' He had had agents doing precisely that ever since the matter began, even though his own attention had certainly been, to some extent, distracted by the sudden alarming complication in the king's affairs.

'We can at least set a limit to the time,' Cadfael said consideringly. 'While the widow was living there it seems highly unlikely others would be up to mischief about the place. They could not use it as a cheap lodging overnight, it is well off any highway, so a chance passerby is improbable, and a couple looking for a quiet place for a roll in the grass would hardly choose the one inhabited spot in a whole range of fields. Once the tenant was out of the place it was solitary enough for any furtive purpose, and before ever she was installed by the canons . . . What was the exact day when Generys walked away and left the cottage door wide and the ashes on the hearth?'

'The exact day, within three,' said Hugh, halting at the open wicket in the gate, 'no one knows. A cowman from Longner passed along the river bank on the twenty-seventh day of June, and saw her in the garden. On the last day of June a neighbour from over the north side of the ridge – the nearest neighbours they had, and those best part of a mile away – came round on her way to the ferry. None too direct a way, for that matter, but I fancy she had a nose for gossip, and was after the latest news on a tasty scandal. She found the door open and the place empty and the hearth cold. After that no one saw Ruald's wife again in these parts.'

'And the charter that gave the field to Haughmond was drawn up and witnessed early in October. Which day? You were a witness.'

'The seventh,' said Hugh. 'And the old smith's widow

moved in to take care of the place three days later. There was work to be done before it was fit, there'd been a bit of looting done by then. A cooking pot or so, and a brychan from the bed, and the doorlatch broken to let the thieves in. Oh, yes, there had been visitors in and out of there, but no great damage up to then. It was later they scoured the place clean of everything worth removing.'

'So from the thirtieth of June to the tenth of October,' Cadfael reckoned, pondering, 'murder could well have been done up there, and the dead buried, and no one any the wiser. And when was it the old woman went away to her daughter in the town?'

'It was the winter drove her away,' said Hugh. 'About Christmas, in the frost, she had a fall. Lucky for her, she has a good fellow married to her girl, and when the hard weather began he kept a close eye on how she did, and when she was laid up helpless he fetched her away to the town to live with them. From that time the croft was left empty.'

'So from the beginning of this year it is also true that things mortal could have been done up there, and no witness. And yet,' said Cadfael, 'I think, truly I think, she had been in the ground a year and more, and put there when the soil was workable quickly and easily, not in the frosts. From spring of this year? No, it is too short a time. Look further back, Hugh. Some time between the end of June and the tenth of October of last year, I think, this thing was done. Long enough ago for the soil to have settled, and the root growth to have thickened and matted through the seasons. And if there were vagabonds making use of the cottage in passing, who was to go probing under the headland among the broom bushes? I have been thinking that whoever put her there foresaw that some day that ground might be broken for tillage, and laid her where her sleep should not be disturbed. A pace or two more cautious in the turn, and we should never have found her.'

'I am tempted,' admitted Hugh wryly, 'to wish you never had. But yes, you found her. She lived, and she is dead, and there's no escaping her, whoever she may be. And why it should be of so great import to restore her her name, and demand an account from whoever put her there in your field, I scarcely know, but there'll be small rest for you or me until it's done.'

It was a well-known fact that all the gossip from the countryside around, in contrast to that which seethed merrily within the town itself, came first into the hospital of Saint Giles, the better half of a mile away along the Foregate, at the eastern rim of the suburb. Those who habitually frequented that benevolent shelter were the rootless population of the roads: beggars, wandering labourers hoping for work, pickpockets and petty thieves and tricksters determined, on the contrary, to avoid work, cripples and sick men dependent on charity, lepers in need of treatment. The single crop they gathered on their travels was news, and they used it as currency to enlist interest. Brother Oswin, in charge of the hospice under the nominal direction of an appointed layman who rarely came to visit from his own house in the Foregate, had grown used to the common traffic in and out, and could distinguish between the genuine poor and unfortunate and the small, pathetic rogues. The occasional able-bodied fake feigning some crippling disability was a rarity, but Oswin was developing an eye even for that source of trouble. He had been Cadfael's helper in the herbarium for some time before graduating to his present service, and learned from him more skills than the mere mixing of lotions and ointments.

It was three days after Sulien's revelation when Cadfael put together the medicaments Brother Oswin had sent to ask for, and set off with a full scrip along the Foregate to replenish the medicine cupboard at Saint Giles, a regular task which he undertook every second or third week, according to the need. With autumn now well advanced, the people of the roads would be thinking ahead to the winter weather and considering where they could find patronage and shelter through the worst of it. The numbers of derelicts had not yet risen, but all those on the move would be making their plans to survive. Cadfael went without haste along the highway, exchanging greetings at open house doors, and taking some abstracted pleasure in the contemplation of children playing in the fitful sunshine, accompanied by their constant camp-followers, the dogs of the Foregate. His mood was contemplative, in keeping with the autumnal air and the falling leaves. He had put away from him for the moment all thought of Hugh's problem, and returned with slightly guilty zeal and devotion to the horarium of the monastic day and his own duties therein. Those small, gnawing doubts that inhabited the back of his mind were asleep, even if their sleep might be tenuous.

He reached the place where the road forked, and the long, low roof of the hospital rose beside the highway, beyond a gentle slope of grass and a wattle fence, with the squat tower of its little church peering over all. Brother Oswin came out into the porch to meet him, as large, cheerful and exuberant as ever, the wiry curls of his tonsure bristling from the low branches of the orchard trees, and a basket of the late, hard little pears on his arm, the kind that would keep until Christmas. He had learned to control his own vigorous body and lively mind since he had first come to assist Cadfael in the herb-garden, no longer broke what he handled or fell over his

101

own feet in his haste and ardour to do good. Indeed, since coming here to the hospital he had quite exceeded all Cadfael's hopes. His big hands and strong arms were better adapted to lifting the sick and infirm and controlling the belligerent than to fashioning little tablets and rolling pills, but he was competent enough in administering the medicines Cadfael brought for him and had proved a sensible and cheerful nurse, never out of temper even with the most difficult and ungrateful of his patients.

They filled up the shelves of the medicine cupboard together, turned the key again upon its secrets, and went through into the hall. A fire was kept burning here, with November on the doorstep, and some of the guests too infirm to move about freely. Some would never leave this place until they were carried into the churchyard for burial. The able-bodied were out in the orchard, gleaning the latest of the harvest.

'We have a new inmate,' said Oswin. 'It would be well if you would take a look at him, and make sure I am using the right treatment. A foul old man, it must be said, and foul-mouthed, he came in so verminous I have him bedded in a corner of the barn, away from the rest. Even now that he's cleaned and new-clothed, I think better he should be kept apart. His sores may infect others. His malignancy would certainly do harm, he has a grudge against the whole world.'

'The whole world has probably done enough to him to earn it,' Cadfael allowed ruefully, 'but a pity to take it out on some even worse off than himself. There will always be the haters among us. Where did you get this one?'

'He came limping in four days ago. From his story, he's been sleeping rough around the forest villages, begging his food where he could, and as like as not stealing it when charity ran short. He says he got a few bits of work to do here and there during the fair, but I doubt it was picking pockets on his own account, for by the look of him no respectable merchant would care to give him work. Come and see!'

The hospice barn was a commodious and even comfortable place, warm with the fragrance of the summer's hay and the ripe scent of stored apples. The foul old man, undoubtedly less foul in body than when he came, had his truckle bed installed in the most draught-proof corner, and was sitting hunched upon his straw pallet like a roosting bird, shaggy grey head sunk into once massive shoulders. By the malignant scowl with which he greeted his visitors, there had been no great change in the foulness of his temper. His face was shrunken and lined into a mask of suspicion and despite, and out of the pitted scars of half-healed sores small, malevolent, knowing eyes glittered up at them. The gown they had put on him was over-large for a body diminishing with age, and had been deliberately chosen, Cadfael thought, to lie loosely and avoid friction upon the sores that continued down his wrinkled throat and shoulders. A piece of linen cloth had been laid between to ease the touch of wool.

'The infection is somewhat improved,' said Oswin softly into Cadfael's ear. And to the old man, as they approached: 'Well, uncle, how do you feel this fine morning?'

The sharp old eyes looked up at them sidelong, lingering upon Cadfael. 'None the better,' said a voice unexpectedly full and robust to emerge from such a tattered shell, 'for seeing two of you instead of one.' He shifted closer on the edge of his bed, peering curiously. 'I know you,' he said, and grinned as though the realisation gave him, perhaps not pleasure, but an advantage over a possible opponent.

'Now you suggest it,' agreed Cadfael, viewing the raised

103

face with equal attention, 'I think I also should recall seeing you somewhere. But if so, it was in better case. Turn your face to the light here, so!' It was the outbreak of sores he was studying, but he took in perforce the lines of the face, and the man's eyes, yellowish and bright in their nests of wrinkles, watched him steadily all the while he was examining the broken rash. Round the edges of the infection showed the faint, deformed crust of sores newly healed. 'Why do you complain of us, when you are warm and fed here, and Brother Oswin has done nobly for you? Your case is getting better, and well you know it. If you have patience for two or three weeks more, you can be rid of this trouble.'

'And then you'll throw me out of here,' grumbled the vigorous voice bitterly. 'I know the way of it! That's my lot in this world. Mend me and then cast me out to fester and rot again. Wherever I go it's the same. If I find a bit of a roof to shelter me through the night, some wretch comes and kicks me out of it to take it for himself.'

'They can hardly do that here,' Cadfael pointed out placidly, restoring the protective linen to its place round the scrawny neck. 'Brother Oswin here will see to that. You let him cure you, and give no thought to where you'll lie or what you'll eat until you're clean. After that it will be time to think on such matters.'

'Fine talk, but it will end the same. I never have any luck. All very well for you,' he muttered, glowering up at Cadfael, 'handing out crumbs in alms at your gatehouse, when you have plenty, and a sound roof over you, and good dry beds, and then telling God how pious you are. Much you care where us poor souls lay our heads that same night.'

'So that's where I saw you,' said Cadfael, enlightened. 'On the eve of the fair.'

'And where I saw you, too. And what did I get out of it?
Bread and broth and a farthing to spend.'

'And spent it on ale,' Cadfael guessed mildly, and smiled.
'And where *did* you lay your head that night? And all the
nights of the fair? We had as poor as you snug enough in one
of our barns.'

'I'd as soon not lie inside your walls. Besides,' he said
grudgingly, 'I knew of a place, not too far, a cottage, nobody
living in it. I was there the last year, until that red-haired devil
of a pedlar came with his wench and kicked me out of it. And
where did I end? Under a hedge in the next field. Would he let
me have even a corner by the kiln? Not he, he wanted the place
to himself for his own cantrips with his wench. And then they
fought like wild cats most nights, for I heard them at it.' He
subsided into morose mutterings, oblivious of Cadfael's sudden intent silence. 'But I got it this year. For what it was
worth! Small use it will be now, falling to pieces as it is.
Whatever I touch rots.'

'This cottage,' said Cadfael slowly, 'that had also a kiln –
where is it?'

'Across the river from here, close by Longner. There's no
one working there now. Wrack and ruin!'

'And you spent the nights of the fair there this year?'

'It rains in now,' said the old man ruefully. 'Last year it was
all sound and good, I thought to do well there. But that's my
lot, always shoved out like a stray dog, to shiver under a
hedge.'

'Tell me,' said Cadfael, 'of last year. This man who turned
you out was a pedlar come to sell at the fair? He stayed there
in that cottage till the fair ended?'

'He and the woman.' The old man had sharpened into the
realisation that his information was here of urgent interest,

and had begun to enjoy the sensation, quite apart from the hope of turning it to advantage. 'A wild, black-haired creature she was, every whit as bad as her man. Every whit! She threw cold water over me to drive me away when I tried to creep back.'

'Did you see them leave? The pair together?'

'No, they were still there when I went packman, with a fellow bound for Beiston who had bought more than he could manage alone.'

'And this year? Did you see this same fellow at this year's fair?'

'Oh yes, he was there,' said the old man indifferently. 'I never had any ado with him, but I saw him there.'

'And the woman still with him?'

'No, never a glimpse of her this year. Never saw him but alone or with the lads in the tavern, and who knows where he slept! The potter's place wouldn't be good enough for him now. I hear she was a tumbler and singer, on the road like him. I never did hear *her* name.'

The slight emphasis on the 'her' had not escaped Cadfael's ear. He asked, with a sense of lifting the lid from a jar which might or might not let loose dangerous revelations: 'But his you do know?'

'Oh, everybody about the booths and alehouses knows *his* name. He's called Britric, he comes from Ruiton. He buys at the city markets, and peddles his wares round all this part of the shire and into Wales. On the move, most times, but never too far afield. Doing well, so I heard!'

'Well,' said Cadfael on a long, slow breath, 'wish him no worse, and do your own soul good. You have your troubles, I doubt Britric has his, no easier or lighter. You take your food and your rest, and do what Brother Oswin bids, and your

106

burden can soon be lightened. Let's wish as much to all men.'

The old man, squatting there observant and curious on his bed, watched them withdraw to the doorway. Cadfael's hand was on the latch when the voice behind them, so strangely resonant and full, called after them: 'I'll say this for him, his bitch was handsome, if she was cursed.'

Chapter Seven

O NOW THEY HAD it, a veritable name, a charm with which to prime memory. Names are powerful magic. Within two days of Cadfael's visit to Saint Giles, faithfully reported to Hugh before the end of the day, they had detail enough about the pedlar of Ruiton to fill a chronicle. Drop the name Britric into almost any ear about the market and the horse-fair ground, and mouths opened and tongues wagged freely. It seemed the only thing they had not known about him was that he had slept the nights of last year's fair in the cottage on the Potter's Field, then no more than a month abandoned, and in very comfortable shape still. Not even the neighbouring household at Longner had known that. The clandestine tenant would be off with his wares through the day, so would his woman if she had a living to make by entertaining the crowds, and they would have discretion enough to leave the door closed and everything orderly. If, as the old man declared, they had spent much of their time fighting, they had kept their battles withindoors. And no one from Longner had gone up the field to the deserted croft once Generys was gone. A kind of coldness and desolation had fallen upon the place, for those who had known it living, and they had shunned it, turning their faces

109

away. Only the wretched old man hoping for a snug shelter
for himself had tried his luck there, and been driven away by a
prior and stronger claimant.

The smith's widow, a trim little elderly body with bright
round eyes like a robin, pricked up her ears when she heard
the name of Britric. 'Oh, him, yes, he used to come round
with his pack some years back, when I was living with my man
at the smithy in Sutton. He started in a very small way, but he
was regular round the villages, and you know a body can't be
every week in the town. I got my salt from him. Doing well, he
was, and not afraid to work hard, either, when he was sober,
but a wild one when he was drunk. I remember seeing him at
the fair last year, but I had no talk with him. I never knew he
was sleeping the nights through up at the potter's croft. Well,
I'd never seen the cottage myself then. It was two months later
when the prior put me in there to take care of the place.
My man was dead late that Spring, and I'd been asking
Haughmond to find me some work to do. Smith had worked
well for them in his time, I knew the prior wouldn't turn me
away.'

'And the woman?' said Hugh. 'A strolling tumbler, so I'm
told, dark, very handsome. Did you see him with her?'

'He did have a girl with him,' the widow allowed after a
moment's thought, 'for I was shopping at the fishmonger's
booth close by Wat's tavern, at the corner of the horse fair,
the one day, and she came to fetch him away before, she said,
he'd drunk all his day's gain and half of hers. That I remember. They were loud, he was getting cantankerous then in his
cups, but she was a match for him. Cursed each other blind,
they did, but then they went off together as close and fond as
you please, and her holding him about the body from
stumbling, and still scolding. Handsome?' said the widow,

considering, and sniffed dubiously. 'Some might reckon so. A bold, striding, black-eyed piece, thin and whippy as a withy.'

'Britric was at this year's fair, too, so they tell me,' said Hugh. 'Did you see him?'

'Yes, he was here. Doing quite nicely in the world, by the look of him. They do say there's a good living to be made in pedlary, if you're willing to work at it. Give him a year or two more, and he'll be renting a booth like the merchants, and paying the abbey fees.'

'And the woman? Was she with him still?'

'Not that ever I saw.' She was no fool, and there was hardly a soul within a mile of Shrewsbury who did not know by this time that there was a dead woman to be accounted for, and the obvious answer, for some reason, was not satisfactory, since enquiry was continuing, and had even acquired a sharper edge. 'I was down into the Foregate only once during the three days, this year,' she said. 'There's others would be there all day and every day, they'll know. But I saw nothing of her. God knows what he's done with her,' said the widow, and crossed herself with matronly deliberation, standing off all evil omens from her own invulnerable virtue, 'but I doubt you'll find anyone here who set eyes on her since last year's Saint Peter's Fair.'

'Oh, yes, that fellow!' said Master William Rede, the elder of the abbey's lay stewards, who collected their rents and the tolls due from merchants and craftsmen bringing their goods to the annual fair. 'Yes, I know the man you mean. A bit of a rogue, but I've known plenty worse. By rights he should be paying a small toll for selling here, he brings in as full a man-load as Hercules could have hefted. But you know how it is. A man who sets up a booth for the three days, that's simple, you know where to find him. He pays his dues, and no time wasted. But a fellow who carries his goods on him, he sets eyes on you from a distance, and he's gone elsewhere, and you can waste more time chasing him than his small toll would be worth. Playing hoodman blind in and out of a hundred stalls, and all crowded with folk buying and selling, that's not for me. So he gets off scot-free. No great loss, and he'll come to it in time, his business is growing. I know no more about him than that.'

'Had he a woman with him this year?' Hugh asked. 'Dark, handsome, a tumbler and acrobat?'

'Not that I saw, no. There was a woman last year I noticed ate and drank with him, she could well be the one you mean. There were times I am sure she made him the sign when I came in sight, to make himself scarce. Not this year, though. He brought more goods this year, and I think you'll find he lay at Wat's tavern, for he needed somewhere to store them. You may learn more of him there.'

Walter Renold leaned his folded arms, bared and brawny, on the large cask he had just rolled effortlessly into position in a corner of the room, and studied Hugh across it with placid professional eyes.

'Britric, is it? Yes, he put up here with me through the fair. Came heavy laden this year, I let him put his bits and pieces in the loft. Why not? I know he slips his abbey dues, but the loss of his penny won't beggar them. The lord abbot doesn't cast too harsh an eye on the small folk. Not that Britric is small in any other way, mind you. A big lusty fellow, red-haired, a bit of a brawler sometimes, when he's drunk, but not a bad lad, take him all in all.'

'Last year,' said Hugh, 'he had a woman with him, or so I hear. I've good cause to know he was not lodging with you then, but if he did his drinking here you must have seen something of them both. You remember her?'

Wat was certainly remembering her already, with some pleasure and a great deal of amusement. 'Oh, her! Hard to forget, once seen. She could twist herself like a slip of willow, dance like a March lamb, and play on the little pipe. Easy to carry, better than a rebec unless you're a master. And she was the practical one, keeping a tight hold on the money they made between them. She talked of marriage, but I doubt she'd ever get him to the church door. Maybe she talked of it once too often, for he came alone this year round. Where he's left her there's no knowing, but she'll make her way wherever she is.'

That had a very bitter ring in Hugh's ear, considering the possibility he had in mind. Wat, it seemed, had not made the connection which had already influenced the widow's thinking. But before he could ask anything further Wat surprised him by adding simply: 'Gunnild, he called her. I never knew where she came from – I doubt if he knew it, either – but she's a beauty.'

That, too, had its strange resonance, when Hugh recalled the naked bones. More and more, in imagination, they took on the living aspect of this wild, sinuous, hardworking waif of the roads, darkly brilliant as the admiring gleam she could kindle in a middle-aged innkeeper's eyes after a year and more of absence.

'You have not seen her since, here or elsewhere?'

'How often am I elsewhere?' Wat responded good-humouredly. 'I did my roaming early. I'm content where I am. No, I've never set eyes on the girl again. Nor heard him so much as mention her name this year, now I come to think of it. For all the thought he seemed to be giving to last year's fancy,' said Wat tolerantly, 'she might as well be dead.'

'So there we have it,' said Hugh, summing up briskly for Cadfael in the snug privacy of the workshop in the herb garden. 'Britric is the one man we know to have made himself at home there in Ruald's croft. There may have been others, but none that we can learn of. Moreover, there was a woman with him, and their mating by all accounts tempestuous, she urging marriage on him, and he none too ready to be persuaded. More than a year ago, this. And this year not only does he come to the fair alone, but she is not seen there at all, she who gets her living at fairs and markets and weddings and such jollifications. It is not proof, but it requires answers.'

'And she has a name,' said Cadfael reflectively. 'Gunnild. But not a habitation. She comes from nowhere and is gone, nowhere. Well, you cannot but look diligently for them both, but he should be the easier to find. And as I guess, you already have all your people alerted to look out for him.'

'Both round the shire and over the border,' said Hugh flatly. 'His rounds, they say, go no further, apart from journeys to the towns to buy such commodities as salt and spices.'

'And here are we into November, and the season for markets and fairs over, but the weather still fairly mild and dry. He'll be still on his travels among the villages, but I would guess,' said Cadfael, pondering, 'not too far afield. If he still has a base in Ruiton, come the hard frosts and snow he'll be making for it, and he'll want to be within a reasonable few miles of it when the pinch comes.'

'About this time of year,' said Hugh, 'he remembers he has

114

a mother in Ruiton, and makes his way back there for the winter.'

'And you have someone waiting there for his coming.'

'If luck serves,' said Hugh, 'we may pick him up before then. I know Ruiton, it lies barely eight miles from Shrewsbury. He'll time his journeys to bring him round by all those Welsh villages and bear east through Knockin, straight for home. There are many hamlets close-set in that corner, he can go on with his selling until the weather changes, and still be near to home. Somewhere there we shall find him.'

Somewhere there, indeed, they found him, only three days later. One of Hugh's sergeants had located the pedlar at work among the villages on the Welsh side of the border, and discreetly waited for him on the English side until he crossed and headed without haste for Meresbrook, on his way to Knockin and home. Hugh kept a sharp eye on his turbulent neighbours in Powys, and as he would tolerate no breach of English law his own side of the border, so he was punctilious in giving them no occasion to complain that he trespassed against Welsh law on their side, unless they had first broken the tacit compact. His relations with Owain Gwynedd, to the northwest, were friendly, and well understood on either part, but the Welsh of Powys were ill-disciplined and unstable, not to be provoked, but not to be indulged if they caused him trouble without provocation. So the sergeant waited until his unsuspecting quarry crossed over the ancient dyke that marked the boundary, somewhat broken and disregarded in these parts but still tracable. The weather was still reasonably mild, and walking the roads not unpleasant, but it seemed that Britric's pack was as good as empty, so he was making for home ahead of the frosts, apparently content with his takings. If he had stocks at home in Ruiton, he could still sell to his neighbours and as far afield as the local hamlets.

So he came striding into the shire towards Meresbrook, whistling serenely and swinging a long staff among the road-side grasses. And short of the village he walked into a patrol of two light-armed men from the Shrewsbury garrison, who closed in on him from either side and took him by either arm, enquiring without excitement if he owned to the name of Britric. He was a big, powerful fellow half a head taller than either of his captors, and could have broken away from them had he been so minded, but he knew them for what they were and what they represented, and forbore from tempting providence unnecessarily. He behaved himself with cautious discretion, owned cheerfully to his name, and asked with disarming innocence what they wanted with him.

They were not prepared to tell him more than that the sheriff required his attendance in Shrewsbury, and their reticence, together with the stolid efficiency of their handling of him, might well have inclined him to think better of his co-operation and make a break for it, but by then it was too late, for two more of their company had appeared from nowhere to join them, ambling unhurriedly from the road-side, but both with bows slung conveniently to hand, and the look of men who knew how to use them. The thought of an arrow in the back did not appeal to Britric. He resigned himself to complying with necessity. A great pity, with Wales only a quarter of a mile behind. But if the worst came to the worst, there might be a better opportunity of flight later if he remained docile now.

They took him into Knockin, and for the sake of speed found a spare horse for him, brought him into Shrewsbury before nightfall, and delivered him safely to a cell in the castle. By that time he showed signs of acute uneasiness, but no real fear. Behind a closed and unrevealing face he might be weighing and measuring whatever irregularities he had to account for, and worrying about which of them could have come to light, but if so, the results seemed to bewilder rather than enlighten or alarm him. All his efforts to worm information out of his captors had failed. All he could do now was wait, for it seemed that the sheriff was not immediately on hand.

The sheriff, as it happened, was at supper in the abbot's lodging, together with Prior Robert and the lord of the manor of Upton, who had just made a gift to the abbey of a fishery on the river Tern, which bordered his land. The charter had been drawn up and sealed before Vespers, with Hugh as one of the witnesses. Upton was a crown tenancy, and the consent and approval of the king's officer was necessary to such transactions. The messenger from the castle was wise enough to wait patiently in the ante-room until the company rose from the table. Good news will keep at least as well as bad, and the suspect was safe enough within stone walls.

'This is the man you spoke of?' asked Radulfus, when he heard what the man had to say. 'The one who is known to have made free with Brother Ruald's croft last year?'

'The same,' said Hugh. 'And the only one I can hear of who *is* known to have borrowed free lodging there. And if you'll hold me excused, Father, I must go and see what can be got out of him, before he has time to get his breath and his wits back.'

'I am as concerned as you for justice,' the abbot avowed. 'Not so much that I want the life of this or any man, but I do want an accounting for the woman's. Of course, go. I hope we may be nearer the truth this time. Without it there can be no absolution.'

'May I borrow Brother Cadfael, Father? He first brought

me word of this man, he knows best what the old fellow at Saint Giles said of him. He may be able to pick up details that would elude me.'

Prior Robert looked down his patrician nose at the suggestion, and thinned his long lips in disapproval. He considered that Cadfael was far too often allowed a degree of liberty outside the enclave that offended the prior's strict interpretation of the Rule. But Abbot Radulfus nodded thoughtful agreement.

'Certainly a shrewd witness may not come amiss. Yes, take him with you. I do know his memory is excellent, and his nose for discrepancies keen. And he has been in this business from the beginning, and has some right, I think, to continue with it to the end.'

So it came about that Cadfael, coming from supper in the refectory, instead of going dutifully to Collations in the chapter-house, or less dutifully recalling something urgent to be attended to in his workshop, in order to avoid the dull, pedestrian reading of Brother Francis, whose turn it was, was haled out of his routine to go with Hugh up through the town to the castle, there to confront the prisoner.

He was as the old man had reported him, big, red-haired, capable of throwing out far more powerful intruders than a scabby old vagabond and, to an unprejudiced eye, a personable enough figure of a man to captivate a high-spirited and self-sufficient woman as streetwise as himself. At any rate for a time. If they had been together long enough to fall easily into fighting, he might well use those big, sinewy hands too freely and once too often, and find that he had killed without even meaning to. And if ever he blazed into the real rage his bush of flaming hair suggested, he might kill with intent. Here

118

in the cell where Hugh had chosen to encounter him, he sat with wide shoulders braced back against the wall, stiffly erect and alert, his face as stony as the wall itself, but for the wary eyes that fended off questions and questioners with an unwavering stare. A man, Cadfael judged, who had been in trouble before, and more than once, and coped with it successfully. Nothing mortal, probably, a deer poached here and there, a hen lifted, nothing that could not be plausibly talked out of court, in these somewhat disorganised days when in many places the king's foresters had little time or inclination to impose the rigours of forest law.

As for his present situation, there was no telling what fears, what speculations were going through his mind, how much he guessed at, or what feverish compilations of lies he was putting together against whatever he felt could be urged against him. He waited without protestations, so stiffly tensed that even his hair seemed to be erected and quivering. Hugh closed the door of the cell, and looked him over without haste.

'Well, Britric – that is your name? You have frequented the abbey fair, have you not, these past two years?'

'Longer,' said Britric. His voice was low and guarded, and unwilling to use more words than he need. 'Six years in all.' A small sidelong flicker of uneasy eyes took in Cadfael's habited figure, quiet in the corner of the cell. Perhaps he was recalling the tolls he had evaded paying, and wondering if the abbot had grown tired of turning a blind eye to the small defaulters.

'It's with last year we're concerned. Not so long past that your memory should fail you. The eve of Saint Peter ad Vincula, and the three days afterwards, you were offering your wares for sale. Where did you spend the nights?'

He was astray now, and that made him even more cautious,

but he answered without undue hesitation: 'I knew of a cottage was left empty. They were talking of it in the market, how the potter had taken a fancy to be a monk, and his wife was gone, and left the house vacant. Over the river, by Longner. I thought it was no harm to take shelter there. Is that why I'm brought here? But why now, after so long? I never stole anything. I left all as I found it. All I wanted was a roof over me, and a place to lie down in comfort.'

'Alone?' asked Hugh.

No hesitation at all this time. He had already calculated that the same question must have been answered by others, before ever hand was laid on him to answer for himself. 'I had a woman with me. Gunnild, she was called. She travelled the fairs and markets, entertaining for her living. I met her in Coventry, we kept together a while.'

'And when the fair here was over? Last year's fair? Did you then leave together, and keep company still?'

Britric's narrowed glance flickered from one face to the other, and found no helpful clue. Slowly he said: 'No. We went separate ways. I was going westward, my best trade is along the border villages.'

'And when and where did you part from her?'

'I left her there at the cottage where we'd slept. The fourth day of August, early. It was barely light when I started out. She was going east from there, she had no need to cross the river.'

'I can find no one in the town or the Foregate,' said Hugh deliberately, 'who saw her again.'

'They would not,' said Britric. 'I said, she was going east.'

'And you have never seen her since? Never made effort for old kindness' sake to find her again?'

'I never had occasion.' He was beginning to sweat, for

whatever that might mean. 'Chance met, nothing more than that. She went her way, and I went mine.'

'And there was no falling out between you? Never a blow struck? No loud disputes? Ever gentle and amiable together, were you, Britric? There are some report differently of you,' said Hugh. 'There was another fellow, was there not, had hoped to lie snug in that cottage? An old man you drove away. But he did not go far. Not out of earshot of the pair of you, when you did battle in the nights. A stormy partnership, he made it. And she was pressing you to marry her, was she not? And marriage was not to your mind. What happened? Did she grow too wearisome? Or too violent? A hand like yours over her mouth or about her throat could very easily quiet her.'

Britric had drawn his head hard back against the stone like a beast at bay, sweat standing on his forehead in quivering drops under the fall of red hair. Between his teeth he got out, in a voice so short of breath it all but strangled in his throat: 'This is mad . . . mad . . . I tell you, I left her there snoring, alive and lusty as ever she was. What is this? What are you thinking of me, my lord? What am I held to have done?'

'I will tell you, Britric, what I think you have done. There was no Gunnild at this year's fair, was there? Nor has she been seen in Shrewsbury since you left her in Ruald's field. I think you fell out and fought once too often, one of those nights, perhaps the last, and Gunnild died of it. And I think you buried her there in the night, under the headland, for the abbey plough to turn up this autumn. As it did! A woman's bones, Britric, and a woman's black hair, a mane of hair still on the skull.'

Britric uttered a small, half-swallowed sound, and let out his breath in a great, gasping sigh, as if he had been hit in the breast with an iron fist. When he could articulate, though in a strangled whisper understood rather by the shaping of his lips than by any sound, he got out over and over: 'No . . . no . . . no! Not Gunnild, no!'

Hugh let him alone until he had breath to make sense, and time to consider and believe, and reason about his own situation. For he was quick to master himself, and to accept, with whatever effort, the fact that the sheriff was not lying, that this was the reason for his arrest and imprisonment here, and he had better take thought in his own defence.

'I never harmed her,' he said at length, slowly and emphatically. 'I left her sleeping. I have never set eyes on her since. She was well alive.'

'A woman's body, Britric, a year at least in the ground. Black hair. They tell me Gunnild was black.'

'So she was. So she *is*, wherever she may be. So are many women along these borderlands. The bones you found cannot be Gunnild's.' Hugh had let slip too easily that all they had, virtually, was a skeleton, never to be identified by face or form. Now Britric knew that he was safe from too exact an accusing image. 'I tell you truly, my lord,' he said, with more insinuating care, 'she was well alive when I crept out and left her in the cottage. I won't deny she'd grown too sure of me. Women want to own a man, and that grows irksome. That was why I rose early, while she was deep asleep, and made off westward alone, to be rid of her without a screeching match. No, I never harmed her. This poor creature they found must be some other woman. It is not Gunnild.'

'What other woman, Britric? A solitary place, the tenants already gone, why should anyone so much as go there, let alone die there?'

'How could I know, my lord? I never heard of the place

until the eve of the fair, last year. I know nothing about the neighbourhood that side of the river. All I wanted was a place to sleep snug.' He had himself well in hand now, knowing that no name could ever be confidently given to a mere parcel of female bones, however black the hair on her skull. That might not save him, but it gave him some fragile armour against guilt and death, and he would cling to it and repeat his denials as often and as tirelessly as he must. 'I never hurt Gunnild. I left her alive and well.'

'What did you know of her?' Cadfael asked suddenly, going off at so abrupt a tangent that for a moment Britric was thrown off-balance, and lost his settled concentration on simple denial. 'If you kept company for a while, surely you learned something of the girl, where she came from, where she had kin, the usual pattern of her travelling year. You say she is alive, or at least that you left her alive. Where should she be looked for, to prove as much?'

'Why, she never told much.' He was hesitant and uncertain, and plainly knew little about her, or he would have poured it out readily, as proof of his good intent towards the law. Nor had he had time to put together a neat package of lies to divert attention to some distant region where she might well be pursuing her vagabond living. 'I met her in Coventry. We came from there together, but she was close-mouthed. I doubt she went further south than that, but she never said where she was from, nor a word of any kinsfolk.'

'You said she was going east, after you left her. But how can you know that? She had not said so, and agreed to part there, or you need not have stolen away early to avoid her.'

'I spoke too loosely,' owned Britric, writhing. 'I own it. I believed – I believe – she would turn eastward, when she found me gone. Small use taking her singing and tumbling into Wales, not alone. But I tell you truly, I never harmed her. I left her alive.'

And that was his simple, stubborn answer to all further questions, that and the one plea he advanced between obstinate denials.

'My lord, deal fairly with me. Make it known that she is sought, have it cried in the town, ask travellers to carry the word wherever they go, that she should send word to you, and show she is still living. I have not lied to you. If she hears I am charged with her death she will come forward. I never harmed her. She will tell you so.'

'And so we will have her name put about, and see if she appears,' agreed Hugh, when they had locked Britric in his stone cell and left him to his uneasy repose, and were walking back towards the castle gatehouse. 'But I doubt if a lady who lives Gunnild's style of life will be too eager to come near the law, even to save Britric's neck. What do you think of him? Denials are denials, worth very little by themselves. And he has something on his conscience, and something to do with that place and that woman, too. First thing he cries when we pin him to the place is: "I never stole anything. I left all as I found it." So I take it he did steal. When it came to the mention of Gunnild dead, then he took fright, until he realised I, like a fool, had let it out that she was mere bones. Then he knew how best to deal, and only then did he begin to plead that we seek her out. It looks and sounds well, but I think he knows she will never be found. Rather, he knows all too well that she *is* found, a thing he hoped would never happen.'

'And you'll keep him in hold?' asked Cadfael.

'Very surely! And go on following his traces wherever he's been since that time, and picking the brains of every innkeeper or potman or village customer who's had to deal with him. There must be someone somewhere who can fill in an hour or two of his life – and hers. Now I have him I'll keep him until I know truth, one way or the other. Why? Have you a thing to add that has passed me by? I would not refuse any detail you may have in mind.'

'A mere thought,' said Cadfael abstractedly. 'Let it grow a day or two. Who knows, you may not have to wait too long for the truth.'

On the following morning, which was Sunday, Sulien Blount came riding in from Longner to attend Mass in the abbey church, and brought with him, shaken and brushed and carefully folded, the habit in which he had made his way home after the abbot dismissed him. In his own cotte and hose, linen shirt and good leather shoes, he looked, if anything, slightly less at ease than in the habit, so new was his release after more than a year of the novitiate. He had not yet regained the freedom of a young man's easy stride, unhampered by monastic skirts. Nor, strangely, did he look any the happier or more carefree for having made up his mind. There was a solemn set to his admirable jaw, and a silent crease of serious thought between his straight brows. The ring of hair that had grown overlong on his journey from Ramsey had been trimmed into tidiness, and the down of dark gold curls within it had grown into a respectable length to blend with the brown. He attended Mass with the same grave concentration he had shown when within the Order, delivered up the clothing he had abandoned, paid his reverences to Abbot Radulfus and Prior Robert, and went to find Brother Cadfael in the herb garden.

'Well, well!' said Cadfael. 'I thought you might be looking

in on us soon. And how do you find things out in the world? You've seen no reason to change your mind?'

'No,' said the boy starkly, and for the moment had nothing more to say. He looked round the high-walled garden, its neat, patterned beds now growing a little leggy and bare with the loss of leaves, the bushy stems of thyme dark as wire. 'I liked it here, with you. But no, I wouldn't turn back. I was wrong to run away. I shall not make the same mistake again.'

'How is your mother faring?' asked Cadfael, divining that she might well be the insoluble grief from which Sulien had attempted flight. For the young man to live with the inescapable contemplation of perpetual pain and the infinitely and cruelly slow approach of lingering death might well be unendurable. For Hugh had reported her present condition very clearly. If that was the heart of it, the boy had braced himself now to make reparation, and carry his part of the load in the house, thereby surely lightening hers.

'Poorly,' said Sulien bluntly. 'Never anything else. But she never complains. It's as if she had some hungry beast for ever gnawing at her body from within. Some days are a little better than others.'

'I have herbs that might do something against the pain,' said Cadfael. 'Some time ago she did use them for a while.'

'I know. We have all told her so, but she refuses them now. She says she doesn't need them. All the same,' he said, warming, 'give me some, perhaps I may persuade her.'

He followed Cadfael into the workshop, under the rustling bunches of dried herbs hanging from the roof beams, and sat down on the wooden bench within while Cadfael filled a flask from his supply of the syrup he made from his eastern poppies, calmer of pain and inducer of sleep.

'You may not have heard yet,' said Cadfael, with his back

126

turned, 'that the sheriff has a man in prison for the murder of the woman we thought was Generys, until you showed us that was impossible. A fellow named Britric, a pedlar who works the border villages, and bedded down in Ruald's croft last year, through Saint Peter's Fair.'

He heard a soft stir of movement at his back, as Sulien's shoulders shifted against the timber wall. But no word was said.

'He had a woman there with him, it seems, one Gunnild, a tumbler and singer entertaining at the fairground. And no one has seen her since last year's fair ended. A black-haired woman, they report her. She could very well be the poor soul we found. Hugh Beringar thinks so.'

Sulien's voice, a little clipped and quiet, asked: 'What does this Britric say to that? He will not have admitted to it?'

'He said what he would say, that he left the woman there the morning after the fair, safe and well, and has not seen her since.'

'So he may have done,' said Sulien reasonably.

'It is possible. But no one has seen the woman since. She did not come to this year's fair, no one knows anything of her. And as I heard it, they were known to quarrel, even to come to blows. And he is a powerful man, with a hot temper, who might easily go too far. I would not like,' said Cadfael with intent, 'to be in his shoes, for I think the charge against him will be made good. His life is hardly worth the purchase.'

He had not turned until then. The boy was sitting very still, his eyes steady upon Cadfael's countenance. In a voice of detached pity, not greatly moved, he said: 'Poor wretch! I daresay he never meant to kill her. What did you say her name was, this tumbler girl?'

'Gunnild. They called her Gunnild.'

'A hard life that must be, tramping the roads,' said Sulien reflectively, 'especially for a woman. Not so ill in the summer, perhaps, but what must they do in the winter?'

'What all the jongleurs do,' said Cadfael, practically. 'About this time of year they begin thinking of what manor is most likely to take them in for their singing and playing, over the worst of the weather. And with the Spring they'll be off again.'

'Yes, I suppose a corner by the fire and a dinner at the lowest table must be more than welcome once the snow falls,' Sulien agreed indifferently, and rose to accept the small flask Cadfael had stoppered for him. 'I'll be getting back now, Eudo can do with a hand about the stable. And I do thank you, Cadfael. For this and for everything.'

Chapter Eight

T WAS THREE DAYS later that a groom came riding in at the gatehouse of the castle, with a woman pillion behind him, and set her down in the outer court to speak with the guards. Modestly but with every confidence she asked for the lord sheriff, and made it known that her business was important, and would be considered so by the personage she sought.

Hugh came up from the armoury in his shirt-sleeves and a leather jerkin, with the flush and smokiness of the smith's furnace about him. The woman looked at him with as much curiosity as he was feeling about her, so young and so unexpected was his appearance. She had never seen the sheriff of the shire before, and had looked for someone older and more defensive of his own dignity than this neat, lightly built young fellow in his twenties still, black-haired and black-browed, who looked more like one of the apprentice armourers than the king's officer.

'You asked to speak with me, mistress?' said Hugh. 'Come within, and tell me what you need of me.'

She followed him composedly into the small ante-room in the gatehouse, but hesitated for a moment when he invited her to be seated, as though her business must first be declared

129

and accounted for, before she could be at ease.

'My lord, I think it is you who have need of me, if what I have heard is true.' Her voice had the cadences of the countrywoman, and a slight roughness and rawness, as though in its time it had been abused by over-use or use under strain. And she was not as young as he had at first thought her, perhaps around thirty-five years old, but handsome and erect of carriage, and moved with decorous grace. She wore a good dark gown, matronly and sober, and her hair was drawn back and hidden under a white wimple. The perfect image of a decent burgess's wife, or a gentlewoman's attendant. Hugh could not immediately guess where and how she fitted into his present preoccupations, but was willing to wait for enlightenment.

'And what is it you have heard?' he asked.

'They are saying about the market that you have taken a man called Britric into hold, a pedlar, for killing a woman who kept company with him for some while last year. Is it true?'

'True enough,' said Hugh. 'You have something to say to the matter?'

'I have, my lord!' Her eyes she kept half-veiled by heavy, long lashes, looking up directly into his face only rarely and briefly. 'I bear Britric no particular goodwill, for reasons enough, but no ill will, either. He was a good companion for a while, and even if we did fall out, I don't want him hung for a murder that was never committed. So here am I in the flesh, to prove I'm well alive. And my name is Gunnild.'

'And, by God, so it proved!' said Hugh, pouring out the whole unlikely story some hours later, in the leisure hour of the monastic afternoon in Cadfael's workshop. 'No question,

Gunnild she is. You should have seen the pedlar's face when I brought her into his cell, and he took one long look at the decent, respectable shape of her, and then at her face closely, and his mouth fell open, he found her so hard to believe. But: "Gunnild!" he screeches, as soon as he gets his breath back. Oh, she's the same woman, not a doubt of it, but so changed it took him a while to trust his own eyes. And there was more than he ever told us to that early morning flight of his. No wonder he crept off and left her sleeping. He took every penny of her earnings with him as well as his own. I said he had something on his conscience, and something to do with the woman. So he had, he robbed her of everything she had of value, and a hard time she must have had of it through the autumn and into the winter, last year.'

'It sounds,' said Cadfael, attentive but unsurprised, 'as if their meeting today might well be another stormy one.'

'Well, he was so glad of her coming, he was all thanks and promises of redress, and fawning flattery. And she refuses to press the theft against him. I do believe he had thoughts of trying to woo her back to the wandering life, but she's having none of that. Not she! She calls up her groom, and he hoists her to the pillion, and away they go.'

'And Britric?' Cadfael reached to give a thoughtful stir to the pot he had gently simmering on the grid that covered one side of his brazier. The sharp, warm, steamy smell of horehound stung their nostrils. There were already a few coughs and colds among the old, frail brothers in Edmund's infirmary.

'He's loosed and away, very subdued, though how long that will last there's no knowing. No reason to hold him longer. We'll keep a weather eye on his dealings, but if he's beginning to prosper honestly – well, almost honestly! – he may have got enough wisdom this time to stay within the law.

Even the abbey may get its tolls if he comes to next year's fair. But here are we, Cadfael, left with a history repeating itself very neatly and plausibly, to let loose not one possible murderer, but the second one also. Is that believable?'

'Such things have been known,' said Cadfael cautiously, 'but not often.'

'Do *you* believe it?'

'I believe it has happened. But that it has happened by chance, that has me in two minds. No,' Cadfael amended emphatically, 'more than two minds.'

'That one supposedly dead woman should come back to life, well and good. But the second also? And are we now to expect a third, if we can find a third to die or rise again? And yet we still have this one poor, offended soul waiting for justice, if not by another's death, at least by the grace and remembrance of a name. She *is* dead, and requires an accounting.'

Cadfael had listened with respect and affection to a speech which might as well have come from Abbot Radulfus, but delivered with a youthful and secular passion. Hugh did not often commit himself to indignation, at least not aloud.

'Hugh, did she tell you how and where she heard of Britric's being in your prison?'

'No more than vaguely. Rumoured about in the market, she said. I never thought,' said Hugh, vexed, 'to question more nearly.'

'And it's barely three days since you let it be known what he was suspected of, and put out her name. News travels fast, but how far it should have reached in the time may be much to the point. I take it Gunnild has accounted for herself? For the change in fortunes? You have not told me, yet, where she lives and serves now.'

'Why, it seems that after a fashion Britric did her a favour when he left her penniless, there in Ruald's croft. It was August then, the end of the fair, no very easy way to pick up a profit, and she barely managed to keep herself through the autumn months, fed but with nothing saved, and you'll remember – God knows you should! – that the winter came early and hard. She did what the wandering players do, started early looking for a manor where there might be a place for a good minstrel through the worst of the winter. Common practice, but you gamble, and may win or do poorly.'

'Yes,' agreed Cadfael, rather to himself than to his friend, 'so I told him.'

'She did well for herself. She happened into the manor of Withington in the December snows. Giles Otmere holds it, a crown tenant these days, since FitzAlan's lands were seized, and he has a young family who welcome a minstrel over the Christmas feast, so they took her in. But better still, the young daughter is eighteen just turned, and took a liking to her, and according to Gunnild she has a neat hand with dressing hair, and is good with her needle, and the girl has taken her on as tirewoman. You should see the delicate pace of her now, and the maidenly manners. She's been profitable to her lady, and thinks the world of her. Gunnild will never go back to the roads and the fairgrounds now, she has too much good sense. Truly, Cadfael, you should see her for yourself.'

'Truly,' said Cadfael musingly, 'I think I should. Well, Withington is not far, not much beyond Upton, but unless Mistress Gunnild came into town for yesterday's market, or someone happened in at Withington with the day's news, rumour seems to have run through the grasses and across the river of its own accord. Granted it does fly faster than the birds at times, at least in town and Foregate, it takes a day or so to reach the outlying villages. Unless someone sets out in haste to carry it.'

'Brought home from market or blown on the wind,' said Hugh, 'it travelled as far as Withington, it seems. As well for Britric. I am left with no notion which way to look now, but better that than hound an innocent man. But I would be loath to give up, and let the thing go by default.'

'No need,' said Cadfael, 'to think in such terms yet. Wait but a few more days, and give your mind to the king's business meantime, and we may have one thread left to us yet.'

Cadfael made his way to the abbot's lodging before Vespers, and asked for an audience. He was a little deprecating in advancing his request, well aware of the licence often granted to him beyond what the Rule would normally countenance, but for once none too certain of what he was about. The reliance the abbot had come to place in him was in itself something of a burden.

'Father, I think Hugh Beringar will have been with you this afternoon, and told you what has happened concerning the man Britric. The woman who is known to have been in his company a year and more ago did indeed vanish from her usual haunts, but not by death. She has come forward to show that he has not harmed her, and the man is set free.'

'Yes,' said Radulfus, 'this I know. Hugh was with me an hour since. I cannot but be glad the man is innocent of murder, and can go his ways freely. But our responsibility for the dead continues, and our quest must go on.'

'Father, I came to ask leave to make a journey tomorrow. A few hours would suffice. There is an aspect of this deliverance that raises certain questions that need to be answered. I did not suggest to Hugh Beringar that he should undertake such an enquiry, partly because he has the king's business very much on his mind, but also because I may be wrong in what I believe, and if it proves so, no need to trouble him with it. And if it proves there is ground for my doubts,' said Cadfael very soberly, 'then I must lay the matter in his hands, and there leave it.'

'And am I permitted,' asked the abbot after a moment's thought, and with a shadowy and wry smile touching his lips briefly, 'to ask what these doubts may be?'

'I would as lief say nothing,' said Cadfael frankly, 'until I have the answers myself, yes or no. For if I am become a mere subtle, suspicious old man, too prone to see devious practices where none are, then I would rather not draw any other man into the same unworthy quagmire, nor levy false charges easier to publish than to suppress. Bear with me until tomorrow.'

'Then tell me one thing only,' said Radulfus. 'There is no cause, I trust, in this course you have in mind, to point again at Brother Ruald?'

'No, Father. It points away from him.'

'Good! I cannot believe any ill of the man.'

'I am sure he has done none,' said Cadfael firmly.

'So he at least can be at peace.'

'That I have not said.' And at the sharp and penetrating glance the abbot fixed upon him he went on steadily: 'All we within this house share the concern and grief for a creature laid astray in abbey land without a name or the proper rites of death and absolution. To that extent, until this is resolved, none of us can be at peace.'

Radulfus was still for a long moment, eyeing Cadfael

closely; then he stirred abruptly out of his stillness, and said practically: 'Then the sooner you advance this argument the better. Take a mule from the stables, if the journey is somewhat long for going and returning in a day. Where is it you are bound? May I ask even so far?'

'No great distance,' said Cadfael, 'but it will save time if I ride. It is only to the manor of Withington.'

Cadfael set out next morning, immediately after Prime, on the six-mile ride to the manor where Gunnild had found her refuge from the chances and mischances of the road. He crossed by the ferry upstream from the Longner lands, and on the further side followed the little brook that entered the Severn there, with rising fields on either side. For a quarter of a mile he could see on his right the long crest of trees and bushes, on the far side of which lay the Potter's Field, transformed now into a plateau of new ploughland above, and the gentle slope of meadow below. What remained of the cottage would have been dismantled by now, the garden cleared, the site levelled. Cadfael had not been back to see.

The way was by open fields as far as the village of Upton, climbing very gently. Beyond, there was a well-used track the further two miles or more to Withington, through flat land, rich and green. Two brooks threaded their gentle way between the houses of the village, to merge on the southern edge and flow on to empty into the River Tern. The small church that sat in the centre of the green was a property of the abbey, like its neighbour at Upton, Bishop de Clinton's gift to the Benedictines some years back. On the far side of the village, drawn back a little from the brook, the manor lay within a low stockade, ringed round with its barns and byres and stables. The undercroft was of timber beams, one end of the living floor of stone, and a short, steep flight of steps led up to the hall door, which was standing open at this early working hour of the day, when baker and dairy-maid were likely to be running busily in and out.

Cadfael dismounted at the gate and led the mule at leisure into the yard, taking time to look about him. A woman-servant was crossing with a huge crock of milk from the byre to the dairy and halted at sight of him, but went on about her business when a groom emerged from the stable and came briskly to take the mule's bridle.

'You're early abroad, Brother. How can we serve you? My master's ridden out towards Rodington already. Shall we send after him, if your errand's to him? Or if you have leisure to wait his return, you're welcome within. His door's always open to the cloth.'

'I'll not disrupt the order of a busy man's day,' said Cadfael heartily. 'I'm on a simple errand of thanks to your young mistress for her kindness and help in a certain vexed business, and if I can pay my compliments to the lady, I'll soon be on my way back to Shrewsbury. I don't know her name, for I hear your lord has a flock of children. The lady I want may well be the eldest, I fancy. The one who has a maid called Gunnild.'

By the practical way the groom received the name, Gunnild's place in this household was established and accepted, and if ever there had been whispers and grudges among the other maids over the transformation of a draggle-tailed tumbler into a favoured tirewoman, they were already past and forgotten, which was shrewd testimony to Gunnild's own good sense.

'Oh, ay, that's Mistress Pernel,' said the groom, and turned to call up a passing boy to take the mule from him and see him cared for. 'She's within, though my lady's gone with my lord, at least a piece of the way; she has business with the miller's wife at Rodington. Come within, and I'll call Gunnild for you.'

The to and fro of voices across the yard gave place, as they climbed the steps to the hall door, to shriller voices and a great deal of children's laughter, and two boys of about twelve and eight came darting out from the open doorway and down the steps in two or three leaps, almost bowling Cadfael over, and recovering with breathless yells to continue their flight towards the fields. They were followed in bounding haste by a small girl of five or six years, holding up her skirts in both plump hands and shrieking at her brothers to wait for her. The groom caught her up deftly and set her safely on her feet at the foot of the steps, and she was off after the boys at the fastest speed her short legs could muster. Cadfael turned for a moment on the steps to follow her flight. When he looked round again to continue mounting, an older girl stood framed in the doorway, looking down at him in smiling and wondering surprise.

Not Gunnild, certainly, but Gunnild's mistress. Eighteen, just turned, Hugh had said. Eighteen, and not yet married or, it seemed, betrothed, perhaps because of the modesty of her dowry and of her father's connections, but perhaps also because she was the eldest of this brood of lively chicks, and very valuable to the household. The succession was secured, with two healthy sons, and two daughters to provide for might be something of a tax on Giles Otmere's resources, so that there was no haste. With her gracious looks and evident warmth of nature she might need very little by way of dowry if the right lad came along.

She was not tall, but softly rounded and somehow

138

contrived to radiate a physical brightness, as if her whole body, from soft brown hair to small feet, smiled as her eyes and lips smiled. Her face was round, the eyes wide-set and wide-open in shining candour, her mouth at once generously full and passionate, and resolutely firm, though parted at this moment in a startled smile. She had her little sister's discarded wooden doll in her hand, just retrieved from the floor where it had been thrown.

'Here is Mistress Pernel,' said the groom cheerfully, and drew back a step towards the yard. 'Lady, the good brother would like a word with you.'

'With me?' she said, opening her eyes wider still. 'Come up, sir, and welcome. Is it really me you want? Not my mother?'

Her voice matched the brightness she radiated, pitched high and gaily, like a child's, but very melodious in its singing cadences.

'Well, at least,' she said, laughing, 'we can hear each other speak, now the children are away. Come into the window-bench, and rest.'

The alcove where they sat down together had the weather shutter partially closed, but the lee one left open. There was almost no wind that morning, and though the sky was clouded over, the light was good. Sitting opposite to this girl was like facing a glowing lamp. For the moment they had the hall to themselves, though Cadfael could hear several voices in busy, braided harmony from passage and kitchen, and from the yard without.

'You are come from Shrewsbury?' she said.

'With my abbot's leave,' said Cadfael, 'to give you thanks for so promptly sending your maid Gunnild to the lord sheriff, to deliver the man held in prison on suspicion of causing her death. Both my abbot and the sheriff are in your debt. Their intent is justice. You have helped them to avoid injustice.'

'Why, we could do no other,' she said simply, 'once we knew of the need. No one, surely, would leave a poor man in prison a day longer than was needful, when he had done no wrong.'

'And how did you learn of the need?' asked Cadfael. It was the question he had come to ask, and she answered it cheerfully and frankly, with no suspicion of its real significance.

'I was told. Indeed, if there is credit in the matter it is not ours so much as the young man's who told me of the case, for he had been enquiring everywhere for Gunnild by name, whether she had spent the winter of last year with some household in this part of the shire. He had not expected to find her still here, and settled, but it was great relief to him. All I did was send Gunnild with a groom to Shrewsbury. He had been riding here and there asking for her, to know if she was alive and well, and beg her to come forward and prove as much, for she was thought to be dead.'

'It was much to his credit,' said Cadfael, 'so to concern himself with justice.'

'It was!' she agreed warmly. 'We were not the first he had visited, he had ridden as far afield as Cressage before he came to us.'

'You know him by name?'

'I did not, until then. He told me he was Sulien Blount, of Longner.'

'Did he ask expressly for you?' asked Cadfael.

'Oh, no!' She was surprised and amused, and he could not be sure, by this time, that she was not acutely aware of the curious insistence of his questioning, but she saw no reason to hesitate in answering. 'He asked for my father, but Father was away in the fields, and I was in the yard when he rode in. It was only by chance that he spoke to me.'

At least a pleasant chance, thought Cadfael, to afford some unexpected comfort to a troubled man.

'And when he knew he had found the woman he sought, did he ask to speak with her? Or leave that telling to you?'

'Yes, he spoke with her. In my presence he told her how the pedlar was in prison, and how she must come forward and prove he had never done her harm. And so she did, willingly.'

She was grave now rather than smiling, but still open, direct and bright. It was evident from the intelligent clarity of her eyes that she had recognised some deeper purpose behind his interrogation, and was much concerned with its implications, but also that even in that recognition she saw no cause to withhold or prevaricate, since truth could not in her faith be a means of harm. So he asked the final question without hesitation: 'Did he ever have opportunity to speak with her alone?'

'Yes,' said Pernel. Her eyes, very wide and steady upon Cadfael's face, were a golden, sunlit brown, lighter than her hair. 'She thanked him and went out with him to the yard when he mounted and left. I was within with the children, they had just come in, it was near time for the supper. But he would not stay.'

But she had asked him. She had liked him, was busy liking him now, and wondering, though without misgivings, what this monk of Shrewsbury might want concerning the movements and generosities and preoccupations of Sulien Blount of Longner.

'What they said to each other,' said Pernel, 'I do not know. I am sure it was no harm.'

141

'That,' said Cadfael, 'I think I may guess at. I think the young man may have asked her, when she came to the sheriff at the castle, not to mention that it was he who had come seeking her, but to say that she had heard of Britric's plight and her own supposed death from the general gossip. News travels. She would have heard it in the end, but not, I fear, so quickly.'

'Yes,' said Pernel, flushing and glowing, 'that I can believe of him, that he wanted no credit for his own goodness of heart. Why? Did she do as he wished?'

'She did. No blame to her for that, he had the right to ask it of her.'

Perhaps not only the right, but the need! Cadfael made to rise, to thank her for the time she had devoted to him, and to take his leave, but she put out a hand to detain him.

'You must not go without taking some refreshment in our house, Brother. If you will not stay and eat with us at midday, at least let me call Gunnild to bring us wine. Father bought some French wine at the summer fair.' And she was on her feet and across the width of the hall to the screen door, and calling, before he could either accept or withdraw. It was fair, he reflected. He had had what he wanted from her, ungrudging and unafraid; now she wanted something from him. 'We need say nothing to Gunnild,' she said softly, returning. 'It was a harsh life she used to live, let her put it by, and all reminders of it. She has been a good friend and servant to me, and she loves the children.'

The woman who came in from the kitchen and pantry with flask and glasses was tall, and would have been called lean rather than slender, but the flow of her movements was elegant and sinuous still within the plain dark gown. The oval face framed by her white wimple was olive-skinned and

142

suave, the dark eyes that took in Cadfael with serene but guarded curiosity and dwelt with almost possessive affection upon Pernel, were still cleanly set and beautiful. She served them handily, and withdrew from them discreetly. Gunnild had come into a haven from which she did not intend to sail again, certainly not at the invitation of a vagabond like Britric. Even when her lady married, there would be the little sister to care for, and perhaps, some day, marriage for Gunnild herself, the comfortable, practical marriage of two decent, ageing retainers who had served long enough together to know they can run along cosily for the rest of their days.

'You see,' said Pernel, 'how well worth it was to take her in, and how content she is here. And now,' she said, pursuing without conceal what most interested her, 'tell me about this Sulien Blount. For I think you must know him.'

Cadfael drew breath and told her all that it seemed desirable to him she should know about the sometime Benedictine novice, his home and his family, and his final choice of the secular world. It did not include any more about the history of the Potter's Field than the mere fact that it had passed by stages from the Blounts to the abbey's keeping, and had given up, when ploughed, the body of a dead woman for whose identity the law was now searching. That seemed reason enough for a son of the family taking a personal interest in the case, and exerting himself to extricate the innocent from suspicion, and accounted satisfactorily for the concern shown by the abbot and his envoy, this elderly monk who now sat in a window embrasure with Pernel, recounting briefly the whole disturbing history.

'And his mother is so ill?' said Pernel, listening with wide, sympathetic eyes and absorbed attention. 'At least how glad she must be that he has chosen, after all, to come home.'

'The elder son married in the summer,' said Cadfael, 'so there is a young woman in the household to give her comfort and care. But yes, certainly she will be glad to have Sulien home again.'

'It is not so far,' Pernel mused, half to herself. 'We are almost neighbours. Do you think the lady Donata is ever well enough to want to receive visitors? If she cannot go out, she must sometimes be lonely.'

Cadfael took his leave with that delicate suggestion still in his ears, in the girl's warm, purposeful, buoyant voice, and with her bright and confident face before his eyes, the antithesis of illness, loneliness and pain. Well, why not? Even if she went rather in search of the young man who had touched her generous fancy than for such benefit as her vigour and charm could confer upon a withered gentle-woman, her presence might still do wonders.

He rode back through the autumnal fields without haste, and instead of turning in at the abbey gatehouse, went on over the bridge and into the town, to look for Hugh at the castle.

It was plain, as soon as he began to climb the ramp to the castle gatehouse, that something had happened to cause a tremendous stir within. Two empty carts were creaking briskly up the slope and in under the deep archway in the tower, and within, there was such bustle between hall, sta-bles, armoury and stores, that Cadfael sat his mule unnoticed for many minutes in the midst of the to-ings and fro-ings, weighing up what he saw, and considering its inevitable meaning. There was nothing confused or distracted about it, everything was purposeful and exact, the ordered climax of calculated and well-planned preparations. He dismounted, and Will Warden, Hugh's oldest and most seasoned sergeant, halted for an instant in directing the carters through to the inner yard, and came to enlighten him.

'We're on the march tomorrow morning. The word came only an hour past. Go in to him, Brother, he's in the gate-tower.'

And he was gone, waving the teamster of the second cart through the arch to the inner ward, and vanishing after the cart to see it efficiently loaded. The supply column must be preparing to leave today, the armed company would ride after them at first light.

Cadfael abandoned his mule to a stable boy, and crossed to the deep doorway of the guardroom in the gate-tower. Hugh rose from a littered table at sight of him, shuffled his records together and pushed them aside.

'It's come, as I thought it would. The king had to move against the man, for the saving of his own face he could no longer sit and do nothing. Though he knows as well as I do,' admitted Hugh, preoccupied and vehement, 'that the chances of bringing Geoffrey de Mandeville to pitched battled are all too thin. What, with his Essex supply lines secure even if the time comes when he can wring no more corn or cattle out of the Fens? And all those bleak levels laced with water, and as familiar to him as the lines of his own hand? Well, we'll do him what damage we can, perhaps bolt him in if we can't flush him out. Whatever the odds, Stephen has ordered his muster to Cambridge, and demanded a company of me for a limited time, and a company he shall have, as good as any he'll get from his Flemings. And unless he has the lightning fit on him – it takes him and us by surprise sometimes – we'll be in Cambridge before him.'

Having thus unburdened himself of his own immediate

preoccupations, concerning which there was no particular haste, since everything had been taken care of in advance, Hugh took a more attentive look at his friend's face, and saw that King Stephen's courier had not been the only visitor with news of moment to impart.

'Well, well!' he said mildly. 'I see you have things on your mind, no less than his Grace the king. And here am I about to leave you hefting the load alone. Sit down and tell me what's new. There's time, before I need stir.'

Chapter Nine

HANCE HAD NO PART in it,' said Cadfael, leaning his folded arms upon the table. 'You were right. History repeated itself for good reason, because the same hand thrust it where the same mind wanted it. Twice! It was in my mind, so I put it to the test. I took care the boy should know there was another man suspected of this death. It may even be that I painted Britric's danger blacker than it was. And behold, the lad takes to heart that true word I offered him, that the folk of the roads look round for a warm haven through the winter, and off he goes, searching here and there about these parts, to find out if one Gunnild had found a corner by some manor fire. And this time, mark you, he had no possibility of knowing whether the woman was alive or dead, knowing nothing of her beyond what I had told him. He had luck, and he found her. Now, why, never having heard her name before, never seen her face, why should he bestir himself for Britric's sake?'

'Why,' agreed Hugh, eye to eye with him across the board, 'unless he knew, whatever else he did not know, that our dead woman was not and could not be this Gunnild? And how could he know that, unless he knows all too well who she really is? And what happened to her?'

147

'Or believes he knows,' said Cadfael cautiously.

'Cadfael, I begin to find your failed brother interesting. Let us see just what we have here. Here is this youngster who suddenly, so short a while after Ruald's wife vanished from her home, chooses most unexpectedly to desert his own home and take the cowl, not close here where he's known, with you, or at Haughmond, the house and the order his family has always favoured, but far away at Ramsey. Removing himself from a scene now haunting and painful to him? Perhaps even dangerous? He comes home, perforce, when Ramsey becomes a robber's nest, and it may well be true that he comes now in doubt of his own wisdom in turning to the cloister. And what does he find here? That the body of a woman has been found, buried on lands that once pertained to his family demesne, and that the common and reasonable thought is that this is Ruald's lost wife, and Ruald her murderer. So what does he do? He tells a story to prove that Generys is alive and well. Distant too far to be easily found and answer for herself, seeing the state of that country now, but he has proof. He has a ring which was hers, a ring she sold in Peterborough, long after she was gone from here. Therefore this body cannot be hers.'

'The ring,' said Cadfael reasonably, 'was unquestionably hers, and genuine. Ruald knew it at once, and was glad and grateful beyond measure to be reassured that she's alive and well, and seemingly faring well enough without him. You saw him, as I did. I am sure there was no guile in him, and no falsity.'

'So I believe, too. I do not think we are back to Ruald, though God knows we may be back with Generys. But see what follows! Next, a search throws up another man who may by all the signs be guilty of killing another vanished woman in

148

that very place. And yet again Sulien Blount, when he hears of it so helpfully from you, continues to interest himself in the matter, voluntarily setting out to trace this woman also, and show that she is alive. And, by God, is lucky enough to find her! Thus delivering Britric as he delivered Ruald. And now tell me, Cadfael, tell me truly, what does all that say to you?'

'It says,' admitted Cadfael honestly, 'that whoever the woman may be, Sulien himself is guilty, and means to battle it out for his life, yes, but not at the expense of Ruald or Britric or any innocent man. And that, I think, would be in character for him. He might kill. He would not let another man hang for it.'

'That is how you read the omens?' Hugh was studying him closely, black brows obliquely tilted, and a wry smile curling one corner of his expressive mouth.

'That is how I read the omens.'

'But you do not believe it!'

It was a statement rather than a question, and voiced without surprise. Hugh was well enough versed in Cadfael by now to discern in him tendencies of which he himself was still unaware. Cadfael considered the implications very seriously for a few moments of silence. Then he said judicially: 'On the face of it, it is logical, it is possible, it is even likely. If, after all, this is Generys, as now again seems all too likely, by common consent she was a very beautiful woman. Nearly old enough to be the boy's mother, true, and he had known her from infancy, but he himself as good as said that he fled to Ramsey because he found himself guiltily and painfully in love with her. It happens to many a green boy, to suffer his first disastrous experience of love for a woman long familiarly known, and loved in another fashion, a woman out of his generation and out of his reach. But how if there was more to

149

it than mere flight to escape from insoluble problems and incurable pain? Consider the situation, when a husband she had loved and trusted was wrenching himself away from her as it were in blood, her blood, and yet leaving her bound and lonely! In her rage and bitterness at such a desertion a passionate woman might well have set herself to take revenge on all men, even the vulnerable young. Taken him up, comforted herself in his worshipping dog's eyes, and then cast him off. Such affronts the young in their first throes feel mortally. But the death may have been hers. Reason enough to fly from the scene and from the world into a distant cloister, out of sight even of the trees that sheltered her home.'

'It is logical,' said Hugh, echoing Cadfael's own words, 'it is possible, it is credible.'

'My only objection,' agreed Cadfael, 'is that I find I do not credit it. Not cannot, for good sound reasons – simply do not.'

'Your reservations,' said Hugh philosophically, 'always have me reining in and treading very carefully. Now as ever! But I have another thought: How if Sulien had the ring in his possession all along, ever since he last parted with Generys – living or dead? How if she herself had given it to him? Tossed away her husband's love gift in bitterness at his desertion, upon the most innocent and piteous lover she could ever have had. And she did say that she had a lover.'

'If he had killed her,' said Cadfael, 'would he have kept her token?'

'He might! Oh, yes, he very well might. Such things have been known, when love at its most devilish raises hate as another devil, to fight it out between them. Yes, I think he would keep her ring, even through a year of concealing it from abbot and confessor and all, in Ramsey.'

150

'As he swore to Radulfus,' remarked Cadfael, suddenly reminded, 'that he did not. He could lie, I think, but would not lie wantonly, for no good reason.'

'Have we not attributed to him good reason enough for lying? Then, if all along he had the ring, the time came when it was urgent, for Ruald's sake, to produce it in evidence, with this false story of how he came by it. If indeed it is false. If I had proof it is not,' said Hugh, fretting at the frustrations of chance, 'I could put Sulien almost – *almost* – out of my mind.'

'There is also,' said Cadfael slowly, 'the question of why he did not tell Ruald at once, when they met, that he had heard news of Generys in Peterborough, and she was alive and well. Even if, as he says, his intent was to keep the ring for himself, still he could have told the man what he must have known would come as great ease and relief to him. But he did not.'

'The boy did not know, then,' Hugh objected fairly, 'that we had found a dead woman, nor that any shadow lay over Ruald. He knew of no very urgent need to give him news of his wife, not until he heard the whole story at Longner. Indeed, he might well have thought it better to leave well alone, since the man is blessedly happy where he is.'

'I am not altogether sure,' Cadfael said slowly, peering back into the brief while he had spent with Sulien as helper in the herbarium, 'that he did not know of the case until he went home. The same day that he asked leave to visit Longner and see his family again, Jerome had been with him in the garden, for I met him as he left, and he was at once in haste, and a shade more civil and brotherly than usual. And I wonder now if something had not been said of a woman's bones discovered, and a man's reputation under threat. That same evening Sulien went to the lord abbot, and was given leave to ride to

Longner. When he came back next day, it was to declare his
intent to leave the Order, and to bring forth the ring and the
story of how he got it.'

Hugh was drumming his fingers softly on the table, his eyes
narrowed in thought. 'Which first?' he demanded.

'First he asked and obtained his dismissal.'

'Would it, you think, be easier, to a man usually truthful,
to lie to the abbot after that than before?'

'You have thoughts not unlike mine,' said Cadfael
glumly.

'Well,' said Hugh, shaking off present concerns from his
shoulders, 'two things are certain. The first, that whatever the
truth about Sulien himself, this second deliverance is proven
absolutely. We have seen and spoken with Gunnild. She is
alive, and thriving, and very sensibly has no intent in the
world to go on her travels again. And since we have no cause
to connect Britric with any other woman, away he goes in
safety, and good luck to them both. And the second certainty,
Cadfael, is that the very fact of this second deliverance casts
great doubt upon the first. Generys we have *not* seen. Ring or
no ring, I am in two minds now whether we ever shall see her
again. And yet, and yet – Cadfael does not credit it! Not as it
stands, not as we see it now.'

'There is one more certainty,' Cadfael reminded him seriously, 'that you are bound away from here tomorrow morning, and the king's business will not wait, so our business here
must. What, if anything, do you want done until you can take
the reins again? Which, God willing, may not be too long.'

They had both risen at the sound of the loaded carts moving
briskly out under the archway, the hollow sound of the wheels
beneath the stone echoing back to them as from a cavern. A
detachment of archers on foot went with the supplies on this

152

first stage of their journey, to pick up fresh horses at Coventry, where the lances would overtake them.

'Say no word to Sulien or any,' said Hugh, 'but watch whatever follows. Let Radulfus know as much as you please, he knows how to keep a close mouth if any man does. Let young Sulien rest, if rest he can. I doubt if he'll sleep too easily, even though he has cleared the field of murderers for me, or hopes, believes, prays he has. Should I want him, when time serves, he'll be here.'

They went out together into the outer ward, and there halted to take leave. 'If I'm gone long,' said Hugh, 'you'll visit Aline?' There had been no mention, and would be none, of such small matters as that men get killed even in untidy regional skirmishes, such as the Fens were likely to provide. As Eudo Blount the elder had died in the rearguard after the messy ambush of Wilton, not quite a year ago. No doubt Geoffrey de Mandeville, expert at turning his coat and still making himself valuable and to be courted, would prefer to keep his devious options open by evading battle with the king's forces if he could, and killing none of baronial status, but he might not always be able to dictate the terms of engagement, even on his own watery ground. And Hugh was not a man to lead from behind.

'I will,' said Cadfael heartily. 'And God keep the both of you, yes, and the lads who're going with you.'

Hugh went with him to the gate, a hand on his friend's shoulder. They were much of a height, and could match paces evenly. Under the shadow of the archway they halted.

'One more thought has entered my mind,' said Hugh, 'one that has surely been in yours all this while, spoken or not. It's no very great distance from Cambridge to Peterborough.'

* * *

'So it has come!' said Abbot Radulfus sombrely, when Cadfael gave him the full report of his day's activities, after Vespers. 'The first time Hugh has been called on to join the king's muster since Lincoln. I hope it may be to better success. God grant they need not be absent about this business very long.'

Cadfael could not imagine that this confrontation would be over easily or quickly. He had never seen Ramsey, but Sulien's description of it, an island with its own natural and formidable moat, spanned by only one narrow causeway, defensible by a mere handful of men, held out little hope of an easy conquest. And though de Mandeville's marauders must sally forth from their fortress to do their plundering, they had the advantage of being local men, used to all the watery fastnesses in that bleak and open countryside, and able to withdraw into the marshes at any hostile approach.

'With November already here,' he said, 'and winter on the way, I doubt if more can be done than penning these outlaws into their own Fens, and at least limiting the harm they can do. By all accounts it's already more than enough for the poor souls who live in those parts. But, with the earl of Chester our neighbour here, and so dubious in his loyalty, I fancy King Stephen will want to send Hugh and his men home again, to secure the shire and the border, as soon as they can be spared. He may well be hoping for a quick stroke and a quick death. I see no other end to de Mandeville now, however nimbly he may have learned to turn his coat. This time he has gone too far for any recovery.'

'Bleak necessity,' said Radulfus grimly, 'to be forced to wish for any man's death, but this one has been the death of so many others, souls humble and defenceless, and by such abominable means, I could find it in me to offer prayers for his ending, as a needful mercy to his neighbours. How else can there ever be peace and good husbandry in those desolated lands? In the meantime, Cadfael, we are left for a while unable to move in the matter of this death nearer home. Hugh has left Alan Herbard as castellan in his absence?'

Hugh's deputy was young and ardent, and promised well. He had little experience as yet in managing a garrison, but he had hardened sergeants of the older generation at his back, to strengthen his hand if their experience should be needed.

'He has. And Will Warden will be keeping an ear open for any word that may furnish a new lead, though his orders, like mine, are to keep a still tongue and a placid face, and let sleeping dogs lie as long as they will. But you see, Father, how the very fact of this woman coming forward at Sulien's prompting, as she has, casts doubts on the story he first told us. Once, we said, yes, that's wholly credible, why question it? But twice, by the same hand, the same deliverance? No, that is not chance at work, nor can it be easily believed. No! Sulien will not suffer either Ruald or Britric to be branded as a murderer, and goes to great pains to prove it impossible. How can he be so certain of their innocence, unless he knows who is really guilty? Or at least, believes he knows?'

Radulfus looked back at him with an impenetrable countenance, and said outright what as yet neither Cadfael nor Hugh had put into words:

'*Or is himself the man!*'

'It is the first and logical thought that came to me,' Cadfael owned. 'But I found I could not admit it. The farthest I dare go as yet is to acknowledge that his behaviour casts great doubts on his ignorance, if not his innocence, of this death. In the case of Britric there is no question. This time it is not a matter of any man's bare word, the woman came forward in the flesh and spoke for herself. Living she is, fortunate and thankful she is, no one need look for her in the grave. It's at the first deliverance we must turn and look again. That Generys is still in this world alive, for that we have only Sulien's word. *She* has not come forward. *She* has not spoken. Thus far, all we have is hearsay. One man's word for the woman, the ring, and all.'

'From such small knowledge of him as I have,' said Radulfus, 'I do not think that Sulien is by nature a liar.'

'Neither do I. But all men, even those not by nature liars, may be forced to lie where they see overwhelming need. As I fear he did, to deliver Ruald from the burden of suspicion. Moreover,' said Cadfael confidently, harking back to old experience with fallible men outside this enclave, 'if they lie only for such desperate cause they will do it well, better than those who do it lightly.'

'You argue,' said Radulfus drily, but with the flicker of a private smile, 'as one who speaks from knowledge. Well, if one man's word is no longer acceptable without proof, I do not see how we can advance our enquiries beyond your "thus far". As well we should let well alone while Hugh is absent. Say nothing to any man from Longner, nothing to Brother Ruald. In stillness and quietness whispers are heard clearly, and the rustle of a leaf has meaning.'

'And I have been reminded,' said Cadfael, rising with a gusty sigh to make his way to the refectory, 'by the last thing Hugh said to me, that it is not too far from Cambridge to Peterborough.'

The next day was sacred to Saint Winifred, and therefore an important feast in the abbey of Saint Peter and Saint Paul, though the day of her translation and installation on her present altar in the church, the twenty-second of June, was accorded greater ceremonial. A midsummer holiday provides better weather and longer daylight for processions and festivities than the third of November, with the days closing in and winter approaching.

Cadfael rose very early in the morning, long before Prime, took his sandals and scapular, and stole out from the dark dortoir by the night stairs, where the little lamp burned all night long to light stumbling feet uncertain from sleep down into the church for Matins and Lauds. The long room, lined with its low partitions that separated cell from cell, was full of small human sounds, like a vault peopled with gentle ghosts, soft, sighing breath, the involuntary catch in the throat, close to a sob, that saluted a nostalgic dream, the uneasy stirring of someone half awake, the solid, contented snoring of a big body sleeping without dreams, and at the end of the long room the deep, silent sleeping of Prior Robert, worshipfully satisfied with all his deeds and words, untroubled by doubts, unintimidated by dreams. The prior habitually slept so soundly that it was easy to rise and slip away without fear of disturbing him. In his time, Cadfael had done it for less approved reasons than on this particular morning. So, possibly, had several of these innocent sleepers around him.

He went silently down the stairs and into the body of the church, dark, empty and vast, lit only by the glowworm lamps on the altars, minute stars in a vaulted night. His first destination, whenever he rose thus with ample time in hand, was always the altar of Saint Winifred, with its silver reliquary, where he stopped to exchange a little respectful and affectionate conversation with his countrywoman. He always spoke Welsh to her, the accents of his childhood and hers brought them into a welcome intimacy, in which he could ask her anything and never feel rebuffed. Even without his advocacy, he felt, her favour and protection would go with Hugh to Cambridge, but there was no harm in mentioning the need. It did not matter that Winifred's slender Welsh bones were still in the soil of Gwytherin, many miles away in North Wales, where her ministry had been spent. Saints are not corporeal, but presences, they can reach and touch wherever their grace and generosity desire.

It came into Cadfael's mind, on this particular morning, to say a word also for Generys, the stranger, the dark woman who was also Welsh, and whose beautiful, disturbing shadow haunted the imaginations of many others besides the husband who had abandoned her. Whether she lived out the remnant of her life somewhere far distant from her own country, in lands she had never thought to visit, among people she had never desired to know, or was lying now in that quiet corner of the cemetery here, removed from abbey land to lie in abbey land, the thought of her touched him nearly, and must surely stir the warmth and tenderness of the saint who had escaped a like exile. Cadfael put forward her case with confidence, on his knees on the lowest step of Winifred's altar, where Brother Rhun, when she had led him by the hand and healed his lameness, had laid his discarded crutches.

When he rose, the first faint pre-dawn softening of the darkness had grown into a pallid, pearly hint of light, drawing in the tall shapes of the nave windows clearly, and conjuring pillar and vault and altar out of the gloom. Cadfael passed down the nave to the west door, which was never fastened but in time of war or danger, and went out to the steps to look along the Foregate towards the bridge and the town.

They were coming. An hour and more yet to Prime, and only the first dim light by which to ride out, but he could already hear the hooves, crisp and rapid and faintly hollow on the bridge. He heard the change in their tread as they emerged upon the solid ground of the Foregate, and saw as it were an agitation of the darkness, movement without form, even before faint glints of lambent light on steel gave shape to their harness and brought them human out of the obscurity. No panoply, only the lance-pennants, two slung trumpets for very practical use, and the workmanlike light arms in which they rode. Thirty lances and five mounted archers. The remainder of the archers had gone ahead with the supplies. Hugh had done well by King Stephen, they made a very presentable company and numbered, probably, more than had been demanded.

Cadfael watched them pass, Hugh at the head on his favourite raw-boned grey. There were faces he knew among them, seasoned soldiers of the garrison, sons of merchant families from the town, expert archers from practice at the butts under the castle wall, young squires from the manors of the shire. In normal times the common service due from a crown manor would have been perhaps one esquire and his harness, and a barded horse, for forty days' service against the Welsh near Oswestry. Emergencies such as the present anarchy in East Anglia upset all normalities, but some length of service must have been stipulated even now. Cadfael had not asked for how many days these men might be at risk. There went Nigel Aspley among the lances, well-mounted and comely. That lad had made one tentative assay into treason, Cadfael remembered, only three years back, and no doubt was intent upon putting that memory well behind him by diligent service now. Well, if Hugh saw fit to make use of him, he had probably learned his lesson well, and was not likely to stray again. And he was a good man of his hands, athletic and strong, worth his place.

They passed, the drumming of their hooves dull on the packed, dry soil of the roadway, and the sound ebbed into distance along the wall of the enclave. Cadfael watched them until they almost faded from sight in the gloom, and then at the turn of the highway vanished altogether round the high precinct wall. The light came grudgingly, for the sky hung low in heavy cloud. This was going to be a dark and overcast day, possibly later a day of rain. Rain was the last thing King Stephen would want in the Fens, to reduce all land approaches and complicate all marshland paths. It costs much money to keep an army in the field, and though the king summoned numbers of men to give duty service this time, he would still be paying a large company of Flemish mercenaries, feared and hated by the civilian population, and disliked even by the English who fought alongside them. Both rivals in the unending dispute for the crown made use of Flemings. To them the right side was the side that paid them, and could as easily change to the opposing party if they offered more; yet Cadfael in his time had known many mercenaries who held fast faithfully to their bargains, once struck, while barons and earls like de Mandeville changed direction as nimbly as weathercocks for their own advantage.

They were gone, Hugh's compact and competent little company, even the last fading quiver and reverberation of earth under them stilled. Cadfael turned and went back through the great west door into the church.

There was another figure moving softly round the parish altar, a silent shadow in the dimness still lit only by the constant lamps. Cadfael followed him into the choir, and watched him light a twisted straw taper at the small red glow, and kindle the altar candles ready for Prime. It was a duty that was undertaken in a rota, and Cadfael had no idea at this moment whose turn this day might be, until he had advanced almost within touch of the man standing quietly, with head raised, gazing at the altar. An erect figure, lean but sinewy and strong, with big, shapely hands folded at his waist, and deepset eyes wide and fixed in a rapt dream. Brother Ruald heard the steady steps drawing near to him, but felt no need to turn his head or in any other way acknowledge a second presence. Sometimes he seemed almost unaware that there were others sharing this chosen life and this place of refuge with him. Only when Cadfael stood close beside him, sleeve to sleeve, and the movement made the candles flicker briefly, did Ruald look round with a sharp sigh, disturbed out of his dream.

'You are early up, Brother,' he said mildly. 'Could you not sleep?'

'I rose to see the sheriff and his company set out,' said Cadfael.

'They are gone already?' Ruald drew breath wonderingly, contemplating a life and a discipline utterly alien to his former or his present commitment. Half the life he could expect had been spent as a humble craftsman, for some obscure reason the least regarded among craftsmen, though why honest potters should be accorded such low status was a mystery to Cadfael. Now all the life yet remaining to him would be spent here in the devoted service of God. He had never so much as shot at the butts for sport, as the young bloods of Shrewsbury's merchant families regularly did, or done combat with singlesticks or blunt swords at the common exercise-ground. 'Father Abbot will have prayers said daily for their safe and early return,' he said. 'And so will Father Boniface at the parish services.' He said it as one offering reassurance and comfort to a soul gravely concerned, but by something which touched him not at all. A narrow life his had been, Cadfael reflected, and looked back with gratitude at the width and depth of his own. And suddenly it began to seem to him as though all the passion there had been even in this man's marriage, all the blood that had burned in its veins, must have come from the woman.

'It is to be hoped,' he said shortly, 'that they come back as many as they have set out today.'

'So it is,' agreed Ruald meekly, 'yet they who take the sword, so it's written, will perish by the sword.'

'You will not find a good honest swordsman quarrelling with that,' said Cadfael. 'There are far worse ways.'

'That may well be true,' said Ruald very seriously. 'I do know that I have things to repent, things for which to do penance, fully as dreadful as the shedding of blood. Even in seeking to do what God required of me, did not I kill? Even if she is still living, there in the east, I took as it were the breath of life from her. I did not know it then. I could not even see her face clearly, to understand how I tore her. And here am I, unsure now whether I did well at all in following what I thought was a sacred beckoning, or whether I should not have forgone even this, for her sake. It may be God was putting me to the test. Tell me, Cadfael, you have lived in the world, travelled the world, known the extremes to which men can be driven, for good or ill. Do you think there was ever any man ready to forgo even heaven, to stay with another soul who loved him, in purgatory?'

To Cadfael, standing close beside him, this lean and limited man seemed to have grown taller and more substantial; or it might have been simply the growing strength and clarity of the light now gleaming in at every window, paling the candles on the altar. Certainly the mild and modest voice had never been so eloquent.

162

'Surely the range is so wide,' he said with slow and careful deliberation, 'that even that is possible. Yet I doubt if such a marvel was demanded of you.'

'In three days more,' said Ruald more gently, watching the flames he had lit burn tall and steady and golden, 'it will be Saint Illtud's day. You are Welsh, you will know what is told of him. He had a wife, a noble lady, willing to live simply with him in a reed hut by the River Nadafan. An angel told him to leave his wife, and he rose up early in the morning, and drove her out into the world alone, thrusting her off, so we are told, very roughly, and went to receive the tonsure of a monk from Saint Dyfrig. I was not rough, yet that is my own case, for so I parted from Generys. Cadfael, what I would ask is, was that an angel who commanded it, or a devil?'

'You are posing a question,' said Cadfael, 'to which only God can know the answer, and with that we must be content. Certainly others before you have received the same call that came to you, and obeyed it. The great earl who founded this house and sleeps there between the altars, he, too, left his lady and put on the habit before he died.' Only three days before he died, actually, and with his wife's consent, but no need at this moment to say any word of that.

Never before had Ruald opened up the sealed places within him where his wife was hidden, even from his own sight, first by the intensity of his desire for holiness, then by the human fallibility of memory and feeling which had made it hard even to recall the lines of her face. Conversion had fallen on him like a stunning blow that had numbed all sensation, and now in due time he was coming back to life, remembrance filling his being with sharp and biting pain. Perhaps he never could have wrenched his heart open and spoken about her, except in this timeless and impersonal solitude, with no witness but one.

163

For he spoke as if to himself, clearly and simply, rather recalling than recounting. 'I had no intent to hurt her – Generys . . . I could not choose but go, yet there are ways and ways of taking leave. I was not wise. I had no skills, I did not do it well. And I had taken her from her own people, and she content all these years with little reward but the man I am, and wanting nothing more. I can never have given her a tenth part, not a mere tithe, of all that she gave me.'

Cadfael was motionless, listening, as the quiet voice continued its threnody. 'Dark, she was, very dark, very beautiful. Everyone would call her so, but now I see that none ever knew how beautiful, for to the world outside it was as if she went veiled, and only I ever saw her uncover her face. Or perhaps, to children – to them she might show herself unconcealed. We never had children, we were not so blessed. That made her tender and loving to those her neighbours bore. She is not yet past all hope of bearing children of her own. Who knows but with another man, she might yet conceive.'

'And you would be glad for her?' said Cadfael, so softly as not to break this thread.

'I would be glad. I would be wholly glad. Why should she continue barren, because I am fulfilled? Or bound, where I am free? I never thought of that when the longing came on me.'

'And do you believe she told you truth, the last time, saying that she had a lover?'

'Yes,' said Ruald, simply and without hesitation, 'I do believe. Not that she might not lie to me then, for I was crass and did her bitter offence, as now I understand, even by visiting her then I offended. I believe because of the ring. You remember it? The ring that Sulien brought back with him when he came from Ramsey.'

'I remember it,' said Cadfael.

164

The dormitory bell was just ringing to rouse the brothers for Prime. In some remote corner of their consciousness it sounded very faintly and distantly, and neither of them heeded it.

'It never left her finger, from the time I put it there. I would not have thought it could be eased over her knuckle, after so long. The first time that I visited her with Brother Paul I know she was wearing it as she always did. But the second time . . . I had forgotten, but now I understand. It was not on her finger when I saw her the last time. She had stripped her marriage to me from her finger with the ring, and given it to someone else, as she stripped me from her life, and offered it to him. Yes, I believe Generys had a lover. One worth the loving, she said. With all my heart I hope he has proved so to her.'

Chapter Ten

HROUGHOUT THE ceremonies and services and readings of Saint Winifred's day a morsel of Cadfael's mind, persistent and unrepentant, occupied itself, much against his will, with matters which had nothing to do with the genuine adoration he had for his own special saint, whom he thought of always as she had been when her first brief life was so brutally ended: a girl of about seventeen, fresh, beautiful and radiant, brimming over with kindness and sweetness as the waters of her well brimmed always sparkling and pure, defying frost, radiating health of body and soul. He would have liked his mind to be wholly filled with her all this day, but obstinately it turned to Ruald's ring, and the pale circle on the finger from which Generys had ripped it, abandoning him as he had abandoned her.

It became ever more clear that there had indeed been another man. With him she had departed, to settle, it seemed, in Peterborough, or somewhere in that region, perhaps a place even more exposed to the atrocities of de Mandeville's barbarians. And when the reign of murder and terror began, she and her man had taken up their new, shallow roots, turned what valuables they had into money, and removed further from the threat, leaving the ring for young Sulien to find, and bring home with him for Ruald's deliverance. That, at least, was surely what Ruald believed. Every word he had spoken before the altar that morning bore the stamp of sincerity. So now much depended on the matter of forty miles or so between Cambridge and Peterborough. Not such a short distance, after all, but if all went well with the king's business, and he thought fit soon to dispense with a force that could be better employed keeping an eye on the earl of Chester, a passage by way of Peterborough would not greatly lengthen the way home.

And if the answer was yes, confirming every word of Sulien's story, then Generys was indeed still living, and not abandoned to loneliness, and the dead woman of the Potter's Field was still left adrift and without a name. But in that case, why should Sulien have stirred himself so resolutely to prove Britric, who was nothing to him, as innocent as Ruald? How could he have known, and why should he even have conceived the possibility, that the pedlar was innocent? Or that the woman Gunnild was alive, or even might be alive?

And if the answer was no, and Sulien had never spent the night with the silversmith in Peterborough, never begged the ring of him, but made up his story in defence of Ruald out of whole cloth, and backed it with a ring he had had in his possession all along, then surely he had been weaving a rope for his own neck while he was so busy unpicking someone else's bonds.

But as yet there was no answer, and no way of hastening it, and Cadfael did his best to pay proper attention to the office, but Saint Winifred's feast passed in distracted thought. In the days that followed he went about his work in the herbarium conscientiously but without his usual hearty concentration, and was taciturn and slightly absent-minded with Brother Winfrid, whose placidity of temperament and boyish appetite for work fortunately enabled him to ride serenely through other men's changes of mood without losing his own equilibrium.

Now that Cadfael came to consider the early part of the November calendar, it seemed to be populated chiefly by Welsh saints. Ruald had reminded him that the sixth day was dedicated to Saint Illtud, who had obeyed his dictatorial angel with such alacrity, and so little consideration for his wife's feelings in the matter. No great devotion was paid to him in English houses, perhaps, but Saint Tysilio, whose day came on the eighth, had a rather special significance here on the borders of Powys, and his influence spilled over the frontier into the neighbouring shires. For the centre of his ministry was the chief church of Powys at Meifod, no great way into Wales, and the saint was reputed to have had military virtues as well as sacred, and to have fought on the Christian side at the battle of Maserfield, by Oswestry, where the royal saint, Oswald, was captured and martyred by the pagans. So a measure of respect was paid to his feast day, and the Welsh of the town and the Foregate came to Mass that morning in considerable numbers. But for all that, Cadfael had hardly expected the attendance of one worshipper from further afield.

She rode in at the gatehouse, pillion behind an elderly groom, in good time before Mass, and was lifted down respectfully to the cobbles of the court by the younger groom who followed on a second stout horse, with the maid Gunnild perched behind him. Both women stood shaking out their skirts for a moment before they crossed demurely to the church, the lady before, the maid attentive and dutiful a pace behind her, while the grooms spoke a word or two to the porter, and then led away the horses to the stable yard. The perfect picture of a young woman conforming to every social sanction imposing rules upon her bearing and movements, with her maid for guardian and companion, and her grooms for escort. Pernel was ensuring that this venture out of her usual ambience should be too correct in every detail to attract comment. She might be the eldest of the brood at Withington, but she was still very young, and it was imperative to temper her natural directness and boldness with caution. It had to be admitted that she did it with considerable style and grace, and had an admirable abettor in the experienced Gunnild. They crossed the great court with hands folded and eyes cast down modestly, and vanished into the church by the south door without once risking meeting the gaze of any of these celibates who moved about court and cloister round them.

Now if she has in mind what I think she has, Cadfael reflected, watching them go, she will have need of all Gunnild's worldly wisdom to abet her own good sense and resolution. And I do believe the woman is devoted to her, and will make a formidable protective dragon if ever there's need.

He caught a brief glimpse of her again as he entered the church with the brothers, and passed through to his place in the choir. The nave was well filled with lay worshippers, some standing beside the parish altar, where they could see through to the high altar within, some grouped around the stout round pillars that held up the vault. Pernel was kneeling where the light, by chance, fell on her face through the opening from the lighted choir. Her eyes were closed, but her lips still. Her prayers were not in words. She looked very grave, thus austerely attired for church, her soft brown hair hidden within a white wimple, and the hood of her cloak drawn over all, for it was none too warm in the church. She looked like some very young novice nun, her round face more childlike than ever, but the set of her lips had a mature and formidable firmness. Close at her back Gunnild kneeled, and her eyes, though half veiled by long lashes, were open and bright, and possessively steady upon her lady. Woe betide anyone who attempted affront to Pernel Otmere while her maid was by!

After Mass Cadfael looked for them again, but they were hidden among the mass of people gathering slowly to leave by the west door. He went out by the south door and the cloisters, and emerged into the court to find her waiting quietly there for the procession of the brothers to separate to their various duties. It did not surprise him when at sight of him her face sharpened and her eyes brightened, and she took a single step towards him, enough to arrest him.

'Brother, may I speak with you? I have asked leave of the lord abbot.' She sounded practical and resolute, but she had not risked the least indiscretion, it seemed. 'I made so bold as to accost him just now, when he left,' she said. 'It seems that he already knew my name and family. That can only have been from you, I think.'

'Father Abbot is fully informed,' said Cadfael, 'with all the matter that brought me to visit you. He is concerned for justice, as we are. To the dead and to the living. He will not stand in the way of any converse that may serve that end.'

'He was kind,' she said, and suddenly warmed and smiled. 'And now we have observed all the proper forms, and I can breathe again. Where may we talk?'

He took them to his workshop in the herb garden. It was becoming too chilly to linger and converse outdoors, his brazier was alight but damped down within, and with the timber doors wide open, Brother Winfrid returning to the remaining patch of rough pre-winter digging just outside the enclosure

171

wall, and Gunnild standing at a discreet distance within, not even Prior Robert could have raised his brows at the propriety of this conference. Pernel had been wise in applying directly to the superior, who already knew of the role she had played, and certainly had no reason to disapprove of it. Had she not gone far to save both a body and a soul? And she had brought the one, if not visibly the other, to show to him.

'Now,' said Cadfael, tickling the brazier to show a gleam of red through its controlling turves, 'sit down and be easy, the both of you. And tell me what you have in mind, to bring you here to worship, when, as I know, you have a church and a priest of your own. I know, for it belongs, like Upton, to this house of Saint Peter and Saint Paul. And your priest is a rare man and a scholar, as I know from Brother Anselm, who is his friend.'

'So he is,' said Pernel warmly, 'and you must not think I have not talked with him, very earnestly, about this matter.' She had settled herself decorously at one end of the bench against the wall of the hut, composed and erect, her face bright against the dark timber, her hood fallen back on her shoulders. Gunnild, invited by a smile and a gesture, glided out of shadow and sat down on the other end of the bench, leaving a discreet gap between the two of them to mark the difference in their status, but not too wide, to underline the depth of her alliance with her mistress. 'It was Father Ambrosius,' said Pernel, 'who said the word that brought me here on this day of all days. Father Ambrosius studied for some years in Brittany. You know, Brother, whose day we are celebrating?'

'I should,' said Cadfael, relinquishing the bellows that had raised a red glow in his brazier. 'He is as Welsh as I am, and a close neighbour to this shire. What of Saint Tysilio?'

172

'But did you know that he is said to have gone over to Brittany to fly from a woman's persecution? And in Brittany they also tell of his life, like the readings you will hear today at Collations. But there they know him by another name. They call him Sulien.'

'Oh, no,' she said, seeing how speculatively Cadfael was eyeing her, 'I did not take it as a sign from heaven, when Father Ambrosius told me that. It was just that the name prompted me to act, where before I was only wondering and fretting. Why not on his day? For I think, Brother, that you believe that Sulien Blount is not what he seems, not as open as he seems. I have been thinking and asking about this matter. I think things are so inclining, that he may be suspect of too much knowledge, in this matter of the poor dead woman your plough team found under the headland in the Potter's Field. Too much knowledge, perhaps even guilt. Is it true?'

'Too much knowledge, certainly,' said Cadfael. 'Guilt, that is mere conjecture, yet there is ground for suspicion.' He owed her honesty, and she expected it.

'Will you tell me,' she said, 'the whole story? For I know only what is gossiped around. Let me understand whatever danger he may be in. Guilt or no, he would not let another man be blamed unjustly.'

Cadfael told her the whole of it, from the first furrow cut by the abbey plough. She listened attentively and seriously, her round brow furrowed with thought. She could not and did not believe any evil of the young man who had visited her for so generous a purpose, but neither did she ignore the reasons why others might have doubts of him. At the end she drew breath long and softly, and gnawed her lip for a moment, pondering.

'Do *you* believe him guilty?' she asked then, pointblank.

'I believe he has knowledge which he has not seen fit to reveal. More than that I will not say. All depends on whether he told us the truth about the ring.'

'But Brother Ruald believes him?' she said.

'Without question.'

'And he has known him from a child.'

'And may be partial,' said Cadfael, smiling. 'But yes, he has more knowledge of the boy than either you or I, and plainly expects nothing less than truth from him.'

'And so would I. But one thing I wonder at,' said Pernel very earnestly. 'You say that you think he knew of this matter before he went to visit his home, though *he* said he heard of it only there. If you are right, if he heard it from Brother Jerome before he went to ask leave to visit Longner, why did he not bring forth the ring at once, and tell what he had to tell? Why leave it until the next day? Whether he got the ring as he said, or had it in his possession from long before, he could have spared Brother Ruald one more night of wretchedness. So gentle a soul as he seems, why should he leave a man to bear such a burden an hour longer than he need, let alone a day?'

It was the one consideration which Cadfael had had at the back of his mind ever since the occasion itself, but did not yet know what to make of it. If Pernel's mind was keeping in reserve the same doubt, let her speak for him, and probe beyond where he had yet cared to go. He said simply: 'I have not pursued it. It would entail questioning Brother Jerome, which I should be loath to do until I am more sure of my ground. But I can think of only one reason. For some motive of his own, he wished to preserve the appearance of having heard of the case only when he paid his visit to Longner.'

'Why should he want that?' she challenged.

'I suppose that he might well want to talk to his brother before he committed himself to anything. He had been away more than a year, he would want to ensure that his family was in no way threatened by a matter of which he had only just learned. Naturally he would be tender of their interests, all the more because he had not seen them for so long.'

To that she agreed, with a thoughtful and emphatic nod of her head. 'Yes, so he would. But I can think of another reason why he delayed, and I am sure you are thinking of it, too.'

'And that is?'

'That he had not got it,' said Pernel firmly, 'and could not show it, until he had been home to fetch it.'

She had indeed spoken out bluntly and fearlessly, and Cadfael could not but admire her singlemindedness. Her sole belief was that Sulien was clean of any shadow of guilt, her sole purpose to prove it to the world, but her confidence in the efficacy of truth drove her to go headlong after it, certain that when found it must be on her side.

'I know,' she said, 'I am making a case that may seem hurtful to him, but in the end it cannot be, because I am sure he has done no wrong. There is no way but to look at every possibility. I know you said that Sulien grew to love that woman, and said so himself, and if she did give her ring to another man, for spite against her husband, yes, it could have been to Sulien. But equally it could have been to someone else. And though I would not try to lift the curse from one man by throwing it upon another, Sulien was not the only young man close neighbour to the potter. There is the other brother at home, older than he. Just as likely to be drawn to a woman every account claims was beautiful. If Sulien has guilty knowledge he cannot reveal, he could as well be shielding a brother as protecting himself. I cannot believe,' she said vehemently, 'that you have not thought of that possibility.'

'I have thought of many possibilities,' agreed Cadfael placidly, 'without much by way of fact to support any. Yes, for either himself or his brother he might lie. Or for Ruald. But only if he knows, as surely as the sun will rise tomorrow, that our poor dead lady is indeed Generys. And never forget, there is also the possibility, however diminished since his efforts for Britric, that he was *not* lying, that Generys *is* alive and well, somewhere there in the eastlands, with the man she chose to follow. And we may never, never know who was the dark-haired woman someone buried with reverence in the Potter's Field.'

'But you do not believe that,' she said with certainty.

'I think truth, like the burgeoning of a bulb under the soil, however deeply sown, will make its way to the light.'

'And there is nothing we can do to hasten it,' said Pernel, and heaved a resigned sigh.

'At present, nothing but wait.'

'And pray, perhaps?' she said.

Cadfael could not choose but wonder, none the less, what she would do next, for inaction would be unbearably irksome to her now that her whole energy was engaged for this young man she had seen only once. Whether Sulien had paid as acute attention to her there was no knowing, but it was in Cadfael's mind that sooner or later he would have to, for she had no intention of turning back. It was also in his mind that the boy might do a good deal worse. If, that is, he came out of this web of mystery and deceit with a whole skin and a quiet mind, something he certainly did not possess at present.

From Cambridge and the Fens there was no news. No one had yet expected any. But travellers from eastward reported that the weather was turning foul, with heavy rains and the first frosts of the winter. No very attractive prospect for an army floundering in watery reaches unfamiliar to them but known to the elusive enemy. Cadfael bethought him of his promise to Hugh, by this time more than a week absent, and asked leave to go up into the town and visit Aline and his godson. The sky was overclouded, the weather from the east gradually moving in upon Shrewsbury in a very fine rain, hardly more than mist, that clung in the hair and the fibres of clothing, and barely darkened the slate-grey earth of the Foregate. In the Potter's Field the winter crop was already sown, and there would be cattle grazing the lower strip of pasture. Cadfael had not been back to see it with his own eyes, but with the inner eye he saw it very clearly, dark, rich soil soon to bring forth new life; green, moist turf and tangled briary headland under the ridge of bushes and trees. That it had once held an unblessed grave would soon be forgotten. The grey, soft day made for melancholy. It was pleasure and relief to turn in at the gate of Hugh's yard, and be met and embraced about the thighs by a small, boisterous boy yelling delighted greetings. Another month or so, and Giles would be four years old. He took a first grip on a fistful of Cadfael's habit, and towed him gleefully into the house. With Hugh absent, Giles was the man of the house, and well aware of all his duties and privileges. He made Cadfael free of the amenities of his manor with solemn dignity, seated him ceremoniously, and himself made off to the buttery to fetch a beaker of ale, bearing it back cautiously in both still-rounded, infantile hands, overfilled and in danger of spilling, with his primrose hair erect and rumpled, and the tip of his tongue braced in the corner of his mouth. His mother followed him into the hall at a discreet distance, to avoid upsetting either his balance or his dignity. She was smiling at Cadfael over her son's fair head, and suddenly the radiant likeness between them shone on Cadfael like the sun bursting out of clouds. The round, earnest face with its full childish cheeks, and the pure oval with its wide brow and tapered chin, so different and yet so similar, shared the pale, lustrous colouring and the lily-smooth skin, the refinement of feature and steadiness of gaze. Hugh is indeed a lucky man, Cadfael thought, and then drew in cautious breath on a superstitious prayer that such luck should stand by him still, wherever he might be at this moment.

If Aline had any misgivings, they were not allowed to show themselves. She sat down with him cheerfully as always, and talked of the matters of the household and the affairs at the castle under Alan Herbard, with her usual practical good sense; and Giles, instead of clambering into his godfather's lap as he might well have done some weeks previously, climbed up to sit beside him on the bench like a man and a contemporary.

'Yes,' said Aline, 'there is a bowman of the company has ridden in only this afternoon, the first word we've had. He got a graze in one skirmish they had, and Hugh sent him home, seeing he was fit to ride, and they had left changes of horses along the way. He will heal well, Alan says, but it weakens his drawing arm.'

'And how are they faring?' Cadfael asked. 'Have they managed to bring Geoffrey into the open?'

She shook her head decisively. 'Very little chance of it. The waters are up everywhere, and it's still raining. All they can do is lie in wait for the raiding parties when they venture out to plunder the villages. Even there the king is at a disadvantage, seeing Geoffrey's men know every usable path, and can bog them down in the marshes only too easily. But they have picked off a few such small parties. It isn't what Stephen wants, but it's all he can get. Ramsey is quite cut off, no one can hope to fetch them out of there.'

'And this tedious business of ambush and waiting,' said Cadfael, 'wastes too much time. Stephen cannot afford to keep it up too long. Costly and ineffective as it is, he'll have to withdraw to try some other measure. If Geoffrey's numbers have grown so great, he must be getting supplies now from beyond the Fen villages. His supply lines might be vulnerable. And Hugh? He is well?'

'Wet and muddy and cold, I daresay,' said Aline, ruefully smiling, 'and probably cursing heartily, but he's whole and well, or was when his archer left him. That's one thing to be said for this tedious business, as you called it, such losses as there are have been de Mandeville's. But too few to do him much harm.'

'Not enough,' Cadfael said consideringly, 'to be worth the king's while for much longer. I think, Aline, you may not have to wait long to have Hugh home again.'

Giles pressed a little closer and more snugly into his godfather's side, but said nothing. 'And you, my lord,' said Cadfael, 'will have to hand over your manor again, and give account of your stewardship. I hope you have not let things get out of hand while the lord sheriff's been away.'

Hugh's deputy made a brief sound indicative of scorn at the very idea that his strict rule should ever be challenged. 'I am *good* at it,' he stated firmly. 'My father says so. He says I keep a tighter rein than he does. And use the spur more.'

'Your father,' said Cadfael gravely, 'is always fair and

179

ungrudging even to those who excel him.' He was aware, through some alchemy of proximity and affection, of the smile Aline was not allowing to show in her face.

'Especially with the women,' said Giles complacently.

'Now that,' said Cadfael, 'I can well believe.'

King Stephen's tenacity, in any undertaking, had always been precarious. Not want of courage, certainly, not even want of determination, caused him to abandon sieges after a mere few days and rush away to some more promising assault. It was rather impatience, frustrated optimism and detestation of being inactive that made him quit one undertaking for another. On occasion, as at Oxford, he could steel himself to persist, if the situation offered a reasonable hope of final triumph, but where stalemate was obvious he soon wearied and went off to fresh fields. In the wintry rains of the Fens anger and personal hatred kept him constant longer than usual, but his successes were meagre, and it was borne in upon him by the last week of November that he could not hope to finish the work. Floundering in the quagmires of those bleak levels, his forces had certainly closed in with enough method and strength to compress de Mandeville's territory, and had picked off a fair number of his rogue troops when they ventured out on to drier ground, but it was obvious that the enemy had ample supplies, and could hold off for a while even from raiding. There was no hope of digging them out of their hole. Stephen turned to changed policies with the instant vigour he could find at need. He wanted his feudal levies, especially any from potentially vulnerable regions, such as those neighbour to the Welsh, or to dubious friends like the earl of Chester, back where they were most useful. Here in the Fens he proposed to marshal an army rather of builders than soldiers, throw up a ring of hasty but well-placed strongpoints to contain the outlaw territory, compress it still further wherever they could, and menace Geoffrey's outside supply lines when his stores ran low. Manned by the experienced Flemish mercenaries, familiar with fighting in flat lands and among complex waterways, such a ring of forts could hold what had been gained through the winter, until conditions were more favourable to open manoeuvring.

It was nearing the end of November when Hugh found himself and his levy briskly thanked and dismissed. He had lost no men killed, and had only a few minor wounds and grazes to show, and was heartily glad to withdraw his men from wallowing in the quagmires round Cambridge and set out with them north-westward towards Huntingdon, where the royal castle had kept the town relatively secure and the roads open. From there he sent them on due west for Kettering, while he rode north, heading for Peterborough.

He had not paused to consider, until he rode over the bridge of the Nene and up into the town, what he expected to find there. Better, perhaps, to approach thus without expectations of any kind. The road from the bridge brought him up into the marketplace, which was alive and busy. The burgesses who had elected to stay were justified, the town had so far proved too formidable to be a temptation to de Mandeville while there were more isolated and defenceless victims to be found. Hugh found stabling for his horse, and went afoot to look for Priestgate.

The shop was there, or at least a flourishing silversmith's shop was there, open for business and showing a prosperous front to the world. That was the first confirmation. Hugh went in, and enquired of the young fellow sitting at work in the back of the shop, under a window that lit his workbench, for Master John Hinde. The name was received blithely, and the young man laid down his tools and went out by a rear door to call his master. No question of any discrepancy here, the shop and the man were here to be found, just as Sulien had left them when he made his way west from Ramsey.

Master John Hinde, when he followed his assistant in from his private quarters, was plainly a man of substance in the town, one who might well be a good patron to his favoured religious house, and on excellent terms with abbots. He was perhaps fifty, a lean, active, upright figure in a rich furred gown. Quick dark eyes in a thin, decisive face summed up Hugh in a glance.

'I am John Hinde. How can I help you?' The marks of the wearisome lurking in wet, windswept ambushes, and occasional hard riding in the open, were there to be seen in Hugh's clothes and harness. 'You come from the king's muster? We have heard he's withdrawing his host. Not to leave the field clear for de Mandeville, I hope?'

'No such matter,' Hugh assured him, 'though I'm sent back to take care of my own field. No, you'll be none the worse for our leaving, the Flemings will be between you and danger, with at least one strongpoint well placed to pen them into their island. There's little more or better he could do now, with the winter coming.'

'Well, we live as candles in the breath of God,' said the silversmith philosophically, 'wherever we are. I've known it too long to be easily frightened off. And what's your need, sir, before you head for home?'

'Do you remember,' said Hugh, 'about the first or second day of October, a young monk sheltering here with you overnight? It was just after the sack of Ramsey, the boy came from there, commended to you, he said, by his abbot. Abbot Walter was sending him home to the brother house at Shrewsbury, to take the news of Ramsey with him along the way. You remember the man?'

'Clearly,' said John Hinde, without hesitation. 'He was just at the end of his novitiate. The brothers were scattering for safety. None of us is likely to forget that time. I would have lent the lad a horse for the first few miles, but he said he would do better afoot, for they were all about the open countryside like bees in swarm then. What of him? I hope he reached Shrewsbury safely?'

'He did, and brought the news wherever he passed. Yes, he's well, though he's left the Order since, and returned to his brother's manor.'

'He told me then he was in doubts if he was on the right way,' agreed the silversmith. 'Walter was not the man to hold on to a youngster against his inclination. So what is it I can add, concerning this youth?'

'Did he,' asked Hugh deliberately, 'notice a particular ring in your shop? And did he remark upon it, and ask after the woman from whom you had bought it, only ten days or so earlier? A plain silver ring set with a small yellow stone, and bearing initials engraved within it? And did he beg it of you, because he had known the woman well from his childhood, and kept a kindness for her? Is any part of this truth?'

There was a long moment of silence while the silversmith looked back at him, eye to eye, with intelligent speculation sharpening the lean lines of his face. It is possible that he was considering retreat from any further confidence, for want of knowing what might result from his answers for a young man perhaps innocently entrammelled in some misfortune no fault of his own. Men of business learn to be chary of trusting too many too soon. But if so, he discarded the impulse of denial, after studying Hugh with close attention and arriving, it seemed, at a judgement.

'Come within!' he said then, with equal deliberation and equal certainty. And he turned towards the door from which he had emerged, inviting Hugh with a gesture of his hand. 'Come! Let me hear more. Now we have gone so far, we may as well go further together.'

Chapter Eleven

ULIEN HAD PUT off the habit, but the hourly order that went with it was not so easy to discard. He found himself waking at midnight for Matins and Lauds, and listening for the bell, and was shaken and daunted by the silence and isolation where there should have been the sense of many brothers stirring and sighing, a soft murmur of voices urging the heavy sleepers, and in the dimness at the head of the night stairs the glow of the little lamp to light them down safely to the church. Even the freedom of his own clothes sat uneasily on him still, after a year of the skirted gown. He had put away one life without being able to take up the old where he had abandoned it, and making a new beginning was unexpected effort and pain. Moreover, things at Longner had changed since his departure to Ramsey. His brother was married to a young wife, settled in his lordship, and happy in the prospect of an heir, for Jehane was pregnant. The Longner lands were a very fair holding, but not great enough to support two families, even if such sharing had ever promised well, and a younger son would have to work out an independent life for himself, as younger sons had always had to do. The cloister he had sampled and abandoned. His family bore with him tolerantly and patiently until

185

he should find his way. Eudo was the most open and amiable of young men, and fond of his brother. Sulien was welcome to all the time he needed, and until he made up his mind Longner was his home, and glad to have him back.

But no one could quite be sure that Sulien was glad. He filled his days with whatever work offered, in the stables and byres, exercising hawk and hound, lending a hand with sheep and cattle in the fields, carting timber for fence repairs and fuel, whatever was needed he was willing and anxious to do, as though he had stored within him such a tension of energy that he must at all costs grind it out of his body or sicken with it.

Withindoors he was quiet company, but then he had always been the quiet one. He was gentle and attentive to his mother, and endured stoically hours of her anguished presence, which Eudo tended to avoid when he could. The steely control with which she put aside every sign of pain was admirable, but almost harder to bear than open distress. Sulien marvelled and endured with her, since there was nothing more he could do for her. And she was gracious and dignified, but whether she was glad of his company or whether it added one more dimension to her burden, there was no telling. He had always supposed that Eudo was her favourite and had the lion's share of her love. That was the usual order of things, and Sulien had no fault to find with it.

His abstraction and quietness were hardly noticed by Eudo and Jehane. They were breeding, they were happy, they found life full and pleasant, and took it for granted that a youth who had mistakenly wasted a year of his life on a vocation of which he had thought better only just in time, should spend these first weeks of freedom doing a great deal of hard thinking about his future. So they left him to his thoughts, accommodated him with the hard labour he seemed to need, and waited with easy affection for him to emerge into the open in his own good time.

He rode out one day in mid-November with orders to Eudo's herdsman in the outlying fields of Longner land to eastward, along the River Tern, almost as far afield as Upton, and having discharged his errand, turned to ride back, and then instead wheeled the horse again and rode on very slowly, leaving the village of Upton on his left hand, hardly knowing what it was he had in mind. There was no haste, all his own industry could not convince him that he was needed at home, and the day, though cloudy, was dry, and the air mild. He rode on, gradually drawing a little further from the river bank, and only when he topped the slight ridge which offered the highest point in these flat, open fields did he realise where he was heading. Before him, at no great distance, the roofs of Withington showed through a frail filigree of naked branches, and the squat, square tower of the church just rose above the grove of low trees.

He had not realised how constantly she had been in his mind since his visit here, lodged deep in his memory, unobtrusive but always present. He had only to close his eyes now, and he could see her face as clearly as when she had first caught the sound of his horse's hooves on the hard soil of the courtyard, and turned to see who was riding in. The very way she halted and turned to him was like a flower swaying in the lightest of winds, and the face she raised to him was open like a flower, without reserve or fear, so that at that first glance he had seemed to see deep into her being. As though her flesh, though rounded and full and firm, had been translucent from without and luminous from within. There had been a little pale sunshine that day, and it had gained radiance from her eyes, russet-gold eyes, and reflected light from her broad brow under the soft brown hair. She had smiled at him with that same ungrudging radiance, shedding warmth about her to melt the chill of anxiety from his mind and heart, she who had never set eyes on him before, and must not be made ever to see him or think of him again.

But he had thought of her, whether he willed it or not.

He had hardly realised now that he was still riding towards the further edge of the village, where the manor lay. The line of the stockade rose out of the fields, the steep pitch of the roof within, the pattern of field strips beyond the enclosure, a square plot of orchard trees, all gleaned and almost leafless. He had splashed through the first stream almost without noticing, but the second, so close now to the wide-open gate in the manor fence, caused him to baulk suddenly and consider what he was doing, and must not do, had no right to do.

He could see the courtyard within the stockade, and the elder boy carefully leading a pony in decorously steady circles, with the small girl on its back. Regularly they appeared, passed and vanished, to reappear at the far rim of their circle and vanish again, the boy giving orders importantly, the child with both small fists clutched in the pony's mane. Once Gunnild came into view for a moment, smiling, watching her youngest charge, astride like a boy, kicking round bare heels into the pony's fat sides. Then she drew back again to clear their exercise ground, and passed from his sight. With an effort, Sulien came to himself, and swung away from them towards the village.

And there she was, coming towards him from the direction of the church, with a basket on her arm under the folds of her cloak, and her brown hair braided in a thick plait and tied with a scarlet cord. Her eyes were on him. She had known him before ever he was aware of her, and she approached him without either hastening or lingering, with confident pleasure. Just as he had been seeing her with his mind's eye a moment earlier, except that then she had worn no cloak, and her hair had been loose about her shoulders. But her face had the same open radiance, her eyes the same quality of letting him into her heart.

A few paces from where he had reined in she halted, and they looked at each other for a long moment in silence. Then she said: 'Were you really going away again, now that you've come? Without a word? Without coming in?'

He knew that he ought to claw out of some astute corner of his mind wit enough and words enough to show that his presence here had nothing to do with her or with his former visit, some errand that would account for his having to ride by here, and make it urgent that he should be on his way home again without delay. But he could not find a single word, however false, however rough, to thrust her away from him.

'Come and be acquainted with my father,' she said simply. 'He will be glad, he knows why you came before. Of course Gunnild told him, how else do you think she got horse and groom to bring her into Shrewsbury, to the sheriff? None of us need ever go behind my father's back. I know you asked her to leave you out of it with Hugh Beringar, and so she did, but in this house we don't have secrets, we have no cause.'

That he could well believe. Her nature spoke for her sire, a constant and carefree inheritance. And though he knew it was none the less incumbent upon him to draw away from her, to avoid her and leave her her peace of mind, and relieve her parents of any future grief on her behalf, he could not do it. He dismounted, and walked with her, bridle in hand and still mute and confounded, in at the gate of Withington.

*　　*　　*

189

Brother Cadfael saw them in church together at the sung Mass for Saint Cecilia's day, the twenty-second of November. It was a matter for conjecture why they should choose to attend here at the abbey, when they had parish churches of their own. Perhaps Sulien still kept a precarious fondness for the Order he had left, for its stability and certainty, not to be found in the world outside, and still felt the need to make contact with it from time to time, while he reorientated his life. Perhaps she wanted Brother Anselm's admired music, especially on this day of all the saints' days. Or perhaps, Cadfael reflected, they found this a convenient and eminently respectable meeting-place for two who had not yet progressed so far as to be seen together publicly nearer home. Whatever the reason, there they were in the nave, close to the parish altar where they could see through into the choir and hear the singing unmarred by the mute spots behind some of the massive pillars. They stood close, but not touching each other, not even the folds of a sleeve brushing, very still, very attentive, with solemn faces and wide, clear eyes. Cadfael saw the girl for once grave, though she still shone, and the boy for once eased and tranquil, though the shadow of his disquiet still set its finger in the small furrow between his brows.

When the brothers emerged after service Sulien and Pernel had already left by the west door, and Cadfael went to his work in the garden wondering how often they had met thus, and how the first meeting had come about, for though the two had never looked at each other or touched hands during worship, or given any sign of being aware each of the other's presence, yet there was something about their very composure and the fixity of their attention that bound them together beyond doubt.

It was not difficult, he found, to account for this

ambivalent aura they carried with them, so clearly together, so tacitly apart. There would be no resolution, no solving of the dichotomy, until the one devouring question was answered. Ruald, who knew the boy best, had never found the least occasion to doubt that what he told was truth, and the simplicity of Ruald's acceptance of that certainty was Ruald's own salvation. But Cadfael could not see certainty yet upon either side. And Hugh and his lances and archers were still many miles away, their fortune still unknown, and nothing to be done but wait.

On the last day of November an archer of the garrison, soiled and draggled from the roads, rode in from the east, pausing first at Saint Giles to cry the news that the sheriff's levy was not far behind him, intact as it had left the town, apart from a few grazes and bruises, that the king's shire levies, those most needed elsewhere, were dismissed to their own garrisons at least for the winter, and his tactics changed from the attempt to dislodge and destroy his enemy to measures to contain him territorially and limit the damage he could do to his neighbours. A campaign postponed rather than ended, but it meant the safe return of the men of Shropshire to their own pastures. By the time the courier rode on into the Foregate the news was already flying ahead of him, and he eased his speed to cry it again as he passed, and answer some of the eager questions called out to him by the inhabitants. They came running out of their houses and shops and tofts, tools in hand, the women from their kitchens, the smith from his forge, Father Boniface from his room over the north porch of the abbey church, in a great buzz of relief and delight, passing details back and forth to one another as they had snatched them by chance from the courier's lips.

By the time the solitary rider was past the abbey gatehouse and heading for the bridge, the orderly thudding of hooves and the faint jingle of harness had reached Saint Giles, and the populace of the Foregate stayed to welcome the returning company. Work could wait for an hour or two. Even within the abbey pale the news was going round, and brothers gathered outside the wall unreproved, to watch the return. Cadfael, who had risen to see them depart, came thankfully to see them safely home again.

They came, understandably, a little less immaculate in their accoutrements than they had departed. The lance pennants were soiled and frayed, even tattered here and there, some of the light armour dinted and dulled, a few heads bandaged, one or two wrists slung for support, and several beards where none had been before. But they rode in good order and made a very respectable show, in spite of the travel stains and the mud imperfectly brushed out of their garments. Hugh had overtaken his men well before they reached Coventry, and made a sufficient halt there to allow rest and grooming to men and horses alike. The baggage carts and the foot bowmen could take their time from Coventry on, where the roads were open and good, and word of their safety had gone before them.

Riding at the head of the column, Hugh had discarded his mail to ride at ease in his own coat and cloak. He looked alert and stimulated, faintly flushed with pleasure from the hum and babel of relief and joy that accompanied him along the Foregate, and would certainly be continued through the town. Hugh would always make a wry mock of praise and plaudits, well aware of how narrowly they were separated from the rumblings of reproach that might have greeted him had he lost men, in however desperate an encounter. But it was human to take pleasure in knowing he had lost none. The return from Lincoln, almost three years ago, had not been like this; he could afford to enjoy his welcome.

At the abbey gatehouse he looked for Cadfael among the bevy of shaven crowns, and found him on the steps of the west door. Hugh said a word into his captain's ear, and drew his grey horse out of the line to rein in alongside, though he did not dismount. Cadfael reached up to the bridle in high content.

'Well, lad, this is a welcome sight if ever there was. Barely a scratch on you, and not a man missing! Who would want more?'

'What I wanted,' said Hugh feelingly, 'was de Mandeville's hide, but he wears it still, and devil a thing can Stephen do about it until we can flush the rat out of his hole. You've seen Aline? All's well there?'

'All's well enough, and will be better far when she sees your face in the doorway. Are you coming in to Radulfus?'

'Not yet! Not now! I must get the men home and paid, and then slip home myself. Cadfael, do something for me!'

'Gladly,' said Cadfael heartily.

'I want young Blount, and want him anywhere but at Longner, for I fancy his mother knows nothing about this business he's tangled in. She goes nowhere out to hear the talk, and the family would go out of their way to keep every added trouble from her. If they've said no word to her about the body you found, God forbid I should shoot the bolt at her now, out of the blue. She has grief enough. Will you get leave from the abbot, and find some means to bring the boy to the castle?'

'You've news, then!' But he did not ask what. 'An easier matter to bring him here, and Radulfus will have to hear, now or later, whatever it may be. He was one of us, he'll come if he's called. Radulfus can find a pretext. Concern for a some-time son. And no lie!'

'Good!' said Hugh. 'It will do! Bring him, and keep him until I come.'

He dug his heels into the grey, dappled hide, and Cadfael released the bridle. Hugh was away at a canter after his troop, towards the bridge and the town. Their progress could be followed by the diminishing sound of their welcome, a wave rolling into the distance, while the contented and grateful hum of voices here along the Foregate had levelled into a murmur like bees in a flowering meadow. Cadfael turned back into the great court, and went to ask audience with the abbot.

It was not so difficult to think of a plausible reason for paying a visit to Longner. There was a sick woman there who at one time had made use of his skills at least to dull her pain, and there was the younger son newly returned, who had consented to take a supply of the same syrup, and try to persuade her to employ it again, after a long while of refusing all solace. To enquire after the mother's condition, while extending the abbot's fatherly invitation to the son, so recently in his care, should not strain belief. Cadfael had seen Donata Blount only once, in the days when she was still strong enough to go out and about and willing, then, to ask and take advice. Just once she had come to consult Brother Edmund, the infirmarer, and been led by him to Cadfael's workshop. He had not thought of that visit for some years, and during that time she had grown frailer by infinitely slow and wasting degrees, and was no longer seen beyond the courtyard of Longner, and seldom even there of late. Hugh was right, her menfolk had surely kept from her every ill thing that could add another care to the all-too-grievous burden she already bore. If she must learn of evil in the end, at least let it be only after proof and certainty, when there was no escape.

He remembered how she had looked, that sole time that ever he had set eyes on her, a woman a little taller than his own modest height, slender as a willow even then, her black hair already touched with some strands of grey, her eyes of a deep, lustrous blue. By Hugh's account she was now shrunk to a dry wand, her every movement effort, her every moment pain. At least the poppies of Lethe could procure for her some interludes of sleep, if only she would use them. And somewhere deep within his mind Cadfael could not help wondering if she abstained in order to invite her death the sooner and be free.

But what he was concerned with now, as he saddled the brown cob and set out eastward along the Foregate, was her son, who was neither old nor ailing, and whose pains were of the mind, perhaps even of the soul.

It was early afternoon, and a heavy day. Clouds had gathered since morning, sagging low and blotting out distances, but there was no wind and no sign of rain, and once out of the town and heading for the ferry he was aware of a weighty silence, oppressive and still, in which not even a leaf or a blade of grass moved to disturb the leaden air. He looked up towards the ridge of trees above the Potter's Field as he passed along the meadows. The rich dark ploughland was beginning to show the first faint green shadow of growth, elusive and fragile as a veil. Even the cattle along the river levels were motionless, as if they slept.

He came through the belt of tidy, well-managed woodland beyond the meadows, and up the slight slope of the clearing into the open gates of Longner. A stable boy came running to the cob's bridle, and a maidservant, crossing the yard from the dairy, turned back to enquire his business here, with some surprise and curiosity, as though unexpected visitors were very rare here. As perhaps they were, for the manor was off the main highways where travellers might have need of a roof for the night, or shelter in inclement weather. Those who came visiting here came with a purpose, not by chance.

Cadfael asked for Sulien, in the abbot's name, and she nodded acceptance and understanding, her civility relaxing into a somewhat knowing smile. Naturally the monastic orders do not much like letting go of a young man, once he has been in their hands, and it might be worth a solicitous visit, so soon after his escape, while judgement is still awkward and doubtful, to see if persuasion can coax him back again. Something of the sort she was thinking, but indulgently. It would do very well. Let her say as much to the other servants of the household, and Sulien's departure at the abbot's summons would only confirm the story, perhaps even put the issue in doubt.

'Go in, sir, you'll find them in the solar. Go through, freely, you'll be welcome.'

She watched him climb the first steps to the hall door, before she herself made for the undercroft, where the wide cart-doors stood open and someone was rolling and stacking barrels within. Cadfael entered the hall, dim after the open courtyard, even dimmer by reason of the overcast day, and paused to let his eyes adjust to the change. At this hour the fire was amply supplied and well alight, but turfed down to keep it burning slowly until evening, when the entire household would be gathered within here and glad of both warmth and light. At present everyone was out at work, or busy in kitchen and store, and the hall was empty, but the heavy curtain was drawn back from a doorway in the far corner of the room, and the door it shielded stood half open. Cadfael could hear voices from within the room, one a man's, young and pleasantly low. Eudo or Sulien? He could not be certain. And the woman's . . . No, the women's, for these were two, one steady, deep, slow and clear in utterance, as though an effort was needed to form the words and give them sound; one young, fresh and sweet, with a candid fullness about it. That one Cadfael did recognise. So they had progressed this far, that somehow she or circumstances or fate itself had prevailed upon Sulien to bring her home. Therefore this must be Sulien in the solar with her.

Cadfael drew back the curtain fully, and rapped on the door as he opened it wide, pausing on the threshold. The voices had ceased abruptly, Sulien's and Pernel's with instant recognition and instant reserve, the Lady Donata's with the slightly startled but gracious tolerance of her kind. Intruders here were few and surprising, but her durable, worn dignity would never be disrupted.

'Peace on all here!' said Cadfael. The words had come naturally, a customary benediction, but he felt the instant stab of guilt at having used them, when he was all too conscious that what he brought them might be anything but peace. 'I am sorry, you did not hear me come. I was told to come through to you. May I enter?'

'Enter and be warmly welcome, Brother!' said Donata.

Her voice had almost more body than her flesh, even though it cost her effort and care to use it. She was installed on the wide bench against the far wall, under a single torch that spilled wavering light from its sconce over her. She was propped in cushions carefully piled to support her upright, with a padded footstool under her feet. The thin oval of her face was the translucent bluish colour of shadows in untrodden snow, lit by huge, sunken eyes of the deep, lustrous blue of bugloss. The hands that lay at rest on the pillows were frail as cobweb, and the body within her dark gown and brocaded bliaut little but skin and bone. But she was still the mistress here, and equal to her role.

'You have ridden from Shrewsbury? Eudo and Jehane will be sorry to have missed you, they have ridden over to Father Eadmer at Atcham. Sit here, Brother, close to me. The light's feeble. I like to see my visitors' faces, and my sight is not quite so sharp as it used to be. Sulien, bring a draught of ale for our guest. I am sure,' she said, turning upon Cadfael the thin, tranquil smile that softened the stoical set of her lips, 'that your visit must really be to my son. It is one more pleasure his return has brought me.'

Pernel said nothing at all. She was sitting at Donata's right hand, very quiet and still, her eyes upon Cadfael. It seemed to him that she was quicker even than Sulien to sense a deeper and darker purpose beyond this unexpected visit. If so, she suppressed what she knew, and continued composed and dutiful, the well-conditioned young gentlewoman being respectful and attentive to her elder. A first visit here? Cadfael thought so, by the slight tension that possessed both the young people.

'My name is Cadfael. Your son was my helper in the herb gardens at the abbey, for the few days he spent with us. I was sorry to lose him,' said Cadfael, 'but not sorry that he should return to the life he chose.'

'Brother Cadfael was an easy master,' said Sulien, presenting the cup to him with a somewhat strained smile.

'So I believe,' she said, 'from all that you have told me of him. And I do remember you, Brother, and the medicines you made for me, some years ago. You were so kind as to send a further supply by Sulien, when he came to see you. He has been persuading me to use the syrup. But I need nothing. You see I am very well tended, and quite content. You should take back the flask, others may need it.'

'It was one of the reasons for this visit,' said Cadfael, 'to enquire if you had found any benefit from the draught, or if there is anything besides that I could offer you.'

She smiled directly into his eyes, but all she said was: 'And the other reason?'

'The lord abbot,' said Cadfael, 'sent me to ask if Sulien will ride back with me and pay him a visit.'

Sulien stood fronting him with an inscrutable face, but betrayed himself for a second by moistening lips suddenly dry. 'Now?'

'Now.' The word fell too heavily, it needed leavening. 'He would take it kindly of you. He thought of your son,' said Cadfael, turning to Donata, 'for a short while as his son. He has not withdrawn that paternal goodwill. He would be glad to see and to know,' he said with emphasis, looking up again into Sulien's face, 'that all is well with you. There is nothing we want more than that.' And whatever might follow, that at least was true. Whether they could hope to have and keep what they wanted was another matter.

'Would an hour or two of delay be allowed me?' asked Sulien steadily 'I must escort Pernel home to Withington. Perhaps I should do that first.' Meaning, for Cadfael, who knew how to interpret: It may be a long time before I come back from the abbey. Best to clear up all unfinished business.

'No need for that,' said Donata with authority. 'Pernel shall stay here with me over the night, if she will be so kind. I will send a boy over to Withington to let her father know that

199

she is safe here with me. I have not so many young visitors that I can afford to part with her so soon. You go with Brother Cadfael, and we shall keep company very pleasantly together until you come back.'

That brought a certain wary gleam to Sulien's face and Pernel's. They exchanged the briefest of glances, and Pernel said at once: 'I should like that very much, if you'll really let me stay. Gunnild is there to take care of the children, and my mother, I'm sure, will spare me for a day.'

Was it possible, Cadfael wondered, that Donata, even in her own extremity, was taking thought for her younger son, and welcomed this first sign in him of interest in a suitable young woman? Mothers of strong nature, long familiar with their own slow deaths, may also wish to settle any unfinished business.

He had just realised what it was that most dismayed him about her. This wasting enemy that had greyed her hair and shrunk her to the bone had still not made her look old. She looked, rather, like a frail waif of a young girl, blighted, withered and starved in her April days, when the bud should just have been unfolding. Beside Pernel's radiance she was a blown wisp of vapour, the ghost of a child. Yet in this or any room she would still be the dominant.

'I'll go and saddle up, then,' said Sulien, almost as lightly as if he had been contemplating no more than a canter through the woods for a breath of air. He stooped to kiss his mother's fallen cheek, and she lifted a hand that felt like the flutter of a dead leaf's filigree skeleton as it touched his face. He said no farewells, to her or to Pernel. That might have spilled over into something betrayingly ominous. He went briskly out through the hall, and Cadfael made his own farewells as gracefully as he could, and hurried down to join him in the stables.

They mounted in the yard, and set out side by side without a word being spoken, until they were threading the belt of woodland.

'You will already have heard,' said Cadfael then, 'that Hugh Beringar and his levy came back today? Without losses!'

'Yes, we heard. I did grasp,' said Sulien, wryly smiling, 'whose voice it was summoning me. But it was well done to let the abbot stand for him. Where are we really bound? The abbey or the castle?'

'The abbey. So much was truth. Tell me, how much *does* she know?'

'My mother? Nothing. Nothing of murder, nothing of Gunnild, or Britric, or Ruald's purgatory. She does not know your plough team ever turned up a woman's body, on what was once our land. Eudo never said a word to her, nor has any other. You have seen her,' said Sulien simply. 'There is not a soul about her who would let one more grief, however small, be added to her load. I should thank you for observing the same care.'

'If that can be sustained,' said Cadfael, 'it shall. But to tell the truth, I am not sure that you have done her any service. Have you ever considered that she may be stronger than any one of you? And that in the end, to worse sorrow, she may have to know?'

Sulien rode beside him in silence for a while, his head was raised, his eyes fixed steadily ahead, and his profile, seen clearly against the open sky with its heavy clouds, pale and set with the rigidity of a mask. Another stoic, with much of his mother in him.

'What I most regret,' he said at last, with deliberation, 'is that I ever approached Pernel. I had no right. Hugh Beringar would have found Gunnild in the end, she would have come forward when she heard of the need, without my meddling. And now see what mischief I have done!'

'I think,' said Cadfael, with respectful care, 'that the lady played as full a part as you. And I doubt if she regrets it.'

Sulien splashed ahead of his companion into the ford. His voice came back to Cadfael's ears clear and resolute. 'Something may be done to undo what we have done. And as to my mother, yes, I have considered the ending. Even for that I have made provision.'

Chapter Twelve

N THE ABBOT'S parlour the four of them were gathered after Vespers, with the window shuttered and the door fast closed against the world. They had had to wait for Hugh. He had a garrison to review, levies newly dismissed from feudal service to pay and discharge home to their families, a few wounded to see properly tended, before he could even dismount stiffly in his own courtyard, embrace wife and son, shed his soiled travelling clothes and draw breath at his own table. The further examination of a doubtful witness, however low his credit stood now, could wait another hour or two without disadvantage.

But after Vespers he came, eased and refreshed but weary. He shed his cloak at the door, and made his reverence to the abbot. Radulfus closed the door, and there was a silence, brief but deep. Sulien sat still and mute on the bench built against the panelled wall. Cadfael had drawn aside into the corner by the shuttered window.

'I must thank you, Father,' said Hugh, 'for providing us this meeting place. I should have been sorry to impose upon the family at Longner, and by all counts you have also an interest in this matter, as valid as mine.'

'We have all an interest in truth and justice, I trust,' said the

203

abbot. 'Nor can I discard all responsibility for a son because he has gone forth into the world. As Sulien knows. Proceed as you choose, Hugh.'

He had made room for Hugh beside him behind his desk, cleared now of its parchments and the business of the day. Hugh accepted the place and sat down with a great sigh. He was still cramped from the saddle and had stiffening grazes newly healed, but he had brought back his company intact from the Fens, and that was achievement enough. What else he had brought back with him he was about to sift, and these three in company with him here were about to learn.

'Sulien, I need not remind you, or these who were witnesses, of the testimony you gave concerning Ruald's wife's ring, and how you came by it at the shop of John Hinde, in Priestgate, in Peterborough. Name and place I asked, and you told me. From Cambridge, when we were discharged from service, I went to Peterborough. Priestgate I found. The shop I found. John Hinde I found. I have talked to him, Sulien, and I report his testimony as I heard it from him. Yes,' said Hugh with deliberation, his eyes on Sulien's blanched but composed face, 'Hinde remembers you well. You did come to him with the name of Abbot Walter to commend you, and he took you in for a single night, and set you on your way home next day. That is truth. That he confirms.'

Recalling how readily Sulien had supplied the jeweller's name and the place where his shop was to be found, Cadfael had had little doubt of the truth of that part of the story. It had not seemed likely, then, that the rest of it would ever be tested. But Sulien's face continued as marble-blank as resolution could make it, and his eyes never left Hugh's face.

'But when I asked him of the ring, he asked, what ring was that? And when I pictured it to him, he was absolute that he had never seen such a ring, never bought that or anything else from such a woman as I described. So recent a transaction he could not possibly forget, even if he did not keep good records, as he does. He never gave you the ring, for he never had the ring. What you told us was a fabric of lies.'

The new silence fell like a stone, and seemed to be arrested in Sulien's braced stillness. He neither spoke nor lowered his eyes. Only the small, spasmodic movement of Radulfus's muscular hand upon the desk broke the tension within the room. What Cadfael had foreseen from the moment he had conveyed the abbot's summons, and observed the set of Sulien's face as he received it, came as a shock to Radulfus. There was not much of human behaviour he had not encountered in his life. Liars he had known and dealt with, without surprise, but this one he had not expected.

'Yet you produced the ring,' Hugh continued steadily, 'and Ruald recognised and verified the ring. Since you did not get it from the silversmith, how did you come by it? One story you told is shown to be false. Now you have your chance to tell another and a truer. Not all liars have that grace. Now say what you have to say.'

Sulien opened his lips with a creaking effort, like one turning a key in a lock unwilling to respond.

'I already had the ring,' he said. 'Generys gave it to me. I have told the lord abbot, I tell you now, all my life long I held her in affection, deeper than I knew. Even as I grew a man, I never understood how that affection was changing, until Ruald deserted her. Her rage and grief made me to know. What moved her I hardly know. It may be she was avenging herself upon all men, even me. She did receive and make use of me. And she gave me the ring. It did not last long,' he said, without bitterness. 'I could not satisfy, green as I was. I was

205

not Ruald, nor of sufficient weight to pierce Ruald to the heart.'

There was something strange, Cadfael thought, in his choice of words, as though at times the blood of passion did run in them, and at others they came with detached care, measured and contrived. Perhaps Radulfus had felt the same unease, for this time he did speak, impatient for plainer telling.

'Are you saying, my son, that you were this woman's lover?'

'No,' said Sulien. 'I am saying that I loved her, and she admitted me some small way into her grief, when she was in mortal need. If my torment was any ease to hers, that time was not wasted. If you mean, did she admit me even into her bed, no, that she never did, nor I never asked nor hoped for it. My significance, my usefulness, never came so high.'

'And when she vanished,' Hugh pursued with relentless patience, 'what did you know of that?'

'Nothing, no more than any other man.'

'What did you suppose had become of her?'

'My time,' said Sulien, 'was over by then, she had done with me. I believed what the world believed, that she had taken up her roots and fled the place that had become abhorrent to her.'

'With another lover?' Hugh asked evenly. 'The world believed so.'

'With a lover or alone. How could I know?'

'Truly! You knew no more than any other man. Yet when you came back here, and heard that we had found a woman's body buried in the Potter's Field, you knew that it must be she.'

'I knew,' said Sulien with aching care, 'that it was the

common belief that it must be. I did not know that it was.'

'True, again! You had no secret knowledge, so equally you could not know that it was *not* Generys. Yet you felt it necessary at once to make up your lying story, and produce the ring she had given you, as you now say, in order to prove that she was well alive and far enough away to make confirmation hard, and to lift the shadow of suspicion from Ruald. Without respect to his guilt or innocence, for according to the account you give of yourself now, you did not know whether she was alive or dead, nor whether he had or had not killed her.'

'No!' said Sulien, with a sudden flush of energy and indignation that jerked his braced body forward from the panelled wall. 'That I did know, because I know him. It is inconceivable that he could ever have harmed her. It is not in the man to do murder.'

'Happy the man whose friends can be so sure of him!' said Hugh drily. 'Very well, pass on to what followed. We had no cause to doubt your word then; you had proved, had you not, that Generys was alive? Therefore we looked about us for other possibilities, and found another woman who had frequented there, and not been seen of late. And behold, your hand is seen again moulding matters. From the moment you heard of the pedlar's arrest you began a hunt for some manor where the woman might have found a shelter through the winter, where someone might be able to testify to her being alive well after she parted from Britric. I doubt if you expected to find her still settled there, but I am sure you were glad of it. It meant you need not appear, she could come forward of her own accord, having heard there was a man charged with her murder. Twice, Sulien? Twice are we to accept your hand for the hand of God, with no more pressing motive than pure love of justice? Since you had so infallibly proved the dead woman could not be Generys, why should you be so sure she was not Gunnild? Two such rescues were one too many to be believed in. Gunnild's survival was proven, she came, she spoke, she was flesh and blood beyond doubt. But for the life of Generys we had only your word. And your word is shown to be false. I think we need look no further for a name for the woman we found. By denying her a name, you have named her.'

Sulien had shut his lips and clenched his teeth, as though he would never speak another word. It was too late to deploy any more lies.

'I think,' said Hugh, 'that when you heard what the abbey plough had turned up out of the soil, you were never in a moment's doubt as to her name. I think you knew very well that she was there. And you were quite certain that Ruald was not her murderer. Oh, that I believe! A certainty, Sulien, to which only God can be entitled, who knows all things with certainty. Only God, and you, who knew all too well who the murderer was.'

'Child,' said Radulfus into the prolonged silence, 'if you have an answer to this, speak out now. If there is guilt on your soul, do not continue obdurate, but confess it. If not, then tell us what your answer is, for you have brought this suspicion upon yourself. To your credit, it seems that you would not have another man, be he friend or stranger, bear the burden of a crime not his to answer. That I should expect of you. But the lies are not worthy, not even in such a cause. Better by far to deliver all others, and say outright: I am the man, look no further.'

Silence fell again, and this time lasted even longer, so that Cadfael felt the extreme stillness in the room as a weight upon his flesh and a constriction upon his breath. Outside the window dusk had gathered in thin, low, featureless cloud, a leaden grey sucking out all colour from the world. Sulien sat motionless, shoulders braced back to feel the solid wall supporting him, eyelids half lowered over the dimmed blue of his eyes. After a long time he stirred, and raised both hands to press and flex with stiff fingers at his cheeks, as though the desperation in which he found himself had cramped even his flesh, and he must work the paralysing chill out of it before he could speak. But when he did speak, it was in a voice low, reasonable and persuasive, and he lifted his head and confronted Hugh with the composure of one who has reached a decision and a stance from which he will not easily be shifted.

'Very well! I have lied, and lied again, and I love lies no more than you do, my lord. But if I make a bargain with you, I swear to you I shall keep it faithfully. I have not confessed to anything, yet. But I will give you my confession to murder, upon conditions!'

'Conditions?' said Hugh, with black brows obliquely raised in wry amusement.

'They need not limit in any degree what can be done to me,' said Sulien, as gently as if he argued a sensible case to which all sane men must consent once they heard it. 'All I want is that my mother and my family shall suffer no dishonour and no disgrace by me. Why should not a bargain be struck even over matters of life and death, if it can spare all those who are not to blame, and destroy only the guilty?'

'You are offering me a confession,' said Hugh, 'in exchange for blanketing this whole matter in silence?'

The abbot had risen to his feet, a hand raised in indignant protest. 'There can be no bargaining over murder. You must withdraw, my son, you are adding insult to your offence.'

'No,' said Hugh, 'let him speak. Every man deserves a hearing. Go on, Sulien, what is it you are offering and asking?'

'Something which could very simply be done. I have been summoned here, where I chose to abandon my calling,' Sulien began in the same measured and persuasive voice. 'Would it be so strange if I should change yet again, and return to my vocation here as a penitent? Father Abbot here, I'm sure, could win me if he tried.' Radulfus was frowning at that moment in controlled disapproval, not of the misuse being made of his influence and office, but of the note of despairing levity which had crept into the young man's voice. 'My mother is in her death illness,' said Sulien, 'and my brother has an honoured name, like our father before us, a wife, and a child to come next year, and has done no wrong to any man, and knows of none. For God's sake leave them in peace, let them keep their name and reputation as clean as ever it was. Let them be told that I have repented of my recantation, and returned to the Order, and am sent away from here to seek out Abbot Walter, wherever he may be, submit myself to his discipline and earn my return to the Order. He would not refuse me, they will be able to believe it. The Rule allows the stray to return and be accepted even to the third time. Do this for me, and I will give you my confession to murder.'

'So in return for your confession,' said Hugh, begging silence of the abbot with a warning gesture of his hand, 'I am to let you go free, but back into the cloister?'

'I did not say that. I said let them believe that. No, do this for me,' said Sulien in heavy earnest, and paler than his shirt, 'and I will take my death however you may require it, and you may shovel me into the ground and forget me.'

'Without benefit of a trial?'

210

'What should I want with a trial? I want them to be left in peace, to know nothing. A life is fair pay for a life, what difference can a form of words make?'

It was outrageous, and only a very desperate sinner would have dared advance it to a man like Hugh, whose grip on his office was as firm and scrupulous as it was sometimes unorthodox. But still Hugh sat quiet, fending off the abbot with a sidelong flash of his black eyes, and tapping the finger-tips of one long hand upon the desk, as if seriously consider-ing. Cadfael had an inkling of what he was about, but could not guess how he would set about it. The one thing certain was that no such abominable bargain could ever be accepted. To wipe a man out, murderer or no, in cold blood and in secret was unthinkable. Only an inexperienced boy, driven to the end of his tether, could ever have proposed it, or cherished the least hope that it could be taken seriously. This was what he had meant by saying that he had made provision. These chil-dren, Cadfael thought in a sudden blaze of enlightened indig-nation, how dare they, with such misguided devotion, do their progenitors such insult and offence? And themselves such grievous injury!

'You interest me, Sulien,'said Hugh at length, holding him eye to eye across the desk. 'But I need to know somewhat more about this death before I can answer you. There are details that may temper the evil. You may as well have the benefit of them, for your own peace of mind and mine, what-ever happens after.'

'I cannot see the need,' said Sulien wearily but resignedly.

'Much depends on how this thing happened,' Hugh per-sisted. 'Was it a quarrel? When she rejected and shamed you? Even a mere unhappy chance, a struggle and a fall? For we do know by the manner of her burial, there under the bushes by

211

Ruald's garden . . .' He broke off there, for Sulien had stiff-
ened sharply and turned his head to stare. 'What is it?'

'You are confused, or trying to confuse me,' said Sulien,
again withdrawing into the apathy of exhaustion. 'It was not
there, you must know it. It was under the clump of broom
bushes in the headland.'

'Yes, true, I had forgotten. Much has happened since then,
and I was not present when the ploughing began. We do
know, I was about to say, that you laid her in the ground with
some evidence of respect, regret, even remorse. You buried a
cross with her. Plain silver,' said Hugh, 'we could not trace it
back to you or anyone, but it was there.'

Sulien eyed him steadily and made no demur.

'It leads me to ask,' Hugh pursued delicately, 'whether this
was not simply mischance, a disaster never meant to happen.
For it may take no more than a struggle, perhaps flight, an
angry blow, a fall, to break a woman's skull as hers was
broken. She had no other broken bones, only that. So tell us,
Sulien, how this whole thing befell, for it may go some way to
excuse you.'

Sulien had blanched into a marble pallor, fending him off
with a bleak and wary face. He said between his teeth: 'I have
told you all you need to know. I will not say a word more.'

'Well,' said Hugh, rising abruptly, as though he had lost
patience, 'I daresay it may be enough. Father, I have two
archers with horses outside. I propose to keep the prisoner
under guard in the castle for the present, until I have more
time to proceed. May my men come in and take him? They
have left their arms at the gate.'

The abbot had sat silent all this time, but paying very close
attention to all that was said, and by the narrowed intelligence
of his eyes in the austere face he had missed none of the

implications. Now he said: 'Yes, call them in.' And to Sulien, as Hugh crossed to the door and went out: 'My son, however lies may be enforced upon us, or so we may think, there is in the end no remedy but truth. It is the one course that cannot be evil.'

Sulien turned his head, and the candle caught and illuminated the dulled blue of his eyes and the exhausted pallor of his face. He unlocked his lips with an effort. 'Father, will you keep my mother and my brother in your prayers?'

'Constantly,' said Radulfus.

'And my father's soul?'

'And your own.'

Hugh was at the parlour door again. The two archers of the garrison came in on his heels, and Sulien, unbidden, rose with the alacrity of relief from the bench, and went out between them without a word or a glance behind. And Hugh closed the door.

'You heard him,' said Hugh. 'What he knew he answered readily. When I took him astray he knew he could not sustain it, and would not answer at all. He was there, yes, he saw her buried. But he neither killed nor buried her.'

'I understood,' said the abbot, 'that you put to him points that would have betrayed him . . .'

'That did betray him,' said Hugh.

'But since I do not know all the details, I cannot follow precisely what you got out of him. Certainly there is the matter of exactly where she was found. That I grasped. He set you right. That was something he knew, and it bore out his story. Yes, he was a witness.'

'But not a sharer, nor even a close witness,' said Cadfael. 'Not close enough to see the cross that was laid on her breast, for it was not silver, but made hastily out of two sticks from the bushes. No, he did not bury her, and he did not kill her, because if he had done so, with his bent for bearing the guilt, he would have set us right about her injuries – or want of them. You know, as I know, that her skull was not broken. She had no detectable injuries. If he had known how she died, he would have told us. But he did not know, and he was too shrewd to risk guessing. He may even have realised that Hugh was setting traps for him. He chose silence. What you do not say cannot betray you. But with eyes like those in his head, even silence cannot shield him. The lad is crystal.'

'I am sure it was truth,' said Hugh, 'that he was sick with love for the woman. He had loved her unquestioning, unthinking, like a sister or a nurse, from childhood. The very pity and anger he felt on her account when she was abandoned must have loosed all the strings of a man's passion in him. It must be true, I think, that she did lean on him then, and gave him cause to believe himself elect, while she still thought of him as a mere boy, a child of whom she was fond, offering her a child's comfort.'

'True, also,' the abbot wondered, 'that she gave him the ring?'

It was Cadfael who said at once: 'No.'

'I was still in some doubt,' said Radulfus mildly, 'but you say no?'

'One thing has always troubled me,' said Cadfael, 'and that is the manner in which he produced the ring. You'll recall, he came to ask you, Father, for leave to visit his home. He stayed there overnight, as you permitted, and on his return he gave us to understand that only from his brother, during that visit, had he learned of the finding of the woman's body, and the understandable suspicion it cast upon Ruald. And then he brought forth the ring, and told his story, which we had then no cause to doubt. But I believe that already, before he came to you to ask leave of absence, he had been told of the case. That was the very reason his visit to Longner became necessary. He had to go home because the ring was there, and he must get it before he could speak out in defence of Ruald. With lies, yes, because truth was impossible. We can be sure, now, that he knew, poor lad, who had buried Generys, and where she was laid. Why else should he take flight into the cloister, and so far distant, from a place where he could no longer endure to be?'

'There is no help for it,' said Radulfus reflectively, 'he is protecting someone else. Someone close and dear to him. His whole concern is for his kin and the honour of his house. Can it be his brother?'

Hugh said: 'No. Eudo seems to be the one person who has escaped. Whatever happened in the Potter's Field, not a shadow of it has ever fallen upon Eudo. He is happy, apart from his mother's sickness he has no cares, he is married to a pleasant wife, and looking forward hopefully to having a son. Better still, he is wholly occupied with his manor, with the work of his hands and the fruits of his soil, and seldom looks below, for the dark things that gnaw on less simple men. No, we can forget Eudo.'

'There were two,' said Cadfael slowly, 'who fled from Longner after Generys vanished. One into the cloister, one into the battlefield.'

'His father!' said Radulfus, and pondered in silence for a moment. 'A man of excellent repute, a hero who fought in the king's rearguard at Wilton, and died there. Yes, I can believe that Sulien would sacrifice his own life rather than see that record soiled and blemished. For his mother's sake, and his brother's, and the future of his brother's sons, no less than for his father's memory. But of course,' he said simply, 'we cannot let it lie. And now what are we to do?'

Cadfael had been wondering the same thing, ever since Hugh's springes had caused even obstinate silences to speak with such eloquence, and confirmed with certainty what had always been persistent in a corner of Cadfael's mind. Sulien had knowledge that oppressed him like guilt, but he carried no guilt of his own. He knew only what he had seen. But how much had he seen? Not the death, or he would have seized on every confirming detail, and offered it as evidence against himself. Only the burial. A boy in the throes of his first impossible love, embraced and welcomed into an all-consuming grief and rage, then put aside, perhaps for no worse reason than that Generys had cared for him deeply, and willed him not to be scorched and maimed by her fire more incurably than he already was, or else because another had taken his place, drawn irresistibly into the same furnace, one deprivation fused inextricably with another. For Donata was already, for several years, all too well acquainted with her interminable death, and Eudo Blount in his passionate and spirited prime as many years forced to be celibate as ever was priest or monk. Two starving creatures were fed. And one tormented boy spied upon them, perhaps only once, perhaps several times, but in any event once too often, feeding his own anguish with his jealousy of a rival he could not even hate, because he worshipped him.

It was conceivable. It was probable. Then how successful had father and son been in dissembling their mutual and mutually destructive obsession? And how much had any other in that house divined of the danger?

Yes, it could be so. For she had been, as everyone said, a very beautiful woman.

'I think,' said Cadfael, 'that with your leave, Father, I must go back to Longner.'

'No need,' said Hugh abstractedly. 'We could not leave the lady waiting all night without word, certainly, but I have sent a man from the garrison.'

'To tell her no more than that he stays here overnight? Hugh, the great error has been, throughout, telling her no more than some innocuous half-truth to keep her content and incurious. Or, worse, telling her nothing at all. Such follies are committed in the name of compassion! We must not let her get word of this! We must keep this and this trouble from her! Starving her courage and strength and will into a feeble shadow, as disease has eaten away her body. When if they had known and respected her as they should she could have lifted half the load from them. If she is not afraid of the monster thing with which she shares her life, there is nothing of which she can be afraid. It is natural enough,' he said ruefully, 'for the manchild to feel he must be his mother's shield and defence, but he does her no service. I said so to him as we came. She would far rather have scope to fulfil her own will and purpose and be shield and defence to him, whether he understand it or not. Better, indeed, if he never understands it.'

'You think,' said Radulfus, eyeing him sombrely, 'that she should be told?'

'I think she should have been told long ago everything there was to tell about this matter. I think she should be told, even now. But I cannot do it, or let it be done if I can prevent. Too easily, as we came, I promised him that if the truth could still be kept from her, I would see it done. Well, if you have put off the hour for tonight, so be it. True, it is too late now to trouble them. But, Father, if you permit, I will ride back there early in the morning.'

217

'If you think it necessary,' said the abbot, 'by all means go. If it is possible now to restore her her son with the least damage, and salve her husband's memory for her without publishing any dishonour, so much the better.'

'One night,' said Hugh mildly, rising as Cadfael rose, 'cannot alter things, surely. If she has been left in happy ignorance all this time, and goes to bed this night supposing Sulien to have been detained here by the lord abbot without a shade of ill, you may leave her to her rest. There will be time to consider how much she must know when we have reasoned the truth out of Sulien. It need not be mortal. What sense would it make now to darken a dead man's name?'

Which was good sense enough, yet Cadfael shook his head doubtfully even over these few hours of delay. 'Still, go I must. I have a promise to keep. And I have realised, somewhat late, that I have left someone there who has made no promises.'

Chapter Thirteen

ADFAEL SET OUT with the dawn, and took his time over the ride, since there was no point in arriving at Longner before the household was up and about. Moreover, he was glad to go slowly, and find time for thought, even if thought did not get him very far. He hardly knew whether to hope to find all as he had left it when he rode away with Sulien, or to discover this morning that he was already forsworn, and all secrecy had been blown away overnight. At the worst, Sulien was in no danger. They were agreed that he was guilty of nothing but suppressing the truth, and if the guilt in fact belonged to a man already dead, what need could there be to publish his blemish to the world? It was out of Hugh's writ or King Stephen's now, and no advocates were needed where next his case must be brought to the bar. All that could be said in accusation or extenuation was known to the judge already.

So all we need, Cadfael thought, is a little ingenuity in dealing with Sulien's conscience, and a little manipulating of truth in gradually laying the case to rest, and the lady need never know more or worse than she knew yesterday. Given time, gossip will tire of the affair, and turn to the next small crisis or scandal around the town, and they will forget at last

219

that their curiosity was never satisfied, and no murderer ever brought to book.

And there, he realised, was where he came into headlong collision with his own unsatisfied desire to have truth, if not set out before the public eye, at least unearthed, recognised and acknowledged. How, otherwise, could there be real reconciliation with life and death and the ordinances of God?

Meantime, Cadfael rode through an early morning like any other November morning, dull, windless and still, all the greens of the fields grown somewhat blanched and dried, the filigree of the trees stripped of half their leaves, the surface of the river leaden rather than silver, and stirred by only rare quivers where the currents ran faster. But the birds were up and singing, busy and loud, lords of their own tiny manors, crying their rights and privileges in defiance of intruders.

He left the highroad at Saint Giles, and rode by the gentle, upland track, part meadow, part heath and scattered trees, that crossed the rising ground towards the ferry. All the bustle of the awaking Foregate, the creaking of carts, the barking of dogs and interlacing of many voices fell away behind him, and the breeze which had been imperceptible among the houses here freshened into a brisk little wind. He crested the ridge, between the fringing trees, and looked down towards the sinuous curve of the river and the sharp rise of the shore and the meadows beyond. And there he halted sharply and sat gazing down in astonishment and some consternation at the ferryman's raft in mid-passage below him. The distance was not so great that he could not distinguish clearly the freight it was carrying towards the near shore.

A narrow litter, made to stand on four short, solid legs,

stood squarely placed in the middle of the raft to ride as steadily as possible. A linen awning sheltered the head of it from wind and weather, and it was attended on one side by a stockily built groom, and on the other by a young woman in a brown cloak, her head uncovered, her russet hair ruffled by the breeze. At the rear of the raft, where the ferryman poled his load through placid waters, the second porter held by a bridle a dappled cob that swam imperturbably behind. Indeed, he had to swim only in mid-stream, for the water here was still fairly low. The porters might have been servants from any local household, but the girl there was no mistaking. And who would be carried in litters over a mere few miles and in decent weather but the sick, the old, the disabled or the dead?

Early as it was, he had set out on this journey too late. The Lady Donata had left her solar, left her hall, left, God alone knew on what terms, her careful and solicitous son, and come forth to discover for herself what business abbot and sheriff in Shrewsbury had with her second son, Sulien.

Cadfael nudged his mule out through the crest of trees, and started down the long slope of the track to meet them, as the ferryman brought his raft sliding smoothly in to the sandy level below.

Pernel left the porters leading the horse ashore and lifting the litter safely to land, and came flying to meet Cadfael as he dismounted. She was flushed with the air and her own haste and the improbable excitement of this most improbable expedition. She caught him anxiously but resolutely by the sleeve, looking up earnestly into his face.

'She wills it! She knows what she is doing! Why could they never understand? Did you know she has never been told anything of all this business? The whole household . . . Eudo would have her kept in the dark, sheltered and wrapped in down. All of them, they did what he wanted. All out of tenderness, but what does she want with tenderness? Cadfael, there has been no one free to tell her the truth, except for you and me.'

'I was not free,' said Cadfael shortly. 'I promised the boy to respect his silence, as they have all done.'

'*Respect!*' breathed Pernel, marvelling. 'Where has been the respect for her? I met her only yesterday, and it seems to me I know her better than all these who move all day and every day under the same roof. You have seen her! Nothing but a handful of slender bones covered with pain for flesh and courage for skin. How dare any man look at her, and say of any matter, however daunting: We mustn't let this come to her ears, *she could not bear it*!'

'I have understood you,' said Cadfael, making for the strip of sand where the porters had lifted the litter ashore. 'You were still free, the only one.'

'One is enough! Yes, I have told her, everything I know, but there's more that I don't know, and she will have all. She has a purpose now, a reason for living, a reason for venturing out like this, mad as you may think it – better than sitting waiting for her death.'

A thin hand drew back the linen curtain as Cadfael stooped to the head of the litter. The shell was plaited from hemp, to be light of weight and give with the movement, and within it Donata reclined in folded rugs and pillows. Thus she must have travelled a year and more ago, when she had made her last excursions into the world outside Longner. What prodigies of endurance it cost her now could hardly be guessed. Under the linen awning her wasted face showed

222

livid and drawn, her lips blue-grey and set hard, so that she had to unlock them with an effort to speak. But her voice was still clear, and still possessed its courteous but steely authority.

'Were you coming to me, Brother Cadfael? Pernel supposed your errand might be to Longner. Be content, I am bound for the abbey. I understand that my son has involved himself in matters of moment both to the lord abbot and the sheriff. I believe I may be able to set the record straight, and see an account settled.'

'I will gladly ride back with you,' said Cadfael, 'and serve you in whatever way I can.'

No point now in urging caution and good sense upon her, none in trying to turn her back, none in questioning how she had eluded the anxious care of Eudo and his wife to undertake this journey. The fierce control of her face spoke for her. She knew what she was doing, no pain, no risk could have daunted her. Brittle energy had burned up in her as in a stirred fire. And a stirred fire was what she was, too long damped down into resignation.

'Then ride before, Brother,' she said, 'if you will be so good, and ask Hugh Beringar if he will come and join us at the abbot's lodging. We shall be slower on the road, you and he may be there before us. But not my son!' she added, with a lift of her head and a brief, deep spark in her eyes. 'Let him be! It is better, is it not, that the dead should carry their own sins, and not leave them for the living to bear.'

'It is better,' said Cadfael. 'An inheritance comes more kindly clear of debts.'

'Good!' she said. 'What is between my son and me may remain as it is until the right time comes. I will deal. No one else need trouble.'

One of her porters was busy rubbing down the cob's saddle and streaming hide for Pernel to remount. At foot pace they would be an hour yet on the way. Donata had sunk back in her pillows braced and still, all the fleshless lines of her face composed into stoic endurance. On her deathbed she might look so, and still never let one groan escape her. Dead, all the tension would have been wiped away, as surely as the passage of a hand closes the eyes for the last time.

Cadfael mounted his mule, and set off back up the slope, heading for the Foregate and the town.

'She *knows*?' said Hugh in blank astonishment. 'The one thing Eudo insisted on, from the very day I went to him first, the one person he would not have drawn into so grim a business! The last thing you said yourself, when we parted last night, was that you were sworn to keep the whole tangle from her. And now you have *told* her?'

'Not I,' said Cadfael. 'But yes, she knows. Woman to woman she heard it. And she is making her way now to the abbot's lodging, to say what she has to say to authority both sacred and secular, and have to say it but once.'

'In God's name,' demanded Hugh, gaping, 'how did she contrive the journey? I saw her, not so long since, every movement of a hand tired her. She had not been out of the house for months.'

'She had no compelling reason,' said Cadfael. 'Now she has. She had no cause to fight against the care and anxiety they pressed upon her. Now she has. There is no weakness in her will. They have brought her these few miles in a litter, at cost to her, I know it, but it is what she would have, and I, for one, would not care to deny her.'

'And she may well have brought on her death,' Hugh said, 'in such an effort.'

'And if that proved so, would it be so ill an ending?'

Hugh gave him a long, thoughtful look, and did not deny it.

'What has she said, then, to you, to justify such a wager?'

'Nothing, as yet, except that the dead should carry their own sins, and not leave them a legacy to the living.'

'It is more than we have got out of the boy,' said Hugh. 'Well, let him sit and think a while longer. He had his father to deliver, she has her son. And all of this while sons and household and all have been so busy and benevolent delivering her. If she's calling the tune now, we may hear a different song. Wait, Cadfael, and make my excuses to Aline, while I go and saddle up.'

They had reached the bridge, and were riding so slowly that they seemed to be eking out time for some urgent thinking before coming to this conference, when Hugh said: 'And she would not have Sulien brought in to hear?'

'No. Very firmly she said: Not my son! What is between them, she said, let it rest until the right time. Eudo she knows she can manipulate, lifelong, if you say no word. And what point is there in publishing the offences of a dead man? He cannot be made to pay, and the living should not.'

'But Sulien she cannot deceive. He witnessed the burial. He knows. What can she do but tell him the truth? The whole of it, to add to the half he knows already.'

Not until then had it entered Cadfael's mind to wonder if indeed they knew, or Sulien knew, even the half of it. They were being very sure, because they thought they had discounted every other possibility, that what they had left was truth. Now the doubt that had waited aside presented itself suddenly as a world of unconsidered possibilities, and no amount of thought could rule out all. How much even of what Sulien knew was not knowledge at all, but assumption? How much of what he believed he had seen was not vision, but illusion?

They dismounted in the stable yard at the abbey, and presented themselves at the abbot's door.

It was the middle of the morning when they assembled at last in the abbot's parlour. Hugh had waited for her at the gatehouse, to ensure that she should be carried at once the length of the great court to the very door of Radulfus's lodging. His solicitude, perhaps, reminded her of Eudo, for when he handed her out among the tattered autumnal beds of the abbot's garden she permitted all with a small, tight but tolerant smile, bearing the too-anxious assiduities of youth and health with the hard-learned patience of age and sickness. She accepted the support of his arm through the ante-room where normally Brother Vitalis, chaplain and secretary, might have been working at this hour, and Abbot Radulfus took her hand upon the other side, and led her within, to a cushioned place prepared for her, with the support of the panelled wall at her back.

Cadfael, watching this ceremonious installation without attempting to take any part in it, thought that it had something of the enthronement of a sovereign lady about it. That might even amuse her, privately. The privileges of mortal sickness had almost been forced upon her, what she thought of them might never be told. Certainly she had an imperishable dignity, and a large and tolerant understanding of the concern and even unease she caused in others and must endure graciously. She had also, thus carefully dressed for an ordeal and a social visit, a fragile and admirable elegance.

Her gown was deep blue like her eyes, and like her eyes a little faded, and the bliaut she wore over it, sleeveless and cut down to either hip, was the same blue, embroidered in rose and silver at the hems. The whiteness of her linen wimple turned her drawn cheeks to a translucent grey in the light almost of noon.

Pernel had followed silently into the ante-room, but did not enter the parlour. She stood waiting in the doorway, her golden-russet eyes round and grave.

'Pernel Otmere has been kind enough to bear me company all this way,' said Donata, 'and I am grateful to her for more than that, but she need not be put to the weariness of listening to the long conference I fear I may be forcing upon you, my lords. If I may ask, first . . . where is my son now?'

'He is in the castle,' said Hugh simply.

'Locked up?' she asked pointblank, but without reproach or excitement. 'Or on his parole?'

'He has the freedom of the wards,' said Hugh, and added no further enlightenment.

'Then, Hugh, if you would be kind enough to provide Pernel with some token that would let her in to him, I think they might spend the time more pleasantly together than apart, while we confer? Without prejudice,' she said gently, 'to any proceedings you may have in mind later.'

Cadfael saw Hugh's black, betraying brows twitch, and lift into oblique appreciation, and thanked God devoutly for an understanding rare between two so different.

'I will give her my glove,' said Hugh, and cast one sharp, enjoying glance aside at the mute girl in the doorway. 'No one will question it, no need for more.' And he turned and took Pernel by the hand, and went out with her.

Their plans had been made, of course, last night or this

morning, in the solar at Longner where the truth came forth
so far as truth was known, or on the journey at dawn, before
they ever reached the ferry over Severn, where Cadfael had
met them. A conspiracy of women had been hatched in
Eudo's hall, that kept due consideration of Eudo's rights
and needs, of his wife's contented pregnancy, even as it nur-
tured and advanced Pernel Otmere's determined pursuit of a
truth that would set Sulien Blount free from every haunted
and chivalrous burden that weighed him down. The young
one and the old one – old not in years, only in the rapidity of
her advance upon her death – they had come together like
lodestone and metal, to compound their own justice.

Hugh came back into the room smiling, though the smile
was invisible to all but Cadfael. A burdened smile, none the
less, for he, too, was in pursuit of a truth which might not
be Pernel's truth. He closed the door firmly on the world
without.

'Now, madam, in what particular can we be of service to
you?'

She had composed herself into a settled stillness which
could be sustained through a long conference. Without her
cloak she made so slight a figure, it seemed a man could have
spanned her body with his hands.

'I must thank you, my lords,' she said, 'for granting me
this audience. I should have asked for it earlier, but only
yesterday did I hear of this matter which has been troubling
you both. My family are too careful of me, and their intent
was to spare me any knowledge that might be distressing. A
mistake! There is nothing more distressing than to find out,
very late, that those who rearrange circumstances around
you to spare you pain have themselves been agonising day
and night. And needlessly, to no purpose. It is an indignity,

would not you think, to be protected by people you know, in your own mind, to be more in need of protection than you have ever been, or ever will be. Still, it is an error of affection. I cannot complain of it. But I need no longer suffer it. Pernel has had the good sense to tell me what no one else would. But there are still things I do not know, since she did not yet know them herself. May I ask?'

'Ask whatever you wish,' said the abbot. 'In your own time, and tell us if you need to rest.'

'True,' said Donata, 'there is no haste now. Those who are dead are safe enough, and those still living and wound into this coil, I trust, are also safe. I have learned that my son Sulien has given you some cause to believe him guilty of this death which is come to judgement here. Is he still suspect?'

'No,' said Hugh without hesitation. 'Certainly not of murder. Though he has said, and maintains, and will not be persuaded to depart from it, that he is willing to confess to murder. And if need be, to die for it.'

She nodded her head slowly, unsurprised. The stiff folds of linen rustled softly against her cheeks. 'I thought it might be so. When Brother Cadfael here came for him yesterday, I knew nothing to make me wonder or question. I thought all was as it seemed, and that you, Father, had still some doubts whether he had not made a wrong decision, and should not be advised to think more deeply about abandoning his vocation. But when Pernel told me how Generys had been found, and how my son had set himself to prove Ruald blameless, by proving this could not in fact be Generys . . . And then how he exerted himself, once again, to find the woman Gunnild alive . . . Then I understood that he had brought inevitable suspicion upon himself, as one knowing far too much.

229

So much wasted exertion, if only I had known! And he was willing to take that load upon him? Well, but it seems you have already seen through that pretence, with no aid from me. May I take it, Hugh, that you have been in Peterborough? We heard that you were newly back from the Fen country, and since Sulien was sent for so promptly after your return, I could not fail to conclude the two were connected.'

'Yes,' said Hugh, 'I went to Peterborough.'

'And you found that he had lied?'

'Yes, he had lied. The silversmith lodged him overnight, true. But he never gave him the ring, never saw the ring, never bought anything from Generys. Yes, Sulien lied.'

'And yesterday? Being found out in his lies, what did he tell you yesterday?'

'He said that he had the ring all along, that Generys had given it to him.'

'One lie leads to another,' she said with a deep sigh. 'He felt he had good cause, but there is never cause good enough. Always lies come to grief. I can tell you where he got the ring. He took it from a small box I keep in my press. There are a few other things in it, a pin for fastening a cloak, a plain silver torque, a ribbon . . . All trifles, but they could have been recognised, and given her a name, even after years.'

'Are you saying,' asked Radulfus, listening incredulously to the quiet, detached tone of the voice that uttered such things, 'that these things were taken from the dead woman? That she is indeed Generys, Ruald's wife?'

'Yes, she is indeed Generys. I could have named her at once, if anyone had asked me. I would have named her. I do not deal in lies. And yes, the trinkets were all hers.'

'It is a terrible sin,' said the abbot heavily, 'to steal from the dead.'

'There was no such intent,' she said with unshakable calm. 'But without them, after no very long time, no one would be able to name her. As you found, no one was. But it was not my choice, I would not have gone to such lengths. I think it must have been when Sulien brought my lord's body back from Salisbury, after Wilton, and we buried him and set all his affairs and debts in order, that Sulien found the box. He would know the ring. When he needed his proof, to show that she still lived, then he came home and took it. Her possessions no one has ever worn or touched, otherwise. Simply, they are in safe keeping. I will readily deliver them up to you, or to anyone who has a claim. Until last night I had not opened the box since first it was laid there. I did not know what he had done. Neither did Eudo. He knows nothing about this. Nor never shall.'

From his preferred corner, where he could observe without involvement, Cadfael spoke for the first time. 'I think, also, you may not yet know all you would wish to know about your son Sulien. Look back to the time when Ruald entered this house, abandoning his wife. How much did you know of what went on in Sulien's mind then? Did you know how deeply he was affected to Generys? A first love, the most desperate always. Did you know that in her desolation she gave him cause for a time to think there might be a cure for his? When in truth there was none?'

She had turned her head and fixed her gaunt dark eyes earnestly on Cadfael's face. And steadily she said: 'No, I did not know it. I knew he frequented their croft. So he had from a small child, they were fond of him. But if there was so extreme a change, no, he never said word or gave sign. He was a secret child, Sulien. Whatever ailed Eudo I always knew, he is open as the day. Not Sulien!'

'He has told us that it was so. And did you know that because of this attachment he still went there, even when she had thought fit to put an end to his illusion? And that he was there in the dark,' said Cadfael with rueful gentleness, 'when Generys was buried?'

'No,' she said, 'I did not know. Only now had I begun to fear it. That or some other knowledge no less dreadful to him.'

'Dreadful enough to account for much. For why he made up his mind to take the cowl, and not here in Shrewsbury, but far away in Ramsey. What did you make of that, then?' asked Hugh.

'It was not so strange in him,' she said, looking into distance and faintly and ruefully smiling. 'That was something that could well happen to Sulien, he ran deep, and thought much. And then, there was a bitterness and a pain in the house, and I know he could not choose but feel it and be troubled. I think I was not sorry that he should escape from it and go free, even if it must be into the cloister. I knew of no worse reason. That he had been there, and seen – no, that I did not know.'

'And what he saw,' said Hugh, after a brief and heavy silence, 'was his father, burying the body of Generys.'

'Yes,' she said. 'It must have been so.'

'We could find no other possibility,' said Hugh, 'and I am sorry to have to set it before you. Though I still cannot see what reason there could be, why or how it came about that he killed her.'

'Oh, no!' said Donata. 'No, not that. He buried her, yes. But he did not kill her. Why should he? I see that Sulien believed it, and would not at any cost have it known to the world. But it was not like that.'

'Then who did?' demanded Hugh, confounded. 'Who was her murderer?'

'No one,' said Donata. 'There was no murder.'

Chapter Fourteen

UT OF THE unbelieving silence that followed, Hugh's voice asked: 'If this was not murder, why the secret burial, why conceal a death for which there could be no blame?'

'I have not said,' Donata said patiently, 'that there was no blame. I have not said that there was no sin. It is not for me to judge. But murder there was none. I am here to tell you truth. The judgement must be yours.'

She spoke as one, and the only one, who could shed light on all that had happened, and the only one who had been kept in ignorance of the need. Her voice remained considerate, authoritative and kind. Very simply and clearly she set out her case, excusing nothing, regretting nothing.

'When Ruald turned away from his wife, she was desolated and despairing. You will not have forgotten, Father, for you must have been in grave doubt concerning his decision. She, when she found she could not hold him, came to appeal to my husband, as overlord and friend to them both, to reason with Ruald and try to persuade him he did terrible wrong. And truly I think he did his best for her, and again and again went to argue her case, and tried also, surely, to comfort and reassure her, that she should not suffer loss of house and living by reason of Ruald's desertion. My lord was good to his people. But Ruald would not be turned back from the way he had chosen. He left her. She had loved him out of all measure,' said Donata dispassionately, speaking pure truth, 'and in the same measure she hated him. And all these days and weeks my lord had contended for her right, but could not win it. He had never before been so often and so long in her company.'

A moment she paused, looking from face to face, presenting her own ruin with wide, illusionless eyes.

'You see me, gentlemen. Since that time I may, perhaps, have moved a few short paces nearer the grave, but the change is not so great. I was already what I am now. I had been so for some few years. Three at least, I think, since Eudo had shared my bed, for pity of me, yes, but himself in abstinence to starvation, and without complaint. Such beauty as I ever had was gone, withered away into this aching shell. He could not touch me without causing me pain. And himself worse pain, whether he touched or abstained. And she, you will remember if ever you saw her, she was most beautiful. What all men said, I say, also. Most beautiful, and enraged, and desperate. And famished, like him. I fear I distress you, gentlemen,' she said, seeing them all three held in frozen awe at her composure and her merciless candour, delivered without emphasis, even with sympathy. 'I hope not. I simply wish to make all things plain. It is necessary.'

'There is no need to labour further,' said Radulfus. 'This is not hard to understand, but very hard to hear as it must be to tell.'

'No,' she said reassuringly, 'I feel no reluctance. Never fret for me. I owe truth to her, as well as to you. But enough, then. He loved her. She loved him. Let us make it brief. They loved,

236

and I knew. No one else. I did not blame them. Neither did I forgive them. He was my lord, I had loved him five-and-twenty years, and there was no remission because I was an empty shell. He was mine, I would not endure to share him.

'And now,' she said, 'I must tell something that had happened more than a year earlier. At that time I was using the medicines you sent me, Brother Cadfael, to ease my pain when it grew too gross. And I grant you the syrup of poppies does help, for a time, but after a while the charm fails, the body grows accustomed, or the demon grows stronger within.'

'It is true,' said Cadfael soberly. 'I have seen it lose its hold. And beyond a certain strength treatment cannot go.'

'That I understood. Beyond that there is only one cure, and we are forbidden to resort to that. None the less,' said Donata inexorably, 'I did consider how to die. Mortal sin, Father, I knew it, yet I did consider. Oh, never look aside at Brother Cadfael, I would not have come to him for the means, I knew he would not give them to me if I did. Nor did I ever intend to give my life away easily. But I foresaw a time when the load would become more than even I could bear, and I wished to have some small thing about me, a little vial of deliverance, a promise of peace, perhaps never to use, only to keep as a talisman, the very touch of it consolation to me that at the worst . . . at the last extreme, there was left to me a way of escape. To know that was to go on enduring. Is that reproach to me, Father?'

Abbot Radulfus stirred abruptly out of a stillness so long sustained that he emerged from it with a sharp indrawn breath, as if himself stricken with a shadowy insight into her suffering.

'I am not sure that I have the right to pronounce. You are

here, you have withstood that temptation. To overcome the lures of evil is all that can be required of mortals. But you make no mention of those other consolations open to the Christian soul. I know your priest to be a man of grace. Did you not allow him the opportunity to lift some part of your burden from you?'

'Father Eadmer is a good man and a kind,' said Donata with a thin, wry smile, 'and no doubt my soul has benefited from his prayers. But pain is here in the body, and has a very loud voice. Sometimes I could not hear my own voice say Amen! for the demon howling. Howbeit, rightly or wrongly, I did look about me for other aid.'

'Is this to the present purpose?' Hugh asked gently. 'For it cannot be pleasant to you, and God knows it must be tiring you out.'

'It is very much to the purpose. You will see. Bear with me, till I end what I have begun. I got my talisman,' she said. 'I will not tell you from whom. I was still able to go about, then, to wander among the booths at the abbey fair, or in the market. I got what I wanted from a traveller. By now she may herself be dead, for she was old. I have not seen her since, nor ever expected to. But she made for me what I wanted, one draught, contained in so small a vial, my release from pain and from the world. Tightly stoppered, she said it would not lose its power. She told me its properties, for in very small doses it is used against pain when other things fail, but in this strength it would end pain for ever. The herb is hemlock.'

'It has been known,' said Cadfael bleakly, 'to end pain for ever even when the sufferer never meant to surrender life. I do not use it. Its dangers are too great. There is a lotion can be made to use against ulcers and swellings and inflammations, but there are other remedies safer.'

'No doubt!' said Donata. 'But the safety I sought was of a different kind. I had my charm, and I kept it always about me, and often I set my hand to it when the pain was extreme, but always I withdrew without drawing the stopper. As if the mere having it was buttress to my own strength. Bear with me, I am coming to the matter in hand. Last year, when my lord gave himself utterly to the love of Generys, I went to her cottage, at a time in the afternoon when Eudo was elsewhere about his manor. I took with me a flask of a good wine, and two cups that matched, and my vial of hemlock. And I proposed to her a wager.'

She paused only to draw breath, and ease slightly the position in which she had been motionless so long. None of her three hearers had any mind to break the thread now. All their presuppositions were already blown clean away in the wind of her chill detachment, for she spoke of pain and passion in tones level and quiet, almost indifferent, concerned only with making all plain past shadow of doubt.

'I was never her enemy,' she said. 'We had known each other many years, I felt for her rage and despair when Ruald abandoned her. This was not in hate or envy or despite. We were two women impossibly shackled together by the cords of our rights in one man, and neither of us could endure the mutilation of sharing him. I set before her a way out of the trap. We would pour two cups of wine, and add to one of them the draught of hemlock. If it was I who died, then she would have full possession of my lord, and, God knows, my blessing if she could give him happiness, as I had lost the power to do. And if it was she who died, then I swore to her that I would live out my life to the wretched end unsparing, and never again seek alleviation.'

'And Generys agreed to such a bargain?' Hugh asked incredulously.

239

'She was as bitter, bold and resolute as I, and as tormented by having and not having. Yes, she agreed. I think, gladly.'

'Yet this was no easy thing to manage fairly.'

'With no will to cheat, yes, it was very easy,' she said simply. 'She went out from the room, and neither watched nor listened, while I filled the cups, evenly but that the one contained hemlock. Then I went out, far down the Potter's Field, while she parted and changed the cups as she thought fit, and set the one on the press and the other on the table, and came and called me in, and I chose. It was June, the twenty-eighth day of the month, a beautiful midsummer. I remember how the meadow grasses were coming into flower, I came back to the cottage with my skirts spangled with the silver of their seeds. And we sat down together, there within, and drank our wine, and were at peace. And afterwards, since I knew that the draught brought on a rigor of the whole body, from the extremities inward to the heart, we agreed between us to part, she to remain quiet where she was, I to go back to Longner, that whichever of us God – dare I say God, Father, or must I say only chance, or fate? – whichever of us was chosen should die at home. I promise you, Father, I had not forgotten God, I did not feel that he had stricken me from his book. It was as simple as where you have it written: of two, one shall be taken and the other left. I went home, and I spun while I waited. And hour by hour – for it does not hurry – I waited for the numbness in the hands to make me fumble at the wool on the distaff, and still my fingers spun and my wrist twisted, and there was no change in my dexterity. And I waited for the cold to seize upon my feet, and climb into my ankles, and there was no chill and no clumsiness, and my breath came without hindrance.'

She drew a deep, unburdened sigh, and let her head rest back against the panelling, eased of the main weight of the load she had brought them.

'You had won your wager,' said the abbot in a low and grieving voice.

'No,' said Donata, 'I had lost my wager.' And in a moment she added scrupulously: 'There is one detail I had forgotten to mention. We kissed, sisterly, when we parted.'

She had not done, she was only gathering herself to continue coherently to the end, but the silence lasted some minutes. Hugh got up from his place and poured a cup of wine from the flask on the abbot's table, and went and set it down on the bench beside her, convenient to her hand. 'You are very tired. Would you not like to rest a little while? You have done what you came to do. Whatever this may have been, it was not murder.'

She looked up at him with the benign indulgence she felt now towards all the young, as though she had lived not forty-five years but a hundred, and seen all manner of tragedies pass and lapse into oblivion.

'Thank you, but I am the better for having resolved this matter. You need not trouble for me. Let me make an end, and then I will rest.' But to accommodate him she put out a hand for the cup, and seeing how even that slight weight made her wrist quiver, Hugh supported it while she drank. The red of the wine gave her grey lips, for a moment, the dew and flush of blood.

'Let me make an end! Eudo came home, I told him what we had done, and that the lot had failed to fall on me. I wanted no concealment, I was willing to bear witness truly, but he would not suffer it. He had lost her, but he would not let me be lost, or his honour, or his sons' honour. He went that night, alone, and buried her. Now I see that Sulien, deep in his own pit of grief, must have followed him to an assignation, and discovered him in a funeral rite. But my lord never knew it. Never a word was said of that, never a sign given. He told me how he found her, lying on her bed as if asleep. When the numbness began she must have lain down there, and let death come to her. Those small things about her that gave her a name and a being, those he brought away with him and kept, not secret from me. There were no more secrets between us two, there was no hate, only a shared grief. Whether he removed them for my sake, looking upon what I had done as a terrible crime, as I grant you a man might, and fearing what should fall on me in consequence, or whether he wanted them for himself, as all he could now keep of her, I never knew.

'It passed, as everything passes. When she was missed, no one ever thought to look sidelong at us. I do not know where the word began that she was gone of her own will, with a lover, but it went round as gossip does, and men believed it. As for Sulien, he was the first to escape from the house. My elder son had never had ado with Ruald or Generys, beyond a civil word if they passed in the fields or crossed by the ferry together. He was busy about the manor, and thinking of marriage, he never felt the pain within the house. But Sulien was another person. I felt his unease, before ever he told us he was set on entering Ramsey. Now I see he had better reason for his trouble than I had thought. But his going weighed yet more heavily on my lord, and the time came when he could not bear ever to go near the Potter's Field, or look upon the place where she had lived and died. He made the gift to Haughmond, to be rid of it, and when that was completed, he went to join King Stephen at Oxford. And what befell him afterwards you know.

'I have not asked the privilege of confession, Father,' she said punctiliously, 'since I want no more secrecy from those fit to judge me, whether it be the law or the Church. I am here, do as you see fit. I did not cheat her, living, it was a fair wager, and I have not cheated her now she is dead. I have kept my pledge. I take no palliatives now, whatever my state. I pay my forfeit every day of my remaining life, to the end. In spite of what you see, I am strong. The end may still be a long way off.'

It was done. She rested in quietness, and in a curious content that showed in the comparative ease of her face. Distantly from across the court the bell from the refectory sounded noon.

The king's officer and the representative of the Church exchanged no more than one long glance by way of consultation. Cadfael observed it, and wondered which of them would speak first, and indeed, to which of these two authorities the right of precedence belonged, in a case so strange. Crime was Hugh's business, sin the abbot's, but what was justice here, where the two were woven together so piteously as to be beyond unravelling? Generys dead, Eudo dead, who stood to profit from further pursuit? Donata, when she had said that the dead should carry their own sins, had counted herself among them. And infinitely slow as the approach of death had been for her, it must now be very near.

Hugh was the first to speak. 'There is nothing here,' he said, 'that falls within my writ. What was done, whatever its rights or wrongs, was not murder. If it was an offence to put the dead into the ground unblessed, he who did it is already

243

dead himself, and what would it benefit the king's law or the good order of my shire to publish it to his dishonour now? Nor could anyone wish to add to your grief, or cause distress to Eudo's heir, who is innocent of all. I say this case is closed, unsolved, and so let it remain, to my reproach. I am not so infallible that I cannot fail, like any other man, and admit it. But there are claims that must be met. I see no help but we must make it public that Generys is Generys, though how she came to her death will never be known. She has the right to her name, and to have her grave acknowledged for hers. Ruald has the right to know that she is dead, and to mourn her duly. In time people will let the matter sink into the past and be forgotten. But for you there remains Sulien.'

'And Pernel,' said Donata.

'And Pernel. True, she already knows the half. What will you do about them?'

'Tell them the truth,' she said steadily. 'How else could they ever rest? They deserve truth, they can endure truth. But not my elder son. Leave him his innocence.'

'How will you satisfy him,' Hugh wondered practically, 'about this visit? Does he even know that you are here?'

'No,' she admitted with her wan smile, 'he was out and about early. No doubt he will think me mad, but when I return no worse than I set out, it will not be so hard to reconcile him. Jehane does know. She tried to dissuade me, but I would have my way, he cannot blame her. I told her I had it in mind to offer my prayers for help at Saint Winifred's shrine. And that I will make good, Father, with your leave, before I return. If,' she said, 'I am to return?'

'For my part, yes,' said Hugh. 'And to that end,' he said, rising, 'if the lord abbot agrees, I will go and bring your son to you here.'

He waited for the abbot's word, and it was long in coming. Cadfael could divine something, at least, of what passed in that austere and upright mind. To bargain with life and death is not so far from self-murder, and the despair that might lead to the acceptance of such a wager is in itself mortal sin. But the dead woman haunted the mind with pity and pain, and the living one was there before his eyes, relentlessly stoical in her interminable dying, inexorable in adhering to the penalty she had imposed upon herself when she lost her wager. And one judgement, the last, must be enough, and that was not yet due.

'So be it!' said Radulfus at last. 'I can neither condone nor condemn. Justice may already have struck its own balance, but where there is no certainty the mind must turn to the light and not the shadow. You are your own penance, my daughter, if God requires penance. There is nothing here for me to do, except to pray that all things remaining may work together for grace. There have been wounds enough, at all costs let us cause no more. Let no word be said, then, beyond these few who have the right to know, for their own peace. Yes, Hugh, if you will, go and bring the boy, and the young woman who has shed, it seems, so welcome a light among these grievous shadows. And, madam, when you have rested and eaten here in my house, we will help you into the church, to Saint Winifred's altar.'

'And it shall be my care,' said Hugh, 'to see that you get home safely. You do what is needful for Sulien and Pernel. Father Abbot, I am sure, will do what is needful for Brother Ruald.'

'That,' said Cadfael, 'I will undertake, if I may.'

'With my blessing,' said Radulfus. 'Go, find him after dinner in the frater, and let him know her story ends in peace.'

All of which they did before the day was over.

They were standing under the high wall of the graveyard, in the furthest corner where modest lay patrons found a place, and stewards and good servants of the abbey and, under a low mound still settling and greening, the nameless woman orphaned after death and received and given a home by Benedictine compassion.

Cadfael had gone with Ruald after Vespers, in the soft rain that was hardly more than a drifting dew on the face, chill and silent. The light would not last much longer. Vespers was already at its winter hour, and they were alone here in the shadow of the wall, in the wet grass, with the earthy smells of fading foliage and autumnal melancholy about them. A melancholy without pain, an indulgence of the spirit after the passing of bitterness and distress. And it did not seem strange that Ruald had shown no great surprise at learning that this translated waif was, after all, his wife, had accepted without wonder that Sulien had concocted, out of mistaken concern for an old friend, a false and foolish story to disprove her death. Nor had he rebelled against the probability that he would never know how she had died, or why she had been buried secretly and without rites, before she was brought to this better resting-place. Ruald's vow of obedience, like all his vows, was carried to the ultimate extreme of duty, into total acceptance. Whatever was, was best to him. He did not question.

'What is strange, Cadfael,' he said, brooding over the new turf that covered her, 'is that now I begin to see her face clearly again. When first I entered here I was like a man in fever, aware only of what I had longed for and gained. I could not recall how she looked, it was as if she and all my life aforetime had vanished out of the world.'

'It comes of staring into too intense a light,' said Cadfael, dispassionately, for he himself had never been dazzled. He had done what he had done in his right senses, made his choice, no easy choice, with deliberation, walked to his novitiate on broad bare feet treading solid earth, not been borne to it on clouds of bliss. 'A very fine experience in its way,' he said, 'but bad for the sight. If you stare too long you may go blind.'

'But now I see her clearly. Not as I last saw her, not angry or bitter. As she always used to be, all the years we were together. And young,' said Ruald, marvelling. 'Everything I knew and did, aforetime, comes back with her, I remember the croft, and the kiln, and where every small thing had its place in the house. It was a very pleasant place, looking down from the crest to the river, and beyond.'

'It still is,' said Cadfael. 'We've ploughed it, and brushed back the headland bushes, and you might miss the field flowers, and the moths at midsummer when the meadow grasses ripen. But there'll be the young green starting now along the furrows, and the birds in the headlands just the same. Yes, a very fair place.'

They had turned to walk back through the wet grass towards the chapter-house, and the dusk was a soft blue-green about them, clinging moist in the half-naked branches of the trees.

'She would never have had a place in this blessed ground,' said Ruald, out of the shadow of his cowl, 'but that she was found in land belonging to the abbey, and without any other sponsor to take care of her. As Saint Illtud drove his wife out into the night for no offence, as I, for no offence in her, deserted Generys, so in the end God has brought her back into

247

the care of the Order, and provided her an enviable grave.
Father Abbot received and blessed what I misused and
misprized.'

'It may well be,' said Cadfael, 'that our justice sees as in a
mirror image, left where right should be, evil reflected back as
good, good as evil, your angel as her devil. But God's justice,
if it makes no haste, makes no mistakes.'

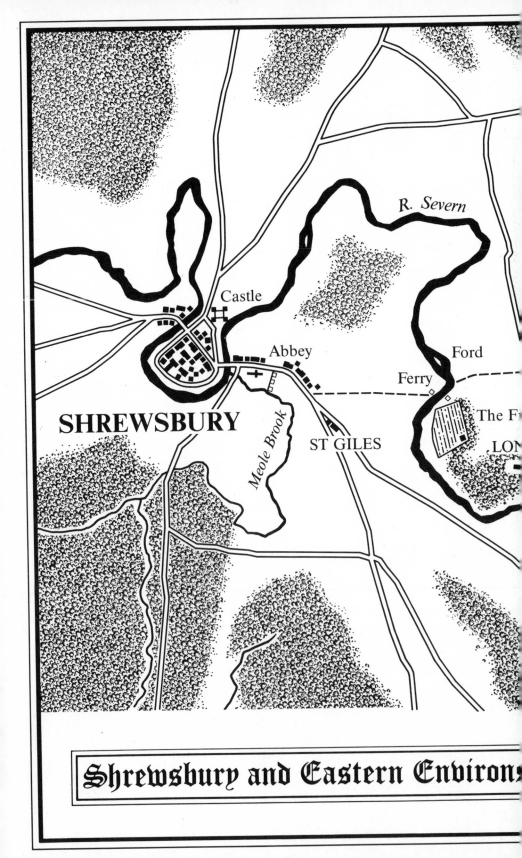

Shrewsbury and Eastern Environs